Changeling MAGIC

MARINA FINLAYSON

FINESSE SOLUTIONS

Cover design by Karri Klawiter
Editing by Larks & Katydids
Formatting by Polgarus Studio

Published by Finesse Solutions Pty Ltd
2018/09
ISBN: 9781925607031

Author's note: This book was written and produced in Australia and
uses British/Australian spelling conventions, such as "colour" instead
of "color", and "-ise" endings instead of "-ize" on words like "realise".

NATIONAL
LIBRARY
OF AUSTRALIA

A catalogue record for this
book is available from the
National Library of Australia

1

You'd think that being granted your heart's deepest desire would make you blissfully happy, but I'm here to tell you: it ain't necessarily so. It had been three weeks since the king had granted me the right—and the power— to enter the Realms of Faerie at will. It was all I had ever wanted, everything I'd dreamed of since I'd first been exiled from my home in the Realm of Autumn. And where had I been for that entire three weeks? Right here, in the mortal world, my powers unused, my golden ticket going to waste.

I bowed my head over my guitar, letting the music carry me away in the dark pub. Rowan's drumbeat reverberated in my chest. The guitar thrummed beneath my hands. And above it all, Willow's astonishing vocals soared. I should have been lost in the music, in the joy of performing. It was our last set of the night, and the songs were familiar enough that I could have played them with my eyes closed, but I was distracted, ill at ease.

When the song finished, I looked up, taking in the

crowd, eager faces turned our way no more than pale ovals under the coloured flashing lights. The Drunken Irishman was only half full tonight, but the patrons, many of them fae, were a rowdy lot, and they made their appreciation of our music known with a roaring and stamping of feet. Willow smiled and took it as her due, red hair tumbling down her back in a flaming waterfall as the sparkles of light from the disco ball in the centre of the room played across her face. Rowan leapt up from his drumkit and planted a smacking kiss on the lips of Sage, our bass guitarist, then grabbed my face in his hands and did the same to me. Willow fended him off and the crowd laughed and jeered.

"That was our best gig yet!" he shouted. I just rolled my eyes and packed my guitar into its case, too tired to deal with his enthusiasm. The room was too dark to make out the time on the clock above the bar, but it felt late. Rowan had taken so many requests tonight that the gig had seemed to last forever. I wanted to go home.

The trouble was, I no longer knew where home was. It definitely wasn't in the little cottage in the Realm of Autumn where I'd grown up anymore, however much I might wish it to be. My mother had made that crystal clear. It was all well and good to have permission to go anywhere in the Realms, but where else would I go if not there?

Maybe the Hawk had been right, and home was right here, where my friends were. At the moment, I was bunking at Willow's, with her and Sage, since the place I'd been living in for the last couple of years had exploded rather spectacularly, almost taking me with it. They were my best friends and it was kind of fun to room together, but it wouldn't work long-term. "Home is where the heart is" was all very well, but it didn't address the practical details of being a human living in what amounted to a bubble of fae magic. I could never give any human friends my address, much less bring anyone home with me. So I was adrift, not sure where I really belonged.

As if thinking of him had summoned him, a dark-haired man, tall and well-muscled, shouldered his way through the crowd to the bar, and my spirits lifted. I may not have seen the Hawk since the ceremony where the king had endowed me with his magic, but I'd sure thought about him plenty. Pretty much constantly, actually. Over and over, I'd replayed that moment when he'd said he wanted to see me again, felt the pressure of his strong body against mine, his arms around me. And now he was here. Finally. I smiled as I met his honey-coloured eyes across the room, my heart soaring. He nodded, but there was no answering smile.

Sage moved closer, so I could hear her over the roar of conversation and the clinking of glasses. "Sir Hot and Steamy is back. I told you he wouldn't be able to stay away."

I shrugged, feigning nonchalance. "I wasn't expecting him. He's a busy man."

"Of course he is. He's a Knight of the Realms who's just rescued the king from twenty years' imprisonment. He's the flavour of the month. I bet those Court ladies back at Whitehaven are fawning over him."

She was right; I'd seen the beginnings of the Hawk's

newfound popularity when I'd received my reward for my part in the king's release. People who'd spent years sniggering at him behind his back for his "fixation" on finding the king were now lining up to be his best buddies. He'd treated them all with his usual cool politeness.

"And yet here he is, hanging out in a dive in the mortal world. I wonder what could possibly have brought him here?" She grinned, but I ignored her teasing and hopped down off our tiny temporary stage to join him at the bar, sliding onto the stool beside him that had miraculously become free at the exact moment I needed it. Probably not so miraculous—just magic at work. The Hawk had no qualms about using his considerable powers to arrange things to suit himself.

He raised two fingers and Randall, who was behind the bar tonight, nodded and filled two small glasses for us without saying anything, which was even more miraculous than the empty bar stool. Randall liked to chat. Perhaps he was awed by the man at my side.

"Hi." My voice came out a little breathless, and I immediately flushed. I may have been hanging out to see him, but there was no need to make it quite so obvious. I had my pride. "Long time no see."

He frowned at me, an expression I had admittedly seen more than a few times before on his face. The man managed to make even disapproval look sexy. "I had expected to see you before this. As had the king."

My smile faltered. Why the cool tone? Had he had second thoughts about starting a relationship with a mere changeling? Randall slid the two shot glasses in front of us, then moved away discreetly, though many of the bar's patrons were watching us. The Hawk, of course, had always been famous, but my notoriety was new.

"Did you miss me?" I asked, taking refuge in smart-arsery.

"His Majesty is curious as to why you haven't yet availed yourself of his gracious gift. He sent me to make sure that all is in order."

Funny how politeness could sound like a rebuke in the right hands. He'd definitely changed his mind about us. I fiddled with the glass in front of me, surprised at how much it hurt. I'd let myself get carried away again, hadn't I? We'd never even kissed, yet I'd been busy dreaming of a future with my beautiful winged knight.

Except, he wasn't my knight, as it turned out. I swirled the rich honey-gold liquid, wondering how fast I could get out of here. When would I learn?

"There's nothing wrong with King Rothbold's gift. I just haven't used it yet." A slight shudder ran down my spine at the thought that the king had noticed and, apparently, been miffed enough to send his knight to make enquiries. I was in the good books right now, because I'd helped save Rothbold from a drugged imprisonment in a dementia unit in the mortal world. Twenty years of that would be enough to make anyone grateful. But gratitude could turn to rancour if he thought I hadn't appreciated his gift, and I did *not* want to make an enemy of the King of the Thirteen Realms. I'd be better off jumping off a building right now and saving myself some anguish.

"Can I ask why?" His voice was clipped, impersonal, as if I was someone he'd only just met. Someone who meant nothing to him.

I took a sip of my drink to try and pull myself together. I wouldn't give him the satisfaction of knowing how much he'd hurt me. The liquid slid down my throat like silk and lit a fire in my belly that spread through my limbs, bringing an amazing sense of wellbeing in its wake.

"What in the name of the Tree is that?" I asked as the pain of rejection receded. Whatever it was, I wanted more. I downed the rest of the glass, licking my lips so as not to waste a single, precious drop. "And can I have some more?"

He pushed his glass across to me. "It's called Courage. Do you need it? Are you scared?"

"What would I be scared of?" Those tawny eyes of his sometimes saw more than I would have liked. I guess that came from counting your age in centuries rather than years—along the way, you learned a thing or two about what made people tick. But I didn't want him psychoanalysing me. I drank the second glass down, and the sense of warmth spread right through my body. I felt so good I almost didn't care about my dashed hopes anymore. Who needed men, anyway?

"You tell me," he said. "You weren't scared when we were lost in the Wilds and faced those dharrigals. You weren't scared when a troll tried to kill you."

Actually, I had been—on both those occasions—but if he thought I was brave, I wasn't going to disabuse him of the notion. Let him believe I was all that and a box of matches. I was practically a superhero these days. I even had a magic cape, courtesy of the mysterious Raven. Now, with the king's gift of the power to open the Way to the Realms, my blood was almost as good as if I'd been born a fae, not just a lowly human. I had the right to call the Realms home. Such irony.

"I'm not scared," I said, and with the Courage burning in my bloodstream, I almost believed it.

"What, then? Is this some perverse form of delayed gratification? Three weeks ago, you were so eager to get back into the Realms that I believe you would have done anything to win that right." A muscle jumped in his jaw, as if he was grinding his teeth. "And now the king has all but laid out a welcome mat, and you won't go? I don't understand."

I sighed, wishing I had another glass—or maybe a whole bottle—of Courage. "Okay. Maybe I am, a little. Well, not scared, exactly." That sounded childish. "More … uncertain of my welcome."

"I just told you, the king—"

"Not from the king."

"Who, then? You're the hero of the hour. Your name is on everyone's lips."

"I highly doubt that. Who's going to talk about the changeling nobody when the Hawk is in the picture? It's such a great story—the knight who never gave up on his quest, rewarded at last for his loyalty and persistence." Unable to resist a little dig, I added, "You know, it makes you sound almost likeable."

He refused to take the bait. "Almost likeable? That's

high praise, coming from you." He sounded almost bitter as he signalled to Randall, who came over to refill the glasses with that liquid gold. "Who has you so uncertain?"

I shrugged. "No one in particular. I just don't really have a place to go." My mother hadn't even waited until I was eighteen to kick me out of the Realms, as if she couldn't bear to put it off a moment longer. I hated that the memory of that pain still had such power to wound me. I should be over my abandonment issues by now.

Rothbold may have given me right of entry, but once I was in, what then? The only place I wanted to go was back to the cottage where I'd grown up, back to the forests of my childhood. But how would my mother receive her prodigal daughter? And if she so clearly didn't want me around, what was the point, anyway? It wouldn't be the same. The feeling of belonging had been part of the pull those woods and that cottage had exerted on me all these lonely years. Funny how it wasn't until I'd won the right to return that I realised that you could never really go back. The past was a country whose borders were closed to all comers.

"Right." He nodded, as if his suspicions had just been confirmed, and I had the distinct feeling that he'd heard everything I hadn't said, despite my feeble attempt to deflect him. Then he pushed the glass toward me. "Drink up. You'll need it."

"What for?" I eyed him suspiciously over the rim of the glass.

"To do what you should have done three weeks ago."

I drained the glass and set it back down on the bar, a

pleasant buzz filling my head. Courage was well named. It made me brave enough to challenge him, to ask the question that most puzzled me. "Why do you care?"

"I don't. I'm Robinson Crusoe, remember? No human feelings at all." Tawny eyes glittered dangerously, as if daring me to argue. I must have struck a deeper nerve than I'd thought with that comment, though it had been meant to help. He seemed in a filthy mood. "I merely act, as always, on my king's command. King Rothbold desires that you should use his gift, so you're going to use it."

He took my hand and all but dragged me off the stool. There were callouses on his skin from sword work, and my hand was engulfed in his larger one. Even in heels, I came no higher than his bearded chin.

"What, now?" It was one o'clock in the morning. That didn't bother the fae patrons of The Drunken Irishman. Fae needed very little sleep and most of the ones living in the mortal world preferred to operate at night, when the pesky humans were out of the way. I, on the other hand, had been looking forward to hitting my pillow back at Willow's sith.

"Yes, now, while the Courage is strong in your veins. Hiding from your fears will only help them grow."

Sage raised an eyebrow as the Hawk pulled me toward the door. I shrugged helplessly and mouthed, "See you later." The Hawk was not the kind of man who took no for an answer, especially not in his current mood.

2

He dropped my hand as soon as he'd hustled me out into the street and strode off, as if he couldn't wait to be away from here. Or away from me.

"Is something wrong?" Maybe he'd decided not to take our relationship any further, but in the past, he'd always been polite, at least. This tight-lipped, hard-eyed man was a stranger, and after all we'd been through together, I deserved a little more than that.

"What could possibly be wrong?" he bit out without even glancing at me.

I hurried to catch up with him and caught at his arm. "I don't know, but you're being kind of a jerk right now. Will you look at me?"

He whirled on me, a dangerous glint in his eye. "Why? One man not enough for you now?"

What the hell? His body was taut with fury, and I only just managed to hold my ground. Every instinct in my body was urging me to step back, to get out of the path of that storm in his eyes before it broke.

"One man …? What in the name of the Lady are you talking about?"

He moved closer, backing me up against the brick wall of the pub. "You. And Rowan."

Seriously? Was he jealous of my friends now? "Rowan's just a friend. What is your problem?"

"Just a friend? It didn't look that way when I arrived tonight."

"You mean that kiss? That was nothing." For God's sake, Rowan had kissed Sage, too. Or hadn't he seen that part? "Any of my friends could kiss me like that."

"So anyone can just grab you" —he jerked me against him, making me gasp— "and kiss you—and it means nothing?"

He swooped down and claimed my lips in a furious kiss. I opened to his onslaught, dizzy with a wave of passion that swept through my body, igniting every nerve ending. I kissed him back with such enthusiasm that all the fury drained from our embrace, and for a few long moments, I was lost in the taste and feel of him. My arms twined around his neck, while his hands roamed hungrily over my body.

At last, he raised his head.

I blinked up at him in a daze. "That was *nothing* like the way Rowan kissed me."

"Did it mean nothing?"

"You know it didn't."

"I know nothing. You're a mystery to me, Allegra."

At least he didn't seem angry anymore, but there was a

wariness about him that kept me at a distance. Already, he was acting as if the kiss had never happened. Something hard bumped against my thigh as he stepped back.

I fell back on humour, always a refuge when I felt uncertain. "Is that a sword in your pocket or are you just happy to see me?"

He snorted and laid his hand on a sword hilt, which became visible at his touch. "It's Ecfirrith. Yriell went hunting for it and the Wilds gave it back to her."

"That's great." Yriell was the king's sister, and a powerful Earthcrafter. Nothing she did could surprise me. "Now you can gate directly into and out of the Realms again."

"Yes." He took my hand and urged me down the road a little further. There was a narrow alley a few doors down from The Drunken Irishman. I'd walked past it hundreds of times but had never had a reason to enter it. Now, the Hawk led me into it.

"Wow, you really know how to show a girl a good time." The alley wasn't particularly grimy or terrifying—it looked like a service way for delivery trucks. No monsters lurking or ominous shadows. Just not a place I'd choose to spend my Friday night. "Where are you taking me?"

"Nowhere." He put some distance between us and the street we'd left, then stopped. "*You're* taking *me*."

"If I'd realised you were so keen on dominant women, I would have brought my whip and handcuffs."

His tawny eyes gleamed with sudden amusement. "You have handcuffs?"

I let out an exasperated sigh. I would never understand this man and his sudden changes of mood. "What are we doing here, Kyrrim? I thought we were going to the Realms." When he'd given me permission to use his name—an honour few enjoyed—he probably hadn't envisaged being scolded with it.

"We are. Open the Way."

"Here? But the park—"

"Is easier, I know. For people whose magic isn't very strong. You are no longer one of those people."

"Right." I was so used to thinking of Hyde Park, with its optimal positioning on a Fold, as *the* place to attempt a crossing to the Realms, that I hadn't considered that the king's gift wouldn't need a turbo assist. Fae didn't give gifts often, but when they did, they weren't stingy about it. My new power to open a Way through the Wilds would be the most powerful, bells and whistles, all-singing, all-dancing power there was. Anything less would shame the king himself. "But why are we in this alley?"

"You'd rather open a Way in plain sight in the middle of the street?"

"No, of course not."

He didn't have to look at me as if he thought I was stupid. I glanced around, the darkness no barrier to my night vision. Jumpers, those fae like Jaxen, the Lord of Autumn's brother, lucky enough to be born with the power to teleport, could literally jump between the mortal world and the faerie one without having to slog through the Wilds first. Their power was rare and much prized. Some artefacts, like the Hawk's sword, Ecfirrith, could create the same kind of gates, allowing instantaneous transition from one plane to the other. Everyone else, whether using their own power or a talisman such as the gate glyph Eldric had once given me, had to make use of the latent power of thresholds to create an opening into the Wilds.

In a place such as Hyde Park, which was on a Fold—a place where the two worlds were closer than usual to each other—almost anything could qualify as a "threshold", as long as the person wishing to travel had enough power to open the Way. An archway formed by the branches of two trees leaning toward each other would do. Further from a Fold, an actual doorway, arch, or window was needed. So, I searched the alleyway for a door I could use.

I'd never done it before myself, but I'd seen others do it. They made it look easy, merely opening a door and stepping through into the Wilds, their feet set on a path that would lead them to the Realms. What I'd never understood, though, was why that ordinary door suddenly opened into the Wilds instead of wherever it was supposed to go in the mortal world. There must be some extra step that I wasn't seeing.

I located a fire door halfway down the alley, but the Hawk shook his head. "Not iron."

Iron and magic didn't mix. I knew that, of course, but my nerves had got the better of me. Feeling like an amateur, I kept walking.

A big metal roller door that probably led to underground parking had the same problem. I headed deeper into the darkness, the Hawk's firm tread at my back, searching for a plain old wooden door that I could use. I finally found one right at the end of the alley, tucked into a shabby old building that looked as though it could have been there since Europeans settled Australia. The door was undoubtedly locked, but that had never seemed to stop anyone before. Hesitantly, I laid my hand on the door handle and looked over my shoulder at the Hawk.

"Do I have to—?"

"Just open it. The magic will do the rest."

I pushed down on the handle, feeling a heat in my fingers that hadn't been there a moment before. Golden light flared around my hand as my fingers tingled, and the door opened easily. Mist billowed out, catching me by surprise, as I'd been half-expecting to see the interior of the building.

"Go on," the Hawk said, so I stepped through, feeling the shiver of threshold magic across my skin, as if tiny insects were crawling on me.

Beyond the door, the mist cleared, and a path beckoned. A path that was clearly outdoors, shadowed by dark trees. It was just as dark there as it was here, but I could make out the sky above the trees. This was the Wilds, that dangerous zone between the two worlds.

"The Realms await," the Hawk said behind me, a note of satisfaction in his voice.

There was no sign, now, of the door. Only the path stretched off into the dark before us.

I shook out my tingling fingers. So weird. "It just … happened. I didn't feel as though I did anything."

"Do you feel as though you must do something to make your lungs breathe, or your heart beat? Magic doesn't come with an instruction manual. It is as much a part of you as your muscles. Did you have to teach your biceps how to contract before you could move your arm?"

I started walking. "It's just strange. I've never been able to do magic before. I thought it would be more ... momentous, somehow."

His chuckle sounded in the dark behind me. "The king himself gifts you a part of his royal magic, and you complain it's not *momentous* enough."

"I'm not complaining! Just saying."

"I forget, sometimes, how young you are."

"Okay, Grandad. I know you're, like, a million years old and all, but no need to rub it in." At least the tension between us had eased, though I could still feel the pressure of his lips on mine. What was I supposed to think about that kiss? Apart from the fact that I wanted more just like it, of course. I touched my bruised lips and smiled into the darkness.

We walked in silence for a while. It might have been peaceful, except for the memories of our last visit to the Wilds. That was an experience I had no desire to repeat, and I watched the dark forest on both sides of the path, my ears straining for any unusual sound. With the Hawk at my back, I had no fear of being taken by surprise from that direction, but I still jumped like a scalded cat when a branch off to our right cracked with a sharp retort.

The Hawk's hands closed on my shoulders. "Be easy.

Your friend Edgar is not here to push us off the path this time. You are perfectly safe." His breath tickled my ear, and a little shiver ran through me. "Unless, of course, you make any more cracks about grandfathers. In which case I may push you off the path myself."

A smile tugged at my lips. "That would be an awful waste of the king's generous gift. You could get into a lot of trouble." He was standing very close, the heat of his body pressed against my back. "Grandfathers are the last thing on my mind right now," I added.

I was getting such mixed signals from him that I didn't know what to think. Right on cue, he stepped away, leaving me even more confused than before.

The rest of the journey passed without incident, though my feet ached long before we reached our destination. It had been a long day—and now we'd spent what felt like half the night walking the Greenways. We followed the twists and turns of the path until it ended in an archway where the trees on either side met overhead. When we stepped through the arch, I gasped at the familiar sight that met my eyes.

"Last time I came to Autumn, the path led me to Eldric's halls." I glanced uncertainly up at the Hawk, who stopped at my side.

"I think the Wilds like you now." There was no hint of a smile, so he must have been serious. Given what I had learned of the Wilds from Yriell, it might even be possible. These remnants of the old Realm of Earth, now called the Wilds, were not exactly sentient, but there was some kind of awareness there. "But the magic the king gave you is strong. If your will matches it, the Greenways should deliver you wherever you wish to go." He stared at the small cottage tucked into the sheltering embrace of a grove of pine trees in front of us, his face giving away nothing of what he was thinking.

I turned back to that familiar view myself, my stomach churning with a welter of emotions. The sun was just beginning to rise behind us, and the clearing was bathed in a soft, grey light. The cottage itself was made of undressed timbers cut long ago from trees just like the pines that crowded behind it. No smoke rose from its chimney, which wasn't all that surprising, given the early hour.

A small stream chattered over smooth pebbles at the bottom of the hill behind us on its way to join the River Ivon, which was only a short walk away. Its noise formed a gentle counterpoint to the birds who were waking in the forest all around.

No flowers bobbed their perfumed heads in the garden beds in front of the cottage, which were wild and overgrown with weeds. A feeling of dread stirred inside me at the sight of those gardens, which had always been a source of pride to my mother.

With quick steps, I led the way up the path. Weeds grew in the cracks between the paving stones.

"Should we knock?" the Hawk asked as we gained the small porch. "We don't want to alarm her."

But my hand was already on the door. It opened to my touch, revealing a small but cosy room, full of bright cushions on every chair, and a magnificent rug that glowed in all the colours of Autumn in front of the stone fireplace. But the house was cold and silent.

Panic rose into my throat as I hurried down the hall to the bedrooms. I threw open her bedroom door so hard it bounced off the wall and would have smacked me in the face if the Hawk hadn't reached around me and caught it. But there was no body in the bed. I breathed out shakily.

"What's wrong?" the Hawk asked.

"I thought she must be dead."

He stepped away from me and checked the other bedroom, and then the small bathroom. "There's no one here."

"She would never have let the gardens get into such a state if she were here. But where would she have gone?" I opened the door of her wardrobe and found the inside all but bare. Only her apron and two dresses hung there.

Back in the main room, the fireplace had been swept clean, and no new logs had been laid. I gazed around the room, finding more signs of a planned departure, and my heart rate began to slow. She hadn't died, and she hadn't been attacked and dragged away—though who would do such a thing, I couldn't imagine. She'd meant to leave.

I hurried outside and walked all around the property, seeing signs of abandonment everywhere in the untended gardens. I even went around to the back of the house, where my childhood nemesis stood—a pine with gnarled branches and grasping, twiggy fingers. It had given me such nightmares I had always avoided this area of the garden.

Even now, it gave me shivers to look at it, and I moved on quickly. Everything back here looked just as overgrown as out the front, and the henhouse was empty, its door standing open.

"Do you have other family?" the Hawk asked.

"No. It was just the two of us." That fact had made her rejection of me all the harder to bear. All my life, it had been the two of us, alone but not lonely. Not needing anyone's company except each other's. I had never felt unloved—quite the opposite, in fact. I knew that many fae rejected their adult changelings, but I had never expected it to happen to me. "She was a bit of a hermit, in some ways. Didn't like mixing with other people much. Being so far out in the woods here suited her. I can't imagine her just … leaving. Where else would she go?"

I also wasn't sure why I cared, since she'd made it quite clear she never wanted to see me again. But I did. I couldn't shake the feeling that something terrible must have happened to drive her from her beloved home.

"Then we will find her," the Hawk said with conviction.

I gave him a rather shaky smile, glad that he was here despite whatever was going on between us. "Let's hope it's a little easier than finding the king."

3

It would have been a long trek to the Hall of Giseult, the ancestral home of the Lords of Autumn, but the Hawk had Ecfirrith back. He unsheathed it right there in my mother's overgrown yard and drew three slashes in the air in the shape of a rough doorway. The slashes left an afterglow, like the trail of a sparkler through the air, and soon the glow spread, forming a gateway. He took my hand in a firm grip, still holding the sword in his other hand, and led the way through.

There was an instant's disorientation and the feeling of something with tiny, tickly feet crawling on my skin, and we were stepping onto the soft grass in front of the Hall. The guards straightened, their hands going to their own swords at the sight of a man wielding a naked blade stepping out of thin air.

"Sir Hawk," one said, in cautious greeting. "The hearth vow, if you please."

That was unusual. The hearth vow protected the inhabitants

of a home; a visitor who had taken it was bound by his own magic not to do them harm. I'd never heard the guards here ask for it—but then, I'd never arrived here in the company of a sword-wielding man, either. It had been far more common in the days before the fall of Illusion, apparently, since an Illusionist enemy could impersonate a friend to perfection, and there was no way to tell if people really were who they appeared to be.

The Hawk was unfazed. "I vow to bring no harm to those who call this hearth their home."

He sheathed his sword, and both guards followed suit, visibly relaxing. "Welcome to my master's halls," said the first one. "You do us great honour with your presence."

I bet these jokers would have been singing a different tune a few weeks ago. People might have paid lip service to his title, but no Knight of the Realms got sent on a hunt for a stolen garment, however expensive, if he was truly valued. His insistence on keeping up the search for the lost king had earned him a lot of scorn among the nobility, who had all believed the king was dead.

"Is Lord Eldric at home?" the Hawk asked. "My lady and I seek an audience with him."

His lady? I gave him the side-eye, and so did the two guards, though for different reasons. They knew who I was, and I was no Lady. Whenever possible, my mother had opted for solitude, but there had been occasions when all the local fae were expected to present themselves at the Hall, mainly for religious festivals. I'd been running around here since I wore pigtails. I wasn't even fae, just a discarded changeling brat, which was why they hadn't bothered to extract a hearth vow from me.

And I was going to get whiplash from all the sudden changes in the Hawk's mood. First, he'd been angry enough to rage-kiss me, and now he was claiming me as his own?

The guard who had first spoken held aside the silken drapes behind him. They might look flimsy, but they were as good as any castle gate. No one could pass without the blessing of the watch. "Please enter. I will send someone to notify Lord Eldric of your arrival."

The great grassy length of the Hall opened up before us. On either side, massive red-trunked trees marched down its length, forming the bones of the Hall, their branches interlacing above in a canopy. Archways between the tree trunks were mainly closed by silken hangings in rich autumnal tones, though some stood open, allowing glimpses of other spaces where the business of daily life was conducted. Spiral staircases curled around the mighty trees, leading to other levels where private chambers hid among the branches and more silken hangings.

Daylight lanced through gaps in the canopy overhead, supplemented by the soft glow of lamps suspended by magic above the Hall. The whole Hall pulsed with magic; even I could feel it. I had always loved coming here as a child and wished that my mother hadn't been so quick to hurry me away home again. The trees had been coaxed into fantastic shapes, the spiralling stairs grown directly from their trunks. Swooping lengths of brightly coloured silk had, to my childhood self, given the impression of a magical space assembled for a special party, and I had always been relieved to find it still there the next time I visited, as if afraid someone would pack it all up and move on when the party was over.

A long table stood on the dais at the far end of the space. Only one man sat there, his back turned to us. Clearly it wasn't Eldric, since Eldric's hair was the russet colour of autumn leaves, and this man's was as black as Raven's. I wouldn't have minded seeing Raven again, but the man turned at our approach, dooming me to disappointment. It was Jaxen, Eldric's dissolute younger brother.

"Sir Hawk. Come, sit down. Help me drink Eldric's excellent wine." He indicated a chair with a lazy wave of his hand. "And little Allegra, everyone's favourite changeling. Well, everyone except Eldric, of course."

I blinked. "What have I done to upset Lord Eldric?"

He barely remembered I was alive unless he wanted something from the mortal world. I couldn't imagine how I might have upset him.

"We had a visit from a new widow last week. Sexiest damn widow I ever saw." He smiled, as if reminiscing. "Naturally, I did my best to comfort her. You don't know her, but I believe you've met her husband." His smirk implied I should know what he was talking about. He refilled his glass and cocked an eyebrow enquiringly at us both, offering the bottle in his hand.

"No, thanks," I said, seating myself in the chair the Hawk had pulled out for me. His Court manners were exquisite. He sat next to me and refused the offer of wine with a curt shake of his head.

"She was most insistent that Eldric owed her the blood price for her husband's death on your behalf. You can imagine how happy Eldric is at the prospect. You run around killing people and get rewarded for it, while he gets landed with the bill."

"Who is this widow?"

"Her name is Blethna Arbre."

What? "But I didn't kill Dansen Arbre."

He shrugged. "That's not how she sees it. Your involvement in his affairs led to his death. Poor Eldric is livid."

Tosser. Jaxen didn't give a shit about his brother's feelings. Even in our isolated cottage, we'd heard the rumours: how tense the relationship between the two brothers was, how Lord Eldric chafed at supporting a younger brother who did nothing but drink all day.

"Eldric should ignore her," the Hawk said. "The king's own sister killed Dansen Arbre. Blethna knows she'd be laughed out of Whitehaven if she demanded blood price for the death of the man responsible for imprisoning the king. She's mad if she thinks Eldric will take her claim seriously."

"Not mad, just hard up for cash. She's Arbre's second wife, and the heir is from the first marriage. He doesn't get on with his delectable stepmother, apparently. Told her to pack herself up and find somewhere else to live." He leaned back in his chair and put his boots up on the table, legs crossed at the ankle. "Families can be so difficult, can't they?"

He didn't seem to be having any trouble—he had a pretty sweet set-up here. As far as I could tell, he did exactly as he pleased, and spent Eldric's money like there was no tomorrow. He was the last person who should be complaining about his family.

"So how is life for Autumn's most famous child?" He watched me over the rim of his glass. "Exercising your new powers already, I see. Does this mean we'll be seeing more of you now?"

"Perhaps." I wished Eldric would appear. I'd never liked Jaxen, and making small talk with him was not my idea of a good time. Fortunately, he spent long periods travelling, visiting friends in other Realms, so even if I did come back to Autumn permanently, I wouldn't necessarily have to deal with him on a regular basis.

"Don't be shy, sweetheart. I won't tell anyone. I'm good at keeping secrets."

"It's not a secret, I just haven't decided yet."

Jaxen appealed to the Hawk. "Sir Knight, tell her she must come home to Autumn. Surely the mortal world has nothing to equal this?" He waved his glass at the Hall in a generous sweep that sloshed a little ruby liquid over the side.

The Hawk regarded him stonily. "Allegra is free to live wherever she chooses."

"Of course. But she's a celebrity now." His fever-bright gaze returned to me. "That's what you call it in the mortal world, isn't it? You're famous, and everyone wants to get to know you better. Including me." He grinned, his eyes dropping to my cleavage.

"You've had plenty of time to get to know me," I said,

resisting the urge to cross my arms over my breasts. "Nothing's changed."

I knew perfectly well that he disliked me as intensely as I disliked him. On the few occasions that he'd been forced to speak to me, he'd done it with a sneer that left me in no doubt of my status as the lowly changeling. Either this was his idea of a joke, or he could see some personal gain in cultivating me now that I had the king's favour.

"On the contrary, you are *vastly* more interesting these days. I feel sure we have much in common." Again, his eyes strayed, and the Hawk tensed.

"The lady is under my protection," the Hawk growled. If looks could kill, Jaxen would have been a hunk of dead meat on the grass.

"Ah." Jaxen's gaze darted between us, bright with interest. "My apologies, Sir Knight. I didn't realise you had a prior claim."

Feeling my cheeks flush with heat, I glanced at the Hawk, expecting him to explain that he had no claim on me. As if anyone did. They made me sound like a piece of baggage. But he only glared at Jaxen in silence. Before I could say anything, Eldric appeared at the top of one of the spiral staircases.

"Sir Hawk," he said, "and Allegra! To what do I owe the pleasure?"

Well, if he was pissed with me, at least he was hiding it well. But then, Eldric had always been a good actor.

Jaxen dropped his boots off the table and drained the last of his wine as he stood. He winked at me. "Well, it's

27

been nice chatting, but I'll leave you to my brother. If you change your mind, you know where to find me."

It would be a cold day in hell before I chose to spend any time with Jaxen. I watched him disappear through one of the archways, then turned my attention to Lord Eldric. He wore brown velvet, in the traditional style of trousers and tunic, with the leaf sigil of his house embroidered above his breast.

We both rose at his approach, but he waved us back into our seats. "I don't suppose my brother offered you anything? Other than wine, that is. We have coffee, or food if you haven't eaten." He glanced at Jaxen's empty wine glass, his face carefully expressionless, then pushed it aside as he sat down.

"Not for me," said the Hawk.

"I'm not hungry," I said, surprised to find it was true. I was usually ravenous after a gig, and I hadn't had anything to eat since we entered the Realms. "And I don't want to take up too much of your time."

"It's no trouble," Eldric said with a practised smile. He sat back, hooking one velvet-clad arm over the back of his chair. "The saviours of the king will always be welcome in Autumn."

"Thank you," said the Hawk. "But we are only looking for news of Allegra's mother."

"I went home this morning," I said, "but the cottage was abandoned. She obviously hasn't been there in months. Do you know where she is?"

He shook his head. "Sorry. I had no idea she'd gone. Livillia likes to keep to herself, you know."

Yes, I did know. "Have you seen her at all since ... since I left?" *Since I was unceremoniously booted out*, I might have said if I was talking to Willow or Sage. My bitterness wouldn't be well received here. It wasn't as if it was Eldric's fault, and I wanted his help.

He looked up at the branches of the ceiling as he thought. "Midsummer's Eve, perhaps? I think she was here for the ball."

Midsummer's Eve would have been nearly four months ago. It was one of the most important festivals in the fae calendar, and fae lords generally threw a big party for all those living in their domain, which was pretty much compulsory to attend. Judging by the state of her garden, she could easily have been gone since then.

"I know she was definitely here for the one before that, because Geltrin went into labour, and your mother took charge." He smiled at the memory.

That definitely sounded like my mother. I'd often suspected there must be some Earthcrafting blood back in her family line somewhere, because she had a way with herbal remedies that was second to none. Not that birth generally required herbal remedies, but if there was a medical emergency, it attracted my mother like a bee to nectar.

"So, last Midsummer's Eve—did she seem herself? Did she mention anything odd?"

"What kind of odd?"

"I don't know. I'm just trying to think of any reason she would leave. We don't have any other family ... It seems strange that she would take off like that."

"I'm sure there's no reason for you to be alarmed. We fae are long-lived. It's reasonable that we might seek a change of scenery now and again."

"I suppose so."

"Perhaps the cottage felt lonely without you there," the Hawk said.

"It was her own decision to send me away. No one forced her to."

"Have you never made a decision that you knew was right, but it still made you unhappy?" Eldric asked.

I stared at him, swallowing the words of protest that rose like lumps in my throat. Of course he would see it like that. The "right decision"—to discard a child like a used tissue, like one of those thoughtless people that bought a cute puppy for Christmas and then gave it to a shelter in March when they realised how big it was going to grow. How could that be the right decision? Only to a fae.

I looked down at the table's gleaming surface, swallowing my anger as best I could. "Could you ask your people if anyone knows anything?"

"Of course. Will you be staying in the cottage? You're welcome to a bed here at the Hall, if you wish."

I let out a deep breath. "No, I think I'll go home for now."

My mother's disappearance had knocked me for six. I'd known that a joyful reunion was unlikely, but still I'd hoped for something. An apology, maybe? Some kind of reason for what she'd done? Now, for the first time in years, the siren song of the Realms was quiet, buried under a weight of regret and hurt, and just a little stirring of fear. There was no way I should care what had happened to her after what she'd done to me, and yet, here I was, worrying that she was in trouble and I'd come too late to do anything to help her. The heart chooses who it will love, and logic plays no part.

It wasn't until I was back in the mortal world that I realised I'd thought of my borrowed bed in Willow's sith as "home".

A week later, Sage and Rowan were playing snooker in the back room of The Drunken Irishman, a fierce competition that took place most Friday nights if we didn't have a gig. According to Rowan, he was the master. That may have been true a year ago, when he'd taught Sage to play, but he was perilously close to being toppled from his throne. She was a quick learner.

"Nice shot," he said, as Sage sunk a red that had been sitting in an awkward spot behind the pink.

She didn't reply, too focused on her next shot. She was trying to sink the brown into the top corner pocket. From where I was sitting, nursing my beer, it looked pretty straightforward—a lot easier than the fluky shot with the red that she'd just pulled off. Yet the brown ball curved away from her cue and ended up nowhere near the corner.

She straightened, giving Rowan a suspicious glare.

He blinked at her, the picture of innocence. "That's a shame. You gave it too much spin."

"I didn't give it any spin. I hit the ball dead centre."

He bent over the table, lining up his next shot. He was only three points ahead of her, but now he had the chance to stretch his lead. Three balls dropped in quick succession, and Sage's face blackened as she came to sit at the table with me.

"He's cheating," she said.

With his fae hearing, he must have heard her, but he continued to sink balls as if nothing was wrong.

I grinned. "With magic, you mean?"

"Yep. That ball was right on course, and then it curved away for no reason."

Rowan stopped pretending he couldn't hear her. "Maybe you're just not as good as you think you are."

"And maybe you're a cheating scum." Her tone was mild, but I knew Rowan was in for a world of trouble. Sage was a yeller—it was only when she was truly pissed that she got all quiet and measured.

"It's just a game," I said, which was a complete waste of breath. Sage and Rowan were both too competitive to see any contest as "just" a game. Sage had dealt with her many losses as part of the price of learning to play, but now that she was actually getting good at it, her competitive streak was alive and well.

"Yeah, Sage. What she said. No need to get all riled up because I'm beating you."

I rolled my eyes. Now he was goading her, hoping she'd play badly because she was angry. "Rowan, don't be a dick. Even if you win, it won't be worth it. She'll make you pay."

"She won't win," he said, with a confidence that his next shot—a miss—didn't justify.

Sage took a swig of her drink and got up, a grim look on her face. "No more tricks, Rowan. I'm watching you."

"Aah, I'm so scared. The Dark Lord's daughter is *watching* me."

I covered my eyes with my hand. Now he was bringing her *father* into it? "Do you have a death wish, Rowan? 'Cause there are easier ways to die, let me tell you."

Someone sat down in the seat Sage had just vacated as I took my hand away again. I'd expected Rowan, but it was the Hawk.

I smiled at him, striving for nonchalance, though my heart had done a little backflip of excitement at the sight of him. "Hey, there. What are you doing here?"

"Watching someone die, apparently. What's the problem?"

"Rowan is cheating at snooker."

"Am not," Rowan said, without turning around.

We all watched Sage's next shot bounce off another ball and ricochet in an odd direction. She glared balefully at Rowan.

He held up his hands. "That wasn't me, I swear."

I glanced at the Hawk, who was staring at Rowan expressionlessly. If Rowan was using magic, the Hawk would have felt it. "Did he—?" I whispered.

The Hawk nodded, watching Rowan take his next shot. The ball looked like it was going in, but it was moving so slowly. In the end, it teetered on the edge of the hole but didn't fall.

A grin split Sage's face. "Move over, loser. Watch how the pros do it."

I glared at Rowan as she got ready to take the shot, shaking my head at him. He gave me an innocent *who, me?* look in return.

Sage's first ball travelled smoothly toward the pocket and dropped without incident. Maybe Rowan had decided not to misbehave in front of the Hawk. The knight did cut a rather menacing figure. Dressed all in black, he sat very still, watching the game like a predator stalking its prey.

Only three balls remained on the table, and the scores were too close to call it. If Sage could sink these last three, she would win, but if she missed her next shot, Rowan could still take the game. She lined up her next shot with more than usual care, all her focus on that blue ball. She hit the cue ball cleanly and the blue sailed toward the pocket she'd lined it up with—until it skipped, as if it had hit some tiny bit of debris on the table, and wobbled off course. I glanced sharply at Rowan.

Then Sage gasped, and I looked back at the ball to see it make a sharp left turn and head straight for the middle pocket. What the—?

Then it veered again, and my lips twitched as I finally realised what was going on. The Hawk had intervened. His face was stony as he watched the ball traverse the baize, but it corrected course again and fell obediently into the centre pocket.

Sage whooped with delight. Rowan gave the Hawk an uncertain look. The knight didn't look the type to play magical tug-of-war with Sage's ball, but he was the only one here with the power to do it.

Sage's next shot wandered all over the table as Rowan and the Hawk fought over the ball. Sage could hardly stop laughing.

"You should see your face," she said to Rowan, and then she turned to the Hawk. "Do I even need to line up the last one?"

A reluctant smile tugged at his lips. "Are you suggesting there is any other way to win?"

She grinned at him. "No, of course not."

The last ball visited every corner of the table, with Sage cheering it on, before it finally fell into a pocket.

"Now *that* was a game of snooker," Sage said. "Hey, loser, don't feel bad. Maybe next time I'll let you win."

"Maybe next time I'll make sure there are no powerful spectators," he muttered.

"Or you could try not cheating," the Hawk offered coolly.

"Or that," Rowan agreed cheerfully, not at all fazed by the knight's evident disapproval. "Can I buy you a drink?"

My phone rang while Rowan was taking drink orders. I didn't recognise the number. "Hello?"

"Allegra? It's Jamison."

Something about his voice sounded off. "Are you all right?"

"I need to see you. Can you come to the shop tonight?"

"Tonight?" This was weird. Jamison had never called me before. How did he even have my number? I occasionally ran into him at The Drunken Irishman, but mostly I only saw him at the pharmacy. Why on earth would he need me to go to the pharmacy now? "Is something wrong?"

"I don't want to talk like this. Come to the shop. Please."

There was such tension in his voice I couldn't help but say yes. He sounded desperate. "I'll be there in ten minutes."

I hung up and found the Hawk staring at me intently. "Trouble?"

"I don't know. That was kind of weird. Jamison wants to see me right now, but he wouldn't say why."

"Jamison? The pharmacist?"

"Yes." I stood up to leave, and he rose with me.

"I doubt it's about medication. I'll come with you."

"You don't have to do that."

He said nothing, merely followed me as I walked out to the main room and found Rowan and Sage at the bar. I tapped Sage on the shoulder. "Just got a strange phone call from Jamison. We're going over there to see what's wrong."

"I just ordered you a beer," Rowan said.

"You'll have to drink it for me."

"I can manage that."

"I'll drink the Hawk's whiskey," Sage offered. Such a selfless move.

"Thanks," he said drily.

"Maybe Jamison's just discovered he's been accidentally poisoning you all these years."

I rolled my eyes. "Yeah, maybe. Hopefully, this won't take long."

She shrugged. "You know where to find us. Otherwise, I'll see you at home."

Outside, a warm breeze was blowing, and the night was quiet after the noise of the pub. The Hawk and I were the only two people on the street, our footsteps the only sound. My mind worried at the problem of Jamison as we walked. The only real contact I had with him was on my regular visits to get my asthma medication, and there was no way he was demanding to see me so urgently over that. What other reason could there be? I was drawing a complete blank.

As long as it was nothing too serious, perhaps I'd use the opportunity to have him make up some more medicine for me. I would have had to drop in some time in the next few days anyway, as my supply was running low. It only took about three weeks for my inhaler to run out.

The Hawk seemed relaxed enough as he walked at my side. He was a puzzle—why had he come? Last time I'd seen him, he'd acted all possessive in front of Jaxen, but there was nothing loverlike about him now. Maybe that had just been a kindness, to stop Jaxen harassing me. He didn't speak, but then he wasn't like Sage—he didn't have to fill every moment of silence. Thoughts of Sage brought the snooker game to my mind.

"That was pretty funny, watching you and Rowan zigzag that ball all over the table."

"I'm glad it amused you." His tawny eyes rested thoughtfully on my face. "You seem tense."

"Just confused about what Jamison could possibly want."

"We'll know soon enough."

True. Already, we had reached the street where Jamison's Pharmacy was located, a long stretch of little shops, all dark at this time of night. Even the pharmacy was unlit, its sign flipped to "Closed". I banged on the glass door until Jamison emerged from the shadows at the back of the shop to let us in.

He opened the door, but blocked the entry with his body. "Sir Hawk, I wasn't expecting you."

The Hawk said nothing, merely gazing at him impassively.

"He was with me when you called," I explained.

"The world owes you a great debt for restoring the king to his throne," Jamison said to the Hawk, as if I hadn't spoken. "I'm truly grateful for what you have done, and hate to seem inhospitable, but ... this is a private matter."

The Hawk stared at him for a long moment. "I am her protector."

Really? This again? I glanced at him in surprise. "Jamison is hardly a threat."

The Hawk said nothing, continuing to stare down the little pharmacist. Jamison turned to me, desperation in his eyes. "Allegra, I'm sorry, but I must insist ..."

The whole situation was ludicrous. The Hawk was twice Jamison's size; if he wanted to, he could walk through Jamison as if he wasn't even there. Jamison was tiny. What could possibly be so private that the pharmacist was prepared to stand up to the most famous Knight of the Realms?

And why in all the thirteen Realms had the Hawk

suddenly decided to appoint himself my protector? The only person I needed protecting from right now was him.

I laid a hand on his arm. "Kyrrim, it's all right. Jamison is a friend."

"So was Edgar, and he tried to kill you."

"It wasn't like that, and you know it."

He continued to favour me with that hard stare. "You're not Robinson Crusoe, either. You need back-up."

I looked back at Jamison, tempted to tell him I'd come back tomorrow if this was such a problem, but I noticed a bead of sweat running down the side of his face.

It wasn't a hot night. The man was terrified.

"Okay, this is getting ridiculous. Jamison, let us into the shop, at least. Maybe the Hawk will consent to wait in the shop while we go into your sith."

He stopped in front of the door, giving the Hawk another anxious look.

The knight looked at my pleading expression and sighed. "Very well. I will wait here." He favoured Jamison with a stern look. "But leave the door ajar. If I hear anything untoward, I will come in."

Jamison pushed the door almost shut behind us, blocking the Hawk's view. "This way," he said.

Jamison's sith was nowhere near as big as Willow's, and reminded me very much of my childhood home. It had the same timbered walls, the same rough stone fireplace, and a view of wild greenery out the windows that echoed the forests of Autumn.

What was different about it was the shelf after shelf of

jars and bottles filled with the ingredients of the apothecary's trade. But these were not the sterile pill bottles of the shop outside; these contained everything from frog legs to unidentifiable organs, and every manner of dried and fresh greenery. Many of the herbs were familiar to me, though some I only knew from books, being rare even in the fabulous lands of the Realms.

I followed him across the room to a closed door. I had never been through it before, despite the many times I had sat in this room watching Jamison work, but I knew it led to his bedroom. This was getting weirder by the moment.

The room was plainly furnished, containing a bookshelf, a chest of drawers, a striped rug, and a bed. It smelled of blood and vomit.

Shockingly, a woman lay in the bed. I had never seen her before, but she looked terrible, racked by some disease. Her lips were blue, and her breath came in quick little gasps, her head moving restlessly on the pillow. Once she had no doubt been beautiful—the bones of her thin face were very fine, but her eyes were now deeply sunken, and her skin had a terrible pallor. Her long hair, straggling limply across the pillow, was as black as Raven's, but damp with sweat.

I stared at Jamison in confusion. He was looking at me as though there was something significant about the woman in the bed.

"I don't understand," I said. "Why did you bring me here?"

"I'm afraid she might not last the night—there's nothing

more I can do for her." He sighed, and the sound was wrenched from somewhere deep in his soul. "I thought you would want to see her."

This was making less and less sense. I glanced back toward the shop, wondering uneasily if Jamison had lost his mind. Should I call in the Hawk?

"Why?" I asked. "Who is she?"

He drew a shaky breath. "Your mother."

5

I must have cried out, though I don't remember. All I was aware of was the Hawk bursting into the room, his sword drawn. Jamison made a sound of distress as the Hawk took in the scene, his eyes roving over the woman in the bed, searching the room for danger before slowly sheathing Ecfirrith.

"What is going on?" he asked.

I wished I knew. I had never seen that woman before in my life. "Jamison said ... he said ..."

I trailed off, beyond confused, and the Hawk turned to the cowering pharmacist.

"Yes?" he ground out between his teeth. "What did you say to her?"

"Sir Hawk, no need for you to concern yourself. Please, wait outside. This is a pri—"

"If you tell me again this is a private matter, they will be the last words you ever speak."

Jamison shut up. The silky menace in the Hawk's voice

even intimidated *me*, and I wasn't the target of that icy stare.

I blew out a shaky breath. "Let's all calm down."

The woman in the bed moaned, and my eyes were drawn unwillingly to her unfamiliar face. She looked like she was in a lot of pain.

I lowered my voice. "Maybe we should talk somewhere else, so we don't disturb her."

Jamison nodded, and led the way back out into the main room, where I sank into a chair at his kitchen table with a grateful sigh. My whole body was tense, and I made an effort to relax my taut muscles, taking several deep breaths. There was no point getting upset; this was just some bizarre misunderstanding. Though how Jamison could confuse that stranger with the golden-haired Livillia, I had no idea. The Hawk remained standing, watching Jamison as if he expected him to produce a weapon out of nowhere.

Jamison brought three glasses and a bottle of whiskey to the table. He poured us all a generous glass full with a slightly shaky hand. He was being very careful not to meet the Hawk's gaze again. He gave me a glass and placed another for the Hawk at the seat opposite me, before taking his own seat at the head of the table. The Hawk didn't sit or touch the glass, and, after waiting a moment, Jamison took a long swig from his drink, as if fortifying himself.

I watched him, waiting for him to speak, but he stared down into his glass. We seemed to be playing a game where the first one to speak lost.

I broke first. "Why did you say that woman was my mother? I know you've met Livillia. That isn't her."

In fact, the one time I'd seen them together, I'd had the impression, from the easy way they chatted, that they knew each other quite well. That had been the day my mother had abandoned me. I'd been so excited for my first trip to the mortal world—I still remembered my amazement at my first sight of cars. Even then, astonished at the noise and smell of the city, I'd been intrigued by those gleaming machines. I'd been almost disappointed when we'd entered Jamison's sith, delightful as it was, and found myself back in a place so much like home. Once the greetings and small talk were over, I'd wandered out into Jamison's garden to check out his herbs while he and my mother chatted.

It wasn't long after that that he'd come out to find me and broken the news that my mother was gone, and she was never coming back.

He looked up now, sadness in his grey eyes. Sadness and … something else. He glanced at the Hawk again. Was that fear? Why should he be afraid of the Hawk? Admittedly, the Hawk was doing a very good line in menacing, but he was a Knight of the Realms, not a criminal. He wouldn't really harm Jamison, not without a good reason. The pharmacist surely knew that.

Seeming to come to a decision, Jamison reached out and covered my hand with one of his own. His skin was crazed with tiny wrinkles, and the veins bulged purple. It was the hand of an old man, browned from a long life spent gathering rare herbs and working in his gardens. "There was a time when I knew Livillia well, though that was not her name then. She came to my shop just as we were closing tonight, begging for my help, and I knew her at once, though it has been many long years since I last saw her in this form, and she is grievously changed. Her real name is Anawen, and the form you saw in there is her real one. The face you grew up with was nothing more than Illusion."

The Hawk stiffened in surprise, but it took me a lot longer to catch his meaning.

"This Anawen is from Illusion?" the Hawk asked.

Jamison nodded, not meeting his eyes. With a screech of wood on wood, the Hawk pulled out a chair and joined us at the table, though he didn't touch the whiskey in front of him.

"But ..." I was still floundering. None of this made any sense.

"She escaped the slaughter the night Summer attacked Illusion," Jamison continued, "and fled to Autumn. She had to disguise herself to stay hidden from Summer's assassins. They were determined to wipe out Illusion completely."

"But ..." I said again, trying to gather my scattered thoughts. "But everyone in Autumn knew Livillia. She may not have been the most sociable person, but there were people there who'd known her since she was a child. She'd been living there for years, long before the king disappeared and Summer started its crusade against Illusion. She wasn't from Illusion; she was Autumn-born and bred."

Jamison sighed, and patted my hand almost apologetically. "Yes, the real Livillia was born in Autumn, before the Night of Swords, as you say. Your mother stole her identity when she fled the swords of Summer."

"Stole her identity?" I repeated. "That's ridiculous. No one would let someone else walk in and take over their life."

"No. They wouldn't."

"You're saying that she *killed* this woman? No." I shook my head vehemently. "My mother wasn't a killer. But even if she was, how could she get away with something like that? The woman's family and friends would have noticed if she suddenly started behaving strangely, or couldn't remember their names."

But even as I said it, I remembered that my mother—or Livillia, if they were not, in fact, the same person—had had no family. And my mother had kept social interactions to the barest minimum. So *maybe* someone could have gotten away with killing Livillia and taking her place, but that was where my willingness to suspend disbelief came up against a brick wall. My mother was no murderer, whatever her failings as a parent.

I stared at Jamison, my mind awhirl.

The Hawk stepped into the silence. "What proof do you have that any of this is true? How do you know all this? And why would this woman come to you now?"

"Because she doesn't want to die, I assume," Jamison snapped.

He was clearly stung by the Hawk's implication that he was lying, but it was a fair question. The story was so far-fetched. Even though I liked Jamison, I found it difficult to swallow. What was that thing the mortals talked about? Occam's Razor? Meaning that usually the simplest explanation was the correct one?

I could believe that my mother was who she said she was,

47

Livillia of Autumn, and that the face I had known was her true face—or I could accept Jamison's story that she was really a fugitive from Illusion called Anawen, who had killed Livillia and taken her place. And I was further expected to believe that no one would have noticed this deception in more than twenty years.

Indeed, how did I even know that this woman lying in Jamison's bed was this Anawen person at all? My head was spinning.

"Allegra," Jamison said. "I know this is hard for you to believe, but ask yourself—what reason would I have to lie to you? My only concern was that you should have a chance to say goodbye to your mother, if it comes to that." He hesitated, as if he would have liked to say more, but one glance at the Hawk's stony face silenced him.

"Do you mean that it might not come to that?" I asked, seizing on the faint hope his words offered. I was so confused—I simply couldn't believe this woman was my mother, but I was still afraid she would die.

He sighed. "I have sent a message, asking Yriell to come, but I am afraid that this may be beyond even her skills."

Yriell. That was good. She was the most powerful fae I'd ever met, and she probably knew more about healing than any mortal doctor. Even Jamison's knowledge and experience paled beside hers.

"Will Yriell be able to confirm your story?" the Hawk asked.

Jamison stiffened. "I don't think she knows Anawen, but I could be wrong."

The Hawk grunted. Clearly, he wasn't buying Jamison's story, and found it convenient that it couldn't be confirmed. I, on the other hand, looked at Jamison's affronted body language and felt my heart sink. He was trying to do me a favour, and finding nothing but disbelief and hostility for his trouble. That unconscious stiffening of his posture did more to convince me of the truth of his story than anything he could say.

Impulsively, I jumped up. "Let me see her again." If that was really my mother in there, unbelievable as that seemed, I didn't want her to suffer alone.

"She's not coherent," Jamison warned, but I was already walking towards the bedroom. He rose, too, at a sharp rap on the outer door. "That's probably Yriell."

He hurried out to let her in, and I paused, waiting for her. She swept into the room like a tiny, fierce whirlwind, carrying a bag from which green stems poked. A twig was caught in her long, grey hair, but that was pretty standard for her. She loved the earth and everything that grew in it, and had absolutely no personal vanity.

She nodded to us, but kept walking, making a beeline for the bedroom door. To Jamison, she said, "All right, let's see how badly you've cocked this up."

She opened the door and we all crowded in behind her. The woman in the bed looked even worse than before, if that was possible. There was blood on the pillow, and a line of it trailed from the corner of her mouth.

"Shit," Yriell said, setting her bag down by the bed. Then she seemed to notice the rest of us. "Lady's tits, give a woman some room to work, can't you? Out!" She made shooing motions and we all began to leave. "Not you, girl. You'd better stay."

The Hawk and Jamison went out, closing the door behind them. Apparently, Yriell was a safe enough person for me to be alone with. I would really have to get to the bottom of this strange new protectiveness on the knight's part, but it would have to wait.

I watched while Yriell examined the woman, opening her mouth to check inside, listening to her heart. The woman stirred, and more blood leaked from her mouth, which Yriell wiped away with calm efficiency.

"Jamison said this is my mother," I said as she inspected the woman's fingernails, which were as blue as her lips.

Yriell gave me an impatient glance. "Well, is she? You know what your own mother looks like, don't you?"

"Not like this. He said she's from Illusion, and that this is her real face."

"Ah." Her face softened into an expression of concern. "Do you believe him?"

"I don't know." I stared miserably at the woman—at Anawen. Whether or not she was my mother, she still had a name.

More blood appeared on her lips, and she started to retch. Suddenly, there was blood everywhere—on the sheets, the pillow, all over Anawen's face and neck. Blood spewed onto Yriell's hands as she turned the woman onto her side, helping support her while she vomited blood everywhere.

I was afraid she would die right then and there. There was so much blood. She gasped and choked, fighting to breathe as her body tried to eject every last drop of her blood through her mouth. At last, the torrent paused. Anawen was deathly pale as Yriell lowered her back onto the pillows.

"Get something to clean this up," Yriell barked, and I moved to obey.

Anawen's eyes fluttered open and fixed on me. "Leggy," she breathed, then her eyes rolled back in her head.

I stood transfixed, unable to move.

"What's the matter with you, girl? Get some towels in here."

"She called me Leggy. My mother used to call me that when I was little."

Yriell snorted, but it wasn't an amused sound. "I guess that answers that question, then."

6

I left the room in a daze. I couldn't believe it. That woman was really my mother?

"What's wrong?" the Hawk asked, as I closed the bedroom door.

"We need towels."

"No. What's wrong with *you*? You look unwell."

"I'm ..."

I burst into tears. Jamison, who'd been about to hand me a pile of clean towels, took them into the bedroom instead and shut the door behind him. The Hawk shoved me into a chair and insisted I swallow two glasses of whiskey. Since he seemed determined to pour whiskey down my throat until I stopped crying, I pulled myself together before I was too drunk to walk.

"She's your mother, isn't she?" There was compassion in his clear golden eyes.

"Yes. No. Shit." I buried my face in my hands. "I think so, but I'm not sure."

We sat in silence until the door opened again, and Jamison peeked out. "You'd better get in here."

I leapt up. The Hawk followed me in, but Yriell made no complaint this time. Anawen had been cleaned up as much as possible. A towel covered the worst of the bloodstains on the sheets and her clothes. She was so pale her whole face had a bluish cast, not just her lips, as if her skin had become translucent and we could see through to the veins beneath. She lay perfectly still, no longer tossing restlessly.

"She won't wake up again. Nothing I can do for her, I'm afraid." There was a smear of blood on Yriell's face that, added to the twigs in her hair, gave her the appearance of a madwoman. But her eyes were full of sympathy as she delivered the news in her usual blunt manner. "It looks like iron poisoning, and she's too far gone."

Iron poisoning? Automatically, my eyes went to Anawen's neck, searching for an iron ward. All fae wore them in the mortal world, to protect them from the lethal effects of iron, which was poisonous to magic. There wasn't one, but she wore a plain silver ring.

"Isn't that an iron ward?" I asked, indicating the ring. I didn't have the ability to sense Charms that fae had, but I knew that any kind of silver jewellery could function as an iron ward.

Yriell shrugged. "That's why I said it *looks like* iron poisoning. The symptoms are classic, yet the ward is functioning. She should be fine, but clearly, she's not." She made a frustrated noise. "A working ward will protect from exposure to the iron-laden atmosphere the humans call home. The only way to cause this much damage is to introduce iron directly into the body, but there are no stab wounds or other marks on her."

"I don't understand."

"That makes two of us, then."

"She only arrived in the mortal world a few hours ago," Jamison added. "But she was already like this."

"So somehow someone poisoned her deliberately," the Hawk said. "While she was still in the Realms."

"That's what it looks like," Yriell agreed.

I stared down at the stranger on the bed, still feeling as though the world were oddly out of alignment. My brain told me that she must be my mother, but my heart couldn't accept it. My mother's hair was a beautiful shade of honey-gold, not black, and her face was rounder than the ravaged features of this Anawen. I couldn't even remember what colour Anawen's eyes were—I'd only seen them open for a brief moment—but I'd have known if they were the clear blue of Livillia's. I'd spent more time with Livillia in my brief life than I had with anyone else, and I knew every angle of her face, every expression. This was not her.

The woman's breathing, which had been so rapid before, now barely stirred her chest. Even as I watched, the intervals between breaths stretched longer and longer, until I was holding my own breath, willing her chest to rise again. No one spoke; everyone in the room focused on the dying woman, keeping the death watch.

Finally, Yriell let out a gusty sigh. "She's gone."

Curiously, this time, I didn't cry. The Hawk's hand rested on my back, offering wordless comfort, but I turned and left the room. I didn't know what I felt, but I couldn't bear to be in that close room anymore, trapped with the smell of sickness and death. The men followed me out, and Yriell appeared a short time later, carrying her bag again, all its contents now carefully packed away.

"I'm drier than a pub with no beer," she said, and Jamison took the hint, pouring her a big glass of whiskey. She downed it in one gulp and sagged into the chair next to the Hawk. "This is a bad business."

Jamison looked up from a bitter contemplation of his own glass. "I thought once the king returned, the vendetta against Illusion would end."

The Hawk's gaze sharpened. "You think that's what this was?"

"What else would it be? How could a woman who lived alone, who barely ever saw another person, have any personal enemies? She was killed simply because of where she was born."

"If she killed to establish her identity in Autumn, I imagine she might quite easily have earned some enemies. If any of the real Livillia's friends ever found out what she'd done, they might well have wanted to kill her."

"After all this time?" Jamison was clearly sceptical. "If she was going to be discovered, it would have happened long ago. No, I see Summer's murderous hand in this."

I felt too numb to have much interest in the conversation, but Jamison's bitterness was so deep it managed to penetrate the fog surrounding me. "Why do you care so much? How do you know her?"

"We met long ago," he said, his eyes sliding away from mine.

That sounded like Jamison himself was from Illusion. There was no point asking him; admitting you were from Illusion these days was a quick way to commit suicide. Although, as Jamison said, that should have ended now that the king had been recovered and it was clear to everyone that Illusion hadn't killed him after all. Perhaps hunting down refugees from the lost Realm had become too much of a way of life in Summer to give it up so easily.

"If this is true, the king must hear of it," the Hawk said.

Yriell snorted. "I doubt Rothbold's got the time to spare from sorting out the snakes' nest in the palace to be bothered about some poor woman getting offed by Summer."

"His Majesty was horrified when he heard what Summer had done to Illusion. The Lord of Illusion was one of his dearest friends."

"And the Lord of Summer is his brother-in-law. Kellith has been running the place in all but name since Rothbold disappeared. He's not going to give that up without a fight. Half the staff has been replaced by Kellith's cronies. Rothbold would be a fool to antagonise Summer until he's had a chance to consolidate. If he's not careful he'll have himself another 'accident' and disappear, only this time no one will ever find the body."

I wandered into the dining room the next morning, coffee already in hand, looking like an extra from *The Walking Dead*. Kel looked up from licking his balls to favour me with a hostile glare, then returned to his task with gusto. Who knew that ball-licking required such dedication? The ginger cat had belonged to my old friend Edgar. Ex-friend? What did you call it when a good friend betrayed you? I still had very confused feelings about that, but it hadn't seemed right to leave Kel to fend for himself after Edgar died. So, even though I wasn't a cat person in general, or a Kel fan in particular, I'd taken him in until I could figure out what to do with him.

"Look what the cat dragged in," Willow said. She was flicking through a magazine. A shaft of sunlight lit her copper hair like flames. "Better than dismembered bird corpses, I guess. Your arsehole cat left one on my bedroom floor this morning."

"Really?" I glared at Kel, who only licked louder and pointedly ignored us both. "He did that to me last week. What happened to the bell I put on his collar?"

"He must have managed to get it off. I swear he was a serial killer in a past life." She shrugged. "Did you hear that Jen is pregnant with Brad's secret love child?"

I glanced at the headlines as I dropped into the chair opposite. "Really? Isn't that, like, the third time this year?"

"Some things never get old," Sage said, walking into the room in a bikini top and shorts. "You guys want to come to the beach with me and Rowan?"

"No, thanks."

"Hey, what did Jamison want?"

I sighed so deeply that Willow looked up from the Hollywood gossip and examined me more carefully. "You really do look like shit, you know. Is something wrong?"

Sensing a story, Sage took a seat at the end of the table, the three of us forming a cosy little triangle. They both waited expectantly.

"You could say that."

"Did you have a fight with your knight errant?" Sage asked.

"He's not *my* knight errant."

"No? Then why is he hanging around?"

"He says he's my protector."

Willow and Sage exchanged significant looks, wearing identical grins.

"Exactly what is he protecting you from?" Willow asked.

"I don't know. I didn't get a chance to ask him. We went to Jamison's and there was this woman there. A dying woman."

My voice wobbled a little on the word *dying*, and the grins died, their expressions shifting to serious and attentive.

"Shit," Sage said. "Who was it?"

I took a deep breath, staring down into my coffee cup. "Jamison said she was my mother."

"Wait, wait, wait." Willow held up her hands imperiously. "Jamison *said*? What the hell does that mean?"

"*Was* it Livillia?" Sage asked.

"I don't know."

For once, neither of them interrupted as I told the whole story.

"Holy Toledo, Batman," Willow said when I'd finished. Sage didn't even comment on the new slang, which showed how distracted she was. "That's one hell of a story. Do you think it was Livillia?"

"I don't know."

"But if she called you Leggy ..." Sage said.

"Maybe I misheard what she said." That sounded lame, even to me, but the whole thing was so hard to accept. My mother, a refugee from Illusion?

"Did you have any idea that your mother might not have been from Autumn?" Willow asked. "Did she ever do anything odd?"

"Odd like what?"

"I don't know. I've never met anyone from Illusion."

We were all so young as fae measured time, Illusion had been no more than a scandalised whisper or an object lesson by the time we were old enough to understand what had happened.

"She did go away sometimes."

"Go away where?"

"I don't know. She would never say. She'd just head off in the morning and I wouldn't see her again until dinner time. Then she'd act like nothing had happened, and ask me about my day like she always did. But she never told me anything about hers." In the end, I'd given up asking, and had just accepted that my mother had an extreme need for solitude.

"Maybe she had a lover," Sage said. "How often did she do this?"

"Not often. Two or three times a year."

"Not much of a love affair, then." Willow closed her magazine and cast it aside. "Sounds like you need to pay another visit to Autumn and see if Eldric has turned up anything yet. Let's assume it wasn't your mother and take it from there."

Maybe I was in denial and clutching at straws—and maybe I'd misheard a dying woman and was stressing unnecessarily. In the cold light of day, it was harder to believe she had really been my mother, but I was sick with the uncertainty. I had to do something to be sure. Livillia had never been close with anyone in Autumn, but surely *someone* must know something. I wasn't ready to believe she was dead until I'd searched everywhere I could.

"Sounds like a plan," I said.

"Do you want me to come with you?" Willow asked.

Sage went still, and I blinked in surprise. Willow had sworn not to return to the Realms until Sage was as welcome in Spring as she was herself. So far, her parents hadn't buckled, and neither had Willow herself. Offering to come with me was a major concession for her. I glanced at Sage, but her face was unreadable.

"Thank you. That's really sweet. But, no. I'll be fine." I made an effort to smile. "I'm the hero of the hour, according to the Hawk. Got my new access-all-areas pass, courtesy of the king."

"I'd come with you if I could," Sage said, her dark eyes fierce.

"I know you would. You guys are the best." The best

friends I'd ever had. I didn't know what I'd done to deserve them, but I was grateful all over again that they'd taken me under their wings when I first arrived, a scared and lonely teenager. I couldn't imagine life without them now.

"Drink your coffee before it gets cold," Willow said. "You're getting mushy."

7

For the second time in as many days, I walked the Greenways of the Wilds. This time, I was alone, but every time I heard a noise in the forest, I reminded myself sternly that my new magic was strong enough to guide me safely through, and nothing could harm me as long as I stayed on the path. My inner voice sounded a lot like the Hawk's.

I kind of wished he was here, despite his on-again, off-again behaviour, but I could hardly ask him to come with me to Autumn again. He wasn't a babysitter, whatever he said about being my protector. And what was with that? Probably just a sense of duty. He'd been acting as if that kiss hadn't happened, but one angry kiss wasn't enough to build a relationship on, anyway. Obviously, I'd misread the signals and he'd thought better of taking our relationship any further.

Company would have been nice, though. I'd decided to check the cottage again before I pestered Eldric, in case there was something I'd missed. A wave of sadness washed over me as I walked up through the trees to the front door and, for a moment, I regretted not taking Willow up on her offer. The signs of neglect were even more poignant today in the full glare of the midday sun. My mother might not ever be coming back to weed those gardens or sweep the cobwebs down from the eaves.

Inside, everything was mostly clean, though grime dulled the view through the windows. It was odd, as though someone had swept and dusted here quite recently, though the outsides showed evidence of months of neglect. But my mother would never have let her beloved gardens get into such a state if she was here.

What was I even looking for? A note, saying where she was going? There was no one to leave a note for—she had no reason to think that I would ever return to this place. Nevertheless, I went carefully through every drawer in her bedroom, the familiar lavender scent of her filling my nostrils as I turned over the few clothes she'd left behind.

Nothing. But why leave these behind if she was leaving for such a long trip? It just wasn't adding up.

I walked out into the garden. The earth smelled fresh and new, as if it had rained just before I arrived, though the sky was as blue as a summer's day overhead, without a cloud in sight. Bees droned among the climbing roses, which had grown leggy and tall, their blowsy pink heads nodding against the front windows of the cottage.

Around the side of the house, the vegetable beds were in no better state than the flowerbeds at the front had been, overgrown with weeds. A few beans still straggled up a trellis, but their size showed how little water they'd been getting. In the herb garden, the story was the same. Here the mint and parsley had overrun the less hardy herbs. Where once there had been segmented rows, each herb in its allotted place, now there was only chaos. Nothing trumpeted my mother's absence more than this. It was she who had taught me all I knew of herb craft. I had sometimes thought her herbs were more her children than I was. She certainly lavished them with enough attention.

The door of our chicken coop was open wide, and the weeds growing up around it showed how long it had stood that way. The inhabitants, of course, were long gone.

I sat down on the grass, discouraged. What should I do now? There seemed no alternative—I'd have to go back to Eldric's Hall and hope he had some answers for me. Surely someone would know something? Because I was stumped.

And in the back of my mind, the thought that I was trying to push away kept whispering. There were no clues, because she was dead. Had died in front of me last night, covered in her own blood in Jamison's bed.

Abruptly, I stood up. No, Jamison was lying, for some bizarre reason of his own. That woman hadn't been my mother. Turning, my eye fell on the pine that had given me childhood nightmares.

I stopped. Something felt different, but it took a long moment before I realised what it was. That feeling of creeping menace, that shiver down my spine that urged me to look away lest I see something peering at me from the shelter of the gnarled branches—that fear was gone. The sun was out, warming my shoulders, filtering through the needles of a perfectly ordinary tree.

I took a step toward it. Nothing. I would have dismissed my fears as those of a child, but I'd felt the same creeping dread last time I'd been here with the Hawk, glad as ever to turn away from the fear the tree represented. And now it was gone.

Well, that wasn't suspicious at all. I sighed and walked toward the tree. My shoulders were hunched, but that was only memories, not anything I was feeling right now. The needles of the tree were long and soft as I brushed my hand over them.

There must have been an Aversion on this tree. It was the only way to explain the strength of the feelings I'd had before. And its sudden disappearance meant ...

Enchantments died with their creator. I closed my eyes for a moment, following that thought to its inevitable conclusion. The most likely person to cast an Aversion here, so near to our home, was my mother. And if she had died between my last visit and this one, her Aversions would be gone. This tree would be just a tree, and not a symbol of childhood terrors.

A crushing weight descended on me, and my heart began to beat wildly. Was it true? Was she really dead? A strong scent of pine tickled my nostrils, and I opened my eyes. I had crushed a handful of the needles, and now my palm was sticky with the residue.

But why put an Aversion on this tree? What was

different about this section of the forest that she wanted to keep people away? I pushed past the tree and found myself on a path that I'd never known was here. It was so overgrown that another might not have realised it had once been a path, but I'd spent my whole life in these woods, and I could see the faint signs. It must have been used quite regularly, years ago, for even these traces to remain.

After only a moment's walk, I found myself in a small, sunlit clearing carpeted in tiny pink flowers. It was so pretty. Why on earth had my mother wanted to hide this?

The flowers brushed against my knees as I waded through them, examining the clearing curiously. It was only a few paces wide. Most of the day, it would be shaded by the surrounding trees. It was only now, with the sun nearly overhead, that the light played on the dancing flower heads. I would have loved a private place like this, to come and read, or to lie back and watch the clouds pass overhead. Was that why my mother had hidden it? Because she wanted such a place, where she could escape from the demands of daily life? Had I been the only person she'd been hiding it from—her sometimes too-loud mortal child? That hurt.

The ground was disturbed at one side of the clearing, the flowers crushed and broken. Something had been digging between two pines that guarded the edge of the clearing. A wild pig, judging by the tracks it had left in the freshly turned earth. Perhaps there were truffles here.

Moving closer, I realised the animal had dug down quite deep, perhaps the length of my forearm in one place. And only recently, too. A worm wiggled through the freshly turned earth as I watched. My coming must have disturbed the pig. I glanced around, scenting the air. I had no wish to meet a wild pig. Even the sows could be nasty, but the boars were something else. Examining the tracks more closely, I realised the prints were too small to be those of a full-grown animal. That was a relief, at least.

My mother would never have tolerated wild pigs so close to her home, which was more proof, if I'd needed any, of how long she must have been gone, for them to unlearn years of caution around her.

I leaned closer, my eye caught by a glint of something at the bottom of the pig's hole. Something pale and honey-gold shone amid the dirt like buried treasure. I knelt among the crushed flowers and scraped away the soil, a terrible dread rising inside me.

It was hair. I swallowed hard and sat back on my heels as if I'd been pushed. Then immediately knelt forward and began to dig in a frenzy. It was hair, and it was the exact shade of my mother's.

Soil flew as I scrabbled in the dirt among the tree roots. More of the soft pink flowers were ripped from the ground, scattered across the clearing. My mind frozen with horror, all I could do was dig. My nails tore and shredded, but I ignored the pain. I had to know.

At last, I let out a shaky breath and stopped, leaning on my hands, head hanging. Crouched over the hole I'd made, I shuddered and shook with reaction. The hair was still soft and lush, but the head it was barely attached to was little more than a skull. This body had been here a long, long time. It wasn't my mother.

And yet ...

I went back to the cottage for a proper shovel, and worked for an hour, gradually uncovering the whole body. There was no telling now how old she'd been. She wore a long dress in a faded blue, with an apron around her waist. The apron had several handy pockets. I knew they were handy, because my mother had had an apron just like it. It was still hanging in her closet. Those pockets could carry eggs, freshly plucked from the straw beneath our hens, or pegs, or scissors and thread—all manner of things. She'd worn it almost every day as she went about her chores.

I stared down at the dead woman, my mind churning. Who was this woman, and why was she buried here? And why had her grave been hidden behind such a strong Aversion? I had to assume my mother had laid the Aversion—who else could it have been? Which made it horribly likely that it was also my mother who had put this woman in her grave.

I sank down on the ground, covered in dirt and sweat. The sun had moved, and the little clearing lay in welcome shade. Why had she hidden this grave? There could only be one answer to that, surely—because she had killed its occupant. I couldn't stop looking at that golden hair. Every time I looked away, my eyes slid straight back to it. I'd spent my whole life looking at that hair. Coiled in a braid around my mother's head, hanging in a long plait down her back, fanned across her pillow in the mornings when I was still young enough to sneak into her bed for a cuddle.

But that wasn't my mother lying in the shallow grave. This body had been here far too long. I was no forensics expert, but I was willing to bet it had lain here since the fall of Illusion, or a little after it.

Jamison hadn't been lying. My mother *was* from Illusion. She was a dark-haired woman called Anawen, and she had killed the real Livillia in order to steal her identity, honey-gold hair and all. All my life, I'd been living with a liar. A killer.

I lay back among the flowers and stared at the sky, unseeing. My hands throbbed from the unaccustomed digging, but I barely noticed the pain. My heart didn't know what to feel. Sorrow that my mother really was dead? Horror at what she'd been, what she'd done? Was it wrong to miss the woman I'd thought she'd been, or just stupid? I wondered if the woman in the grave had befriended her, perhaps taken in a frightened refugee, only to have her kindness repaid with death. Or had Anawen just knifed her in the back one day, emerging from the forest like a wild animal, and Livillia had never known what hit her?

The sky above me was darkening to deep, dark blue by the time it occurred to me that I should rebury Livillia's body. Anawen hadn't buried her deep enough, relying on her Aversion to keep everyone away, which was why the pigs had uncovered her once the Aversion died. Probably, she had been too afraid of being caught to take the time necessary to dig a deep enough grave.

I removed the body from the ground, laying the poor bones in the middle of the pink flowers, then took up my shovel again. It was hard, back-breaking work, but I kept at it. I owed the real Livillia this much at least, for the home she had unwittingly provided for me. Had she loved her little cottage as much as I had? Best not to think too much about it, though it was hard to turn my mind to anything else. Guilt ate at me, though I had never laid a finger on her. I knew I wasn't responsible for my mother's actions, but that didn't make me feel any better.

Grimly, I dug on as the day faded through twilight into full night. The pink flowers closed with the last of the light, hiding their faces from the moon, and crickets began to chirp in the forest around me. It was probably three or four hours before I considered the grave deep enough to keep Livillia safe from pigs or other scavengers. At least my mother had picked a place without too many tree roots, and the ground was soft, dark soil, not rock or hard clay.

By the time I'd laid the body in the grave and covered her over again, the blisters on my hands had burst and blood and other fluids stuck my hands to the shovel. In spite of the pain, I felt a sense of satisfaction as I tamped down the last shovelful of dirt. There would be no hiding that a body was buried here, but who would come here to notice?

Still, as I carried the shovel back to the cottage, I couldn't help a feeling of uneasiness. Somewhere in all the digging, my emotions had calmed. Anawen may have been a killer, but she was still my mother. I could mourn them both—the real Livillia and the fake one. But what to do with this new information I had? Did I really want to announce to the world at large what my mother had done, all those years ago? Was there any connection between that long-ago murder and my mother's death? I would have been happier if I'd had the power to cast an Aversion of my own over the little clearing—I needed to think carefully about this before I told anyone. Once again, I wished the Hawk had been with me. He would have known the best thing to do. As it was, I'd just have to rely on the grave's remoteness to keep my mother's secret.

Once I'd put the shovel away, I drew water from the well. Its chill eased the pain in my hands, and I took my time washing the dirt off. Pity there was no such easy way to remove the ache from my heart, or from my back and shoulders. I was pretty fit, but not grave-digging fit. That had uncovered a whole new set of muscles that were making themselves known in unpleasant ways. City life had made me soft.

I hadn't bothered lighting a lamp; I could see well enough in the dark, and besides, I didn't really want to advertise my presence here. So I nearly jumped out of my skin when a shadow separated from the darkness underneath the trees and stepped into the yard.

"Who's there?" I stood up straight, suddenly alert, water dripping from my face and running down my arms.

"It's me." The figure moved closer, and I saw it was Jaxen.

8

"What are you doing here?" It was late; I didn't know what time exactly, but it had been dark for several hours. I felt suddenly vulnerable, standing in the middle of the yard alone, surrounded by empty forest, in a way I hadn't when I'd been the only one here.

"I could ask you the same thing." He stopped on the other side of the well, close enough for me to see him clearly, but still far enough way that the feeling of threat began to ease, and my heart stopped trying to pound its way out of my chest. "I came to look for Livillia."

"I told your brother two days ago that she was gone. There's no point looking here for her; she hasn't been here in a long while." And I didn't want him poking around, perhaps coming across the grave.

"Then what are you doing here? Gardening?" He looked around at the dismal jungles of weed that had once been orderly flowerbeds. "It's a strange time of day for it."

"I have the freedom of the Realms. I can go where I like."

"And so can Livillia," he pointed out. "She's a grown woman. What makes you think there's something wrong? She might have decided to move to another Realm. She might have fallen hopelessly in love with some lucky fae and gone to live with him. I admit, it seems a little unlikely, given our Livillia's disdain for company, but stranger things have happened."

He wandered around the well, coming a little closer, making me wish I hadn't been so quick to put the shovel away.

"She wouldn't leave this place. She loved it here."

Only she had, of course, and got herself killed in the process. But I wasn't going to tell him that. If my mother hadn't chosen to let anyone know her secret while she was alive, I wouldn't betray it now she was dead. And if Eldric and his brother were still looking for her, perhaps they'd turn up some information that would lead me to her killer.

He sighed. "And so, my brother sends me on a wild goose chase, looking for a woman who doesn't want to be found. At least it brought me here tonight, to see you." He moved closer again, and now only two paces separated us.

I stepped back. "You're just in time to see me leave."

"A pretty girl like you shouldn't be wandering around all alone out here. Anything could happen to her."

My gaze darted to his face. Was he threatening me? There was a note of silken menace in his voice that was at odds with the image I had of him as a lazy drunk. His smile was calculating, and all of a sudden, I was afraid he was calculating where he could hide my body. He was fae, of course, which meant he could wipe the floor with me any time he liked. Now, I wished I'd brought a knife with me. Or even not been in such a hurry to put the shovel away.

"It's kind of you to worry," I said, choosing to brazen it out, hoping he wouldn't notice the frightened pulse beating in my neck. "But the Hawk knows where I am. He'll be meeting me here soon."

"But he's not here now, is he?" He stepped closer, still with that disconcerting smile in place. Frankly, he looked like a serial killer, and I wondered uneasily if psychopathy ran in Eldric's family.

Was it possible that Jaxen knew more about my mother's disappearance than he was letting on? An hour ago, I would have laughed at the idea, but now I was finding him genuinely creepy, and I was prepared to believe anything.

"I'm sure we can find a way to while away the time together while we wait. The night is still young."

I moved to put the well between us. Maybe I could push him in if I caught him by surprise. He had wings, but they wouldn't be any use to him in the tight confines of a well shaft. "I have places to be."

"I thought you were meeting the Hawk?" His eyes glittered with malice in the moonlight, pleased to have caught me out in a lie.

He rounded the well abruptly, but when I stepped back, his hand snaked out and caught my arm.

"Allegra, sweet Allegra. Lying to an old friend? Why are you so unkind?"

"We are not friends. We were never friends." My pulse accelerated as I prepared to defend myself. I was convinced Jaxen had never made friends with anyone unless he wanted something from them. It astonished me that someone like him could be the brother of Eldric, who wasn't bad for a Lord, despite his disdain for changelings. It probably astonished Eldric, too.

"But we could be." He smiled nastily. "I could put in a good word for you with Blethna Arbre. You two should kiss and make up. I'm sure the three of us could be great friends."

Was he actually suggesting a threesome? I began to relax. Why had I felt so threatened? He was just being sleazy. "What do you want, Jaxen?"

"Me? What should I want? Don't I have everything a man should ever need? A place to lay my head, all the wine I can drink. The derision of the Court. I know what they all think of me." He leaned closer, until I could smell the alcohol on his breath.

"Then why are you here?" I shrugged him off and stepped back.

He bared his teeth in an unpleasant smile. "The joys of being a younger brother. The mighty Lord Eldric has only to snap his fingers and I must jump. Eldric told me to check out the cottage, and here I am. Who knows what clues we might find here?"

I began walking away from him, grateful that his dangerous mood had faded as quickly as it had come. Hopefully, if I left, he would, too. I'd already uncovered the only clue the cottage held, and all it did was confirm that my mother was dead. The search was over before it had begun. The only thing left to find now was the identity of her killer, and I suspected that was going to be much harder to uncover.

"There are some weevils in the flour container. Nothing else to find here, but you're welcome to look." I needed to get away before it occurred to him to wonder why I'd been washing myself in the garden, and what I'd been doing to get so dirty. His natural disinclination to exert himself should work in my favour. The faster he could get back to his drinking, the happier he'd be. He could return and tell Eldric with a clear conscience that the cottage was a dead end. If he even had a conscience. Some of the stories I'd heard about him made me wonder, and tonight's little display had convinced me to treat him with a little more respect. I had the feeling he could prove dangerous. "I'm going home."

"Give my regards to the lovely Willow. And that other mongrel friend of yours."

I whirled on him. "Do you mean Sage?"

He grinned, pleased to see he'd managed to get under my skin. "Is that her name? Fallon Domani's get."

"That's her name, and she's a half-breed."

He shrugged. "Half-breed, mongrel—same thing."

I clenched my fists, but managed to stop myself responding. I wouldn't give him the satisfaction. I stormed around the side of the cottage, his mocking laughter echoing in my ears. Eldric would take a very dim view of a mere mortal backhanding his brother across the face, much as I might like to. Better to remove myself from temptation. Back down the slope and away from the cottage I went. I opened a Way as soon as I reached the trees, and stepped through into the blessed solitude of the Wilds with relief.

"She couldn't have lived somewhere that was free to visit?" Sage threw a disgusted look at the sign. *Twelve dollars per car. Gates shut at 8:30pm.*

The driver of the car in front of us was having a long conversation with the woman at the toll booth, who turned and began making sweeping gestures with her arms. He must have been asking for directions, though it shouldn't have been that confusing. The national park was a big place, but it was kind of short on options as far as roads went. Most of it was natural bushland, impassable for cars.

I fished in my wallet and handed her a twenty-dollar note, remembering my first trip to see Yriell with the Hawk, and how he'd handed the man fake money, refusing to pay the toll. "None of the fae are going to pay it, anyway."

"I guess." She still looked grumpy as she handed the money to the woman, as if the price of entry was a personal insult. Once she got the change, she roared away from the toll booth as if she were on a race track and someone had just waved the starting flag.

"Take it easy. Willow won't be happy if you burn all the rubber off the rental's tyres."

Willow's car was still in the body shop, getting the

damage caused by an axe-wielding troll repaired, so she'd hired a replacement. Not having a car of my own was a pain in the arse, especially since Willow wasn't keen on letting me drive hers. I was saving for one, but unless I could find a better-paying job, I wouldn't be able to afford a decent one until I was about eighty-five.

Sage flashed me a grin. "What Willow doesn't know won't hurt her." But she was a model of respectable driving all the way to the car park.

Out of the car, she stretched and looked around with interest. It was a fine morning, and there were several kayaks already out on the river. A group of teenagers was kicking a ball around on the grass, and two women were blowing up balloons and decorating one of the picnic tables for a birthday party.

"It looks a lot more inviting in daylight without a bunch of homicidal trolls breathing down your neck."

"I know, right?"

"I can barely remember any of this. Which way to the scary fairy?"

I headed off down the walking track. "Don't let her hear you calling her that."

She snorted. "Do I *look* stupid?"

"Well, I don't want to hurt your feelings, but …"

She slapped me on the shoulder, and I laughed and skipped out of her reach. This was good. This felt real and normal, and the body I'd found at the cottage and my mother's death was just some horribly vivid nightmare.

I'd gone straight to Jamison's Pharmacy this morning,

desperate to find out what else he knew about my mother, but he wasn't working today, so I'd dragged Sage out here to see Yriell instead.

Neither of us were laughing once we reached the Aversion zone. I'd forgotten just how bad it was. Really, why had I thought this would be a good idea? There was no need to talk to Yriell about my mother's death. I should just go.

I stopped so abruptly that Sage trod on my heel.

"Whoa, whoa, where are you going?" She grabbed my arm as I turned back.

"Back to the car."

Her dark brown eyes bored into mine. "Al, it's just the Aversion. Come on."

Cold fear crawled over my skin as she dragged me forward, past the burned gum tree, towards the thicket of vicious thorns. "It's okay. Jamison obviously has a way to contact her. I could ring her instead."

"Are you kidding me?" Her grip on my arm tightened. "And waste twelve bucks? No way. We're doing this."

If she felt the same fear that I did, she didn't show it. She was half fae; even though her magic was practically non-existent, perhaps her fairy blood helped her resist the Aversion. Suddenly, we were through it, and the relief was immediate. I shook off her hand.

"Thanks. I'm okay now." I blew out a deep breath, releasing the fear and tension. "Remind me never to come here on my own. I'm obviously too weak to resist her spells."

"It's not your fault. You can't help being human."

It was still a relief to come out of the trees at last and see the little house waiting. Smoke curled from the chimney. That was good; she was home. I hadn't even considered that she might not be. Sage would have been even more pissed about the twelve dollars then.

I knocked, expecting a long wait, but the door jerked open immediately.

"Oh, it's you," Yriell said, though she must have seen us coming to answer so quickly. She stood back to let us in. The big, sunny room smelled of bread baking, which was an unexpectedly homey smell, considering the number of peculiar-looking things in jars that lined the walls.

"What do you want?"

"Answers."

A wry smile bloomed on her face. "Then you'd better ask the right questions, girl."

"Okay, here's a question for you: who killed my mother?"

She waved at two overstuffed floral armchairs that faced each other beside the empty fireplace. They looked as though they should belong to someone's harmless grandma, not to a dangerous Earthcrafter like Yriell. Sage and I sat down, while Yriell put the kettle on and began assembling cups and a teapot.

"So, you believe Jamison now? I had the distinct feeling that you weren't convinced that woman was actually your mother the other night." She heaped tea leaves into the pot and poured the boiling water over them. The smell of jasmine and something else I couldn't place filled the room. I half-hoped she would offer some of that bread I could smell, too.

"I changed my mind."

"Changeable as the wind, you mortals," she sniffed. "Never know whether you're coming or going."

I didn't tell her yet *why* I'd changed my mind, though Sage looked at me with one eyebrow raised, as if prompting me to go on. She and Willow knew, of course. They were like sisters to me; there was no need to hide anything from them.

Yriell handed us both a mug brimming with tea. Mine said *I drink coffee for your protection* in big red letters on the side. Sage's had a picture of Santa Claus with his pants around his ankles, but I couldn't see most of the lettering. Probably a good thing. I wondered what other little surprises Yriell had in her cupboard.

The Earthcrafter dragged one of the dining chairs over to join us and planted herself in it with her own cup, this one disappointingly plain. Her eyes were shrewd as they watched me over the rim.

"What else can you tell me about my mother's death?" I asked.

"You were there, girl. You saw it all."

"I saw your powers fail after Jamison had told me you could save her. What happened?"

Her brows drew together. "You blaming me? Because if you've come here to whine at me, you can piss right off again."

Maybe in the depths of the night I'd wondered if she'd truly done all she could, but face to face with her, I couldn't think that. We weren't exactly friends, but there was a bond between us, and she'd told me herself that she owed me for saving her brother. And when a fae admitted to a debt, that meant something. I knew she'd done all she could for my mother—which left the question of why her all hadn't been enough.

"I'm not blaming you. Just confused. Why didn't your magic work?"

"Lady's tits, girl, magic isn't a bloody vending machine. You don't put in your money and out comes your can of Coke. There are variables."

"Such as?"

"The strength of the user, their experience, their attention to detail. The phase of the bloody moon, for all I know."

I made an impatient noise. "All of which you have in spades. You're the king's sister, and you've been Earthcrafting since before Moses was a boy. Why didn't it work?"

She sighed and put her tea down. It was horribly bitter, and could have done with a spoonful or ten of sugar to make it bearable. I was only drinking mine to be polite.

"Sometimes things can block a person's magic. Someone else's spell. Natural resistance. Iron."

"But you said you didn't see how it could be iron poisoning, since she was wearing an iron ward. You think it was caused by magic? A spell someone cast on her?"

"It's possible."

"Did she have any wounds?" Sage asked.

Yriell waved her hand impatiently. "I checked for that. No wounds that I could see, yet she had every symptom of a classic case of iron poisoning."

"Could they have been caused by something else?"

"Sure they could. Half a dozen things. But none of *those* would block my magic."

"And iron poisoning does?" I asked.

"Well, it could—but it takes a while for the symptoms to become that bad. Normally if a fae gets the iron sickness, they only have to retreat to the Realms, or a sith, to recover. It never gets to that extreme—unless the iron has been introduced to the body. And there were no wounds, so … Her body repelled my magic, as if she were soaking in iron, but how the hell does that happen without some whopping great stab wound from a steel sword?"

I took another sip of the bitter tea, sorting through the possibilities. "Then it probably wasn't iron poisoning. It must have been a spell that sickened her and stopped your magic from healing her. The symptoms just happened to look similar to iron poisoning."

Yriell gave me a bland look. "But what enemies would someone like your mother have had? And why are you now convinced that woman was your mother? You all but told Jamison to his face that he was lying on Friday night."

I owed Jamison an apology for that. "Well, he was right. My mother wasn't really Livillia of Autumn. She was from Illusion, and I guess her name was Anawen, just like he said, and she stole Livillia's identity."

"How do you know?"

"I found the body."

She sat up straight. "The real Livillia's body? Where?"

"Buried in a clearing behind the cottage that had such a strong Aversion on it that I never even knew it was there." I didn't have to explain that the Aversion had dissipated with my mother's death; this was Magic 101, and Yriell didn't need a primer. "There's not a lot left of her now—mainly bones and hair—but who else could it be? The hair was the exact same colour as my mother's. A pig had been trying to dig her up."

"Pigs will do that. Eat you as soon as look at you."

"I reburied her deeper. And then that arsehole Jaxen showed up."

"While you were burying the body?"

"No, thank God, just after I'd finished." I hadn't actually meant to tell her about Jaxen, but it seemed as though once I got talking, my tongue just ran away with me. I looked down at my mug of tea, now half empty. "Did you put something in this?"

Yriell snorted. "If I was going to poison you, kid, you'd know about it."

"Not poison. It's like I can't stop blabbing, as if there's something making me talk."

"Oh, good. Tell me about your last sexual experience."

"What? No!"

"Well, there goes that theory. Guess you just wanted to confide in me. What was Jaxen doing there?"

"He said Eldric had asked him to investigate my mother's disappearance."

"Hmm. Doesn't sound very likely. Eldric has far more reliable people than his drunkard brother to run his errands."

That was true. I hadn't thought of that. Usually Dorset got those kind of odd assignments.

"And since when has Jaxen done what Eldric asked him to, anyway?" Sage put in.

"He does sometimes. He brought me the gate glyph on Eldric's orders."

"Only when it suits him," Sage muttered darkly. Her opinion of Jaxen was no better than mine.

I turned back to Yriell. "He might have been telling the truth. But if he wasn't, what was he doing there?"

"Good question. Looking for you? Making sure he'd left no incriminating evidence behind?"

I drew in a sharp breath, all my suspicions flooding back. For a moment there, I'd really felt as if Jaxen meant to do me harm. "You think he could have killed my mother?"

"With no more compunction than swatting a fly. But I don't know of any reason why he would. Do you?"

I shrugged. "It's been four years since I lived in Autumn. We had nothing to do with him then, beyond seeing him at festivals, but anything could have happened since. I don't know."

I didn't know what had happened in my mother's life since she'd thrown me out, but it occurred to me that I really hadn't known what went on in her life even before that, despite how closely we'd lived together. If she'd managed to hide her history from me all those years, what else could she have been hiding?

"Perhaps it was revenge for the real Livillia's death," Sage suggested.

Yriell shook her head decisively. "Too long ago. If anyone was going to catch her out for that, it would have happened years ago. I think we're looking for enemies of Illusion, here."

The fall of Illusion was a long time ago, too, but Summer had never given up the hunt. Every so often, we would hear of another Illusion native discovered and killed, as Summer did their best to wipe every trace of the offending Realm from the world.

"But Illusion has been absolved," I said. "They clearly didn't kill the king, so no one should be killing people just because they're from Illusion any more. The king is back."

Yriell swirled the tea in her cup thoughtfully. "And did Queen Ceinwen look happy to you to have him back?"

The queen hadn't struck me as particularly happy about anything, but I didn't see how that was relevant. "What's that got to do with my mother's death?"

"Maybe nothing," Yriell said. "Maybe something. But I wouldn't trust those Summer bastards as far as I could kick them. They're not going to give up Illusion's territories without a fight."

9

Not even Ricky could lift my black mood the next day, though usually I enjoyed working with him. But the drawer of the register kept getting stuck, and every second customer had a complaint, or did something else to annoy me. The guy who demanded his twenty dollars' worth of change in one-dollar coins was the last straw. I told him where he could stick his one-dollar coins.

"What's the matter?" Ricky asked after the man had stalked out, threatening to report me to my manager. "You look like you threw up a pound and down came sixpence."

That, at least, caught my attention. "*Threw up a pound and down came sixpence*? Are you serious? We've had decimal currency in this country since 1966. You can't possibly be old enough to be saying shit like that, Ricky." Just wait until I told Willow and Sage. They'd seize on the expression with glee, and add it to their "assimilation project" of interesting slang.

"'Course I can. I was only a lad when we changed over,

but I still remember the old money. And me mum used to say that all the time, God bless her."

His eyes softened at the thought of his mum, who must surely have gone to God years ago. I didn't know exactly how old Ricky was, but I knew he was past the normal retiring age of sixty-five. He said he had to keep working to keep up with the payments to all his ex-wives.

"But you're trying to change the subject," he continued. "What's wrong?"

What could I say? His feelings for his mother were clearly way less complicated than mine were. I wasn't even sure *what* I was feeling. Sad? Angry? The sting of rejection was smarting again as strongly as it had the first day my mother had cast me out. I missed her and loved her and hated her all at the same time. And now I could never go back, could never make it right between us. No matter what magic the king had gifted me with, it wouldn't bring back what I'd lost. I guess, somehow, I'd been unconsciously thinking that if I could only get back to Autumn, I would somehow get back my mother's love as well. Autumn just wasn't the same without my mother in it.

And now it turned out my whole life in Autumn had been a lie, too. I wasn't a child of Autumn, but the child of a murderer. Bad enough that I wasn't her real daughter— just a changeling stolen from a human family—but she wasn't the person I'd thought she was, either. Neither of us were who we pretended to be. What did that mean for our relationship? Was any of it real, or had she just been acting a part the whole time?

"I got some bad news," I said at last. In a way, I'd been grieving for my mother for the last four years, so I wasn't as upset by her death as I might have been earlier. I felt curiously numb about it, as if this whole thing was happening to someone else. When Ricky tried to press me for details, I said I didn't want to talk about it, and the rest of the shift passed without any of the chatter I was used to from him.

On my way home, I went to Jamison's Pharmacy again, determined that this time I would get some answers. I strode past displays of makeup and cold and flu medicine to the back of the store where the pharmacists worked, filling prescriptions. A Chinese girl was behind the counter.

"Can I help you?" she asked.

"I'm looking for Jamison."

"He's not in today."

That was odd—Jamison rarely missed a day, let alone two in a row—but typical of the kind of day I was having. I really needed to talk to him. My mother might have told him something before I got there that could help identify her killer. Even if she'd mentioned where she'd gone between leaving the cottage and turning up on his doorstep, that could help.

"Will he be in tomorrow?"

"I'm not sure. Is there something I can help you with instead?"

I was about to say no, but at the rate I went through them, it never hurt to have a spare asthma inhaler. Sometimes Jamison made them up for me in advance. "Has he filled my prescription? My name's Allegra Brooks."

She went off to check and came back with the familiar yellow inhaler in a little tray, which she handed to me. "There you are. Pay up the front. Is there anything else you need?"

A whole lot of things—answers about what kind of person my mother really was and what had happened to her was at the top of a long list—but nothing she could provide. "No, thanks."

I picked up the inhaler. The canister had commercial printing on it. "Are you sure this is the right one?"

Usually, they were plain. Maybe Jamison had decided to add a little Glamour, but I couldn't see why he would. If this was a regular drug, it might not work for me after all the years I'd spent in the Realms. I was mainly human, but that much exposure to magic tended to alter a person. That was why I came to Jamison for personalised fae-type drugs.

She turned the little tray around to show me a sticky label with my name printed on it in Jamison's spidery handwriting. "If you want to leave it, I can check with Jamison next time he's in."

Reassured by the sticky note, I shook my head. "No, I'd better take it. Wouldn't want to run out."

I paid at the front counter and shoved the inhaler in my back pocket as I left the shop. I was about to cross the road when a familiar black Maserati pulled into the kerb. The driver's window slid down, revealing the Hawk's face.

"Want a lift home?"

"Sure." I got in beside him, breathing deeply of the luxurious leather smell.

The Hawk smiled briefly at me, then turned his attention back to the road, but that one look was enough. I'd forgotten how attractive he was. That smile was devastating. It was as much a weapon as the sword he kept hidden, maybe even more lethal.

Get a grip, idiot, I told myself firmly. *He doesn't want you. And he's fae. Of course he's gorgeous.*

Yeah, and so was Jaxen. And Eldric. And Raven, and even Rowan—basically every other fae man I'd ever met. But none of them could make me feel lightheaded with just a smile. I was seriously smitten with King Rothbold's favourite knight, and all I could hope was that it wasn't obvious to him, since he'd clearly decided he wasn't interested in me. That would be too embarrassing. His attentiveness was only duty; probably the king had told him he had to protect me or something.

"What are you doing slumming it in this neck of the woods?" I asked, trying to distract myself with small talk.

"Looking for you, actually," he said, and my heart nearly missed a beat. "I tried at your work, but your friend there said you'd already left, so I was heading over to Willow's when I saw you."

"Oh? Got some other missing royalty you'd like help with?"

That killer smile slipped out again. "Not today. The king sent me."

There it was. Duty again. Some of my joy in seeing him faded. Of course he wasn't seeking me out for himself, but on the king's business.

"Is Rothbold missing me already?"

"So much that he's holding a ball," he said gravely, "just to give him an excuse to invite you."

I raised a sceptical eyebrow. "Really."

"Well, officially, it's to celebrate his return, but I'm sure it's really to see you." He grinned—a genuine, unguarded expression of enjoyment. He seemed so much happier since we'd freed the king, as if it had lifted a burden from his shoulders. I guess that figured—the poor bastard had spent years looking for his king, never giving up hope of finding him or belief that he was still alive to be found. He'd been the laughing stock of the Court. Now he seemed a different person to the serious knight I'd first met. And I had to admit, the difference only added to his attractiveness.

"Who else is invited?"

He rolled his eyes. "Your friends, Willow and Sage, plus about half the kingdom. All the Lords and Ladies, of course; all the members of the Court; every last relative of the king and queen; representatives of all the major guilds—you name it, and they're probably invited."

"So Yriell will be there?" As the sister of the king, her name should be near the top of the list.

"Yriell is invited. As to whether she'll bother attending, your guess is as good as mine. She seems to prefer being Yriell to her role as Princess Orina. She's never been much interested in the politics of rule."

"And this is politics?"

"Of course. Rothbold's been gone too long." Some of the light faded from his eyes, his expression growing serious as he pulled up for a red light. "It's important to reassert his position."

I could read between the lines just fine. "You mean he's got to show his brother-in-law who's boss before Kellith decides he preferred life without a king?"

He frowned, staring at the car in front as if it were a dragon he'd like to slay. "Officially, Kellith is considered blameless for the actions of a rogue member of his Court."

"And unofficially?"

His hands tightened on the steering wheel, his knuckles white. "Unofficially, I would kill the traitorous bastard tomorrow if the king would only give the word."

"What's stopping him?"

"The fact that the snake is his wife's brother? The naïve hope that the breach between them can still be mended? The fear that such action might cause open revolt among the other Lords? Who knows? The king doesn't confide in me to such an extent."

We turned a corner and he pulled up outside the rundown property that hid the entry to Willow's sith. I paused, my hand on the door handle. "But you think he's making a mistake."

Stern golden eyes met mine. "Kellith is a rabid dog, and there is no reasoning with such. He needs to be put down before he attacks again."

<hr />

The king's ball was only three days away. Apparently, if you were royalty, you didn't worry that people might already have other engagements, you just scheduled things to suit yourself and expected them to drop everything to come to your party.

"Do you think your parents will be there?" Sage asked Willow.

The three of us were in the garden again—Willow spent most of her time in the sith's garden. A Spring thing, I guess. They liked their nature as much as any Earthcrafter. Sage had a book in her lap, but she hadn't turned a page for a while. She'd just been sitting there, gnawing at her bottom lip. Now I knew what was eating at her.

"Of course they will," Willow replied. "They're the Lord and Lady of Spring. But that doesn't make any difference. The king himself has invited you. You have just as much right to be there as they do."

"I know, I know," she said hurriedly, "It's just—"

"Just nothing," I cut in. Sage was normally so ballsy, but mention the Lord and Lady of Spring, or anything about her father, and she shrank into herself.

Willow's parents had thrown her out with the same callousness as my mother had shown me, and with even less cause. Sage was no changeling—no one was required to give up part of their power to allow her to stay in the Realms. She could have stayed there forever, but they'd cast her out simply because of who her father was, which was a raging injustice as far as I was concerned. As far as Willow was concerned, too, which was why she had left with Sage. It wasn't as if Sage had had any choice in her parents, or control over what her father did.

"You don't have to speak to them if you don't want to. They have no power over you anymore."

"Make sure they see you speaking to the king, though," Willow said. "That will drive my father insane."

That drew a grin from her. She sighed. "I wish I didn't have to go."

"Well, you can hardly refuse an invitation from the king himself."

"I know, but it will be so awkward. All the nobles will be trying to avoid me. No one will ask me to dance, and I'll probably spend the night getting drunk in the corner."

Willow shrugged. "Sounds perfect. I'll join you." I envied Willow her assurance. She didn't give a shit what people thought of her.

"I'm with you," I said to Sage. "I'd much rather stay home. What on earth am I going to wear?"

"Oh, that's no problem. We can go shopping," Willow said.

"Hello? No money here, remember? Lost all possessions in a fire and all that?"

"Don't be silly. I'll buy you something. Spoilt rich girl here, remember?"

I shifted uncomfortably. "I can't let you spend your money on a ball gown. That shit's expensive, and you've already given me so much."

Sage laid down her book, giving up all pretence of reading. "That's what friends are for, right?"

"What, to live off like a parasite? No."

"Then what will you wear?"

I lay back in my chair and stared up at the leaves dancing above my head. "Stuffed if I know. I'll think of something."

"Borrow something of mine, then, if you won't let me buy you anything," Willow said. "I have more Court gowns than you could poke a stick at." She cast a triumphant smile at Sage, pleased with her use of the mortal idiom, but Sage wasn't paying attention.

"That green one with the slit might work." Sage had obviously been doing a mental review of Willow's wardrobe. "The colour would suit her."

They both stared at me appraisingly.

"Uh, guys, I don't know if you've noticed, but Willow has a little more in the boob department than I do." Okay, a lot more. And serious hips. Willow had a classic hourglass figure, and people still asked me for ID at pubs because I was built like a twelve-year-old. "I'll look like a kid playing dress ups in her mother's clothes."

"Not the green one," Willow said, as if I hadn't spoken. "The blue satin would bring out her eyes more."

"Let's try it and see," Sage said, and they hustled me into Willow's bedroom before I could object.

Willow's room was a bigger version of mine, open on two sides to the garden, the floor covered in soft grass rather than carpet. But the walk-in closet was all modern, and organised within an inch of its life. Everything was hung in colour order, with like items grouped with like, including a rainbow of evening gowns, some slippery satin or silk, others frothing with tulle or lace. All beautiful, and so expensive looking that I was afraid even to touch them.

Sage pulled out the green dress she'd mentioned and held it up against me for Willow's inspection. It was covered in tiny embroidered flowers with little crystals at their centre. The slit up one side went nearly to the waist. Willow shook her head decisively and reached for a dress the dark blue of the sky as it faded to night. It had no straps, and I was the one who shook her head this time. I could imagine how well a bodice cut for Willow's generous size would stay up on me.

"Try it." Willow thrust the hanger at me.

I rolled my eyes, but pulled my shirt off over my head. I figured it would save time arguing if I just showed them. Gingerly, I stepped into the gown and pulled its liquid folds up over my hips.

"You could have taken your jeans off first," Sage said, appalled, but I ignored her.

I caught a glimpse of myself in the full-length mirror on the wall. Willow was right—the colour did bring out the blue of my eyes, and its deep shade worked well with my pale skin and blonde hair. But, dear God, I was right, too. Even after Sage had done up the zipper, I had to hold the bodice up for fear the whole thing would slide right down to my hips. There was room for me and a friend in the elegant top of this thing.

Willow laid her hands on my waist as I opened my mouth to say *I told you so*. I felt the tingle of magic in the air and caught a whiff of rose perfume as Willow ran her hands up my sides. In their wake, the fabric tightened, conforming to my meagre curves. And not only conforming, but pushing and enhancing. For the first time in my life, I had serious cleavage happening.

"Wow. What did you do?"

"Just a little reshaping. Doesn't that look better?"

"Yes, but …" I couldn't help doing a little twirl in front of the mirror. Of course, my jeans sticking out the bottom didn't exactly add to the look, but I could see that, in this dress, I needn't be ashamed to hobnob with the great and powerful of the Realms. Even the Hawk might look twice, and that thought brought a surge of colour to my face and a thrill of excitement to my heart. "But you won't be able to change it back to fit you, will you?"

Willow's magic could do amazing things, like turn glass back into sand, or cause a flower to bloom or a tree to grow in mere seconds. But I'd never seen her return anything to its original state once she'd used her magic on it. As far as I knew, it was a one-time process only.

Willow waved an airy hand at the rack of gorgeous gowns. "Look at all these others I have. As if I'm going to miss one."

"But—"

"Forget it. Consider it my present to you."

I gave her a quick hug, though I still felt guilty. The idea had been for Willow *not* to spend money on me, but she'd be offended if I rejected her gift now, and it wouldn't fit her anymore anyway. "Thank you. It's an awesome present."

"You look great," Sage said. "That dress should rock the Hawk right out of his socks. And maybe a few other items of clothing."

"Don't be ridiculous," I said, as if I hadn't been just thinking something along the same lines myself.

But I was looking forward to the ball a whole lot more than I had been.

10

On the evening of the ball, the Hawk arrived to escort us to the palace. I didn't ask if that was on the king's orders. There was no need to spoil my good mood. And besides, the look of appreciation in his eyes when he saw me made me think that my hopes for the evening might not be so far-fetched after all. He'd been interested once before—surely he could be again?

He took my hand, in the old-fashioned courtly manner, and bowed over it. I shivered a little as his lips brushed my skin. He was wearing a tuxedo, or at least appeared to be. More likely that was a Glamour laid over the top of what he was really wearing. Fae men didn't go in much for suits. I resolved to enjoy the view while it lasted, though. A good-looking man in a suit is a thing of beauty—only that same man in a uniform could possibly beat the effect.

Hurriedly, I brushed aside any lingering images of the Hawk in a fireman's uniform, or possibly naval whites. He was distracting enough in the flesh.

He drew his sword which, as usual, was concealed at his side, only becoming visible as it slid from its sheath. Then he glanced at Willow. "I assume there is no barrier to gating from here?"

"Not leaving," she said. "But I have wards against unexpected visitors coming in."

He gave an approving nod and slashed a doorway in the air. The interior boiled with a kind of fog, giving no hint of what lay on the other side. I wondered if the palace also had wards against incoming gates.

My question was answered as the four of us stepped through the fog and found ourselves outside the magnificent gates of Whitehaven. They were flung wide tonight, and extra guards stood at attention, welcoming the throng of noble visitors. The Hawk led us through, onto the pebbled path that wound through the gardens surrounding the palace. Sage walked on one side of me, and Willow on the other, all of us in finery borrowed from Willow's extensive wardrobe. Ahead of us, the palace's mighty towers pierced the night sky. A thousand globes of light hovered about the castle walls, making the gardens almost as bright as day, and cheerful bunting hung from every window.

Sage glanced nervously around, as if expecting assassins to jump out at us from under the delicate drapery of willow branches. "Do you think my father will be here?"

"Stop worrying about it," Willow said. "The king didn't like him before he disappeared, and that won't have changed. You're not going to suddenly run into Daddy Dearest in the hallway."

"Have you seen your parents yet?"

Willow rolled her eyes. "Honey, we've barely arrived. Relax, would you?"

We reached the forecourt, which was full of people. The towers and spires of the castle loomed above us in a gleaming white stone that glowed softly in the lamp light. I'd heard that in the full sun, the walls were so bright it was impossible to look at them, and they sparkled with flecks of quartz embedded in the stone. Just as well the fae were a night-loving people.

Floating balls of light, held aloft by magic, illuminated a glittering stream of fae climbing the wide marble steps to the great doors of the castle, now standing open. Music floated down the stairs from inside, a waltz, though the instruments would have sounded odd to human ears. The waterfall of liquid sound from the harp was easy to pick out, and the wooden flute so beloved of the fae was also familiar, but I couldn't tell what the other instruments were.

I was more than a little anxious as we climbed the wide steps to the main entrance. Around us were all the high and mighty of the Realms. I didn't know any of them, but Willow was kept busy greeting people, exchanging air kisses amid cries of how long it had been since they'd seen each other.

Yeah, that happened when your parents were arseholes so you stormed off to the mortal world and didn't come back for five years. She wouldn't have come back now, but, as she'd pointed out to Sage, no one refused an invitation from the king. It was strange to see her like this, working the crowd like a politician as we made our slow procession up the stairs and through the crowded foyer.

When she was lazing around at home, or rocking out in the band, it was easy to forget she was virtually royalty herself. They called the rulers of the separate Realms Lords and Ladies, but they were more like kings and queens of their own little domains, answerable to the High King in Whitehaven, but pretty free to do whatever they wished. Which made Willow a princess, in a way, and she looked every inch of it tonight. Her unruly red curls had been tamed into an upswept hairstyle that made her neck appear even longer and more graceful than usual. Diamonds dripped from her earlobes, and her pale green dress sparkled with stones that may have been diamonds as well, for all I knew.

Sage wore a deep red gown that clung to her athletic figure and set off her darker skin to perfection. Her hair was too short to style, but none of the men were looking at her face, their gaze drawn by the plunging neckline of her dress, which reached almost to her navel. She looked amazing, and moved with an easy confidence that gave no sign of her inner nerves.

My own borrowed finery clung from breasts to hips, then flared out into a skirt that swished against my legs as I walked. Willow had worked a miracle with my hair—it wasn't really long enough to put up, but she'd managed it with some clever work with the hairpins. When I'd looked in the mirror, I'd been surprised at how regal I looked. The high heels helped a little with that, too.

I clung to the Hawk's arm, feeling like this was a fairy tale I didn't belong in. A woman in a deep red dress the colour of fresh blood turned to stare at me, then whispered something to the man to whose arm she clung. He laughed. Another group at the top of the stairs turned as if the laugh were a signal, and looked me up and down as if I were a cow for sale at the stock markets.

I ran my hand nervously over the slippery satin of my dress, feeling it slide across my thighs with each step. Sage had lent me a necklace of dark blue stones, almost the same colour as the dress, which lay heavy against my pale skin. I straightened my shoulders, my heart beating faster as we approached the doors. Screw them and the horse they rode in on, as Sage would say. They could look down their noses all they liked, but I was the one on the arm of the handsomest man there. I might only be a changeling, but, unlike them, I'd actually gotten off my arse to help the king. I deserved my place here. I'd earned it.

Rows of guards lined each side of a narrow white carpet. They must use magic to keep it so clean. We passed under the guards' watchful eyes, through an archway, into a larger vestibule, where busy servants were taking cloaks and wraps. I kept a firm grip on my tiny clutch purse, though other women were abandoning their jewelled bags to the staff. My asthma puffer was in mine. Although I rarely needed an extra dose, my mother had drummed it into me from childhood: always keep your medicine with you.

I realised that the Hawk was now wearing a cream silk shirt, nicely fitted across his broad chest but with full sleeves, set off by dark blue pants tucked into high black boots. With his dark beard, he looked like a pirate. I added "pirate" to my mental catalogue of sexy looks for men, wondering if Willow had told him what colour my dress was. His pants were an exact match.

The noise level increased as we passed through another set of doors into a long, narrow room. We were almost at the ballroom; I could see it through the doors at the end of the room. Here, a row of dignitaries waited beside the white carpet, greeting each guest who funnelled through. The Hawk presented me to various palace functionaries, whose names I promptly forgot in my nervousness, and then we were on to the royal family.

Lord Kellith and his Lady stood beside his sister, the queen. The siblings shared the same white-blond hair and icy blue eyes.

The Lord of Summer took my hand with a cool smile. "The conquering hero and her gallant knight," he said, bringing my hand to his lips. "So lovely to see you again."

The Hawk gave a stiff nod, but said nothing. My skin crawled at having Kellith touch me. This was the man who was indirectly responsible for my mother's death. Perhaps even directly. I seethed at having to play polite games. How did the king stand it? I wanted nothing more than to smash my fist into his fake smile.

"You must save a dance for me," he said.

"Of course," I said, hating myself for playing along. What was wrong with all these people? Couldn't they see what he was? Why did no one call him on his bullshit?

His wife gave me a wintry nod as we moved on to the queen. I barely restrained myself from wiping my hand on my dress. Maybe tonight I might find some information that would help lead me to the killer.

The queen wore silver, every inch of her form-fitting gown crusted with diamonds. The only way she could have made a bigger statement of her wealth was if she'd worn rainbow drake skin. That was probably a sensitive topic in the palace right now, considering the role that drake skin had played in sedating the king during his captivity.

"Sir Kyrrim." She gave the Hawk a regal nod, making the diamonds in her tiara flash as they reflected the lamplight. Her hair, piled up on her head in a series of intricate braids, was so pale it was almost white. She looked as if she were made of frosted glass.

"Your Majesty." He swept into a deep bow, elegant but with no more feeling than there had been in her nod. It didn't take a genius to figure out that these two didn't like each other.

Her gaze was no warmer when she turned to me. "And Miss Brooks. I hope you enjoy the ball."

"Thank you, Your Majesty."

And then we were on to the king. Here, at least, there was no doubt of our welcome.

He grinned at the Hawk. "Well done, Sir Kyrrim. You managed to spirit her away from the mortals for us."

"Not exactly an unpleasant task, sire."

"No, I can see that. You look magnificent, Allegra." Rothbold's gaze held an appreciative gleam as he took in the glory of Willow's dress. "I will die a broken man if you don't dance with me tonight."

That attracted the queen's attention. "It seems our little changeling is to be the belle of the ball."

"And why should she not be? Doesn't she look beautiful tonight?"

"Quite charming." The queen's face was expressionless as she turned to greet Willow.

Rothbold took my hand and squeezed it. "I'm glad you could join us, my dear."

As if I'd had a choice. "I'm honoured to be invited, Your Majesty."

The queen cleared her throat. Behind us, the line had stopped.

Reluctantly, Rothbold let go of my hand. "Don't let that knight of mine monopolise you all night. Make sure you save me a dance."

Free of the formalities, we entered the ballroom, where no one was dancing yet. The musicians were set up in an area to one side, but they were playing soft background music as the crowd milled around, waiting for something. A long strip of white carpet led from the door to a pair of thrones on a dais at the far end of the room.

Sage looked around with her usual impatience. She seemed calmer now we'd made it in without having to confront anyone from Spring. "What's the hold-up? I thought we were here to dance?"

"The king has a little something planned first," the Hawk said. "It won't be long; we were nearly the last ones through the receiving line."

Sure enough, only a few minutes later, the musicians stopped playing abruptly and everyone bowed as the king entered with the glittering queen on his arm. An expectant hush fell on the room as they paraded down the white carpet and seated themselves on their thrones. The Dragon and the Wolf had come in on the heels of the royal couple, but they had joined us instead of following the king and queen.

"Lady Willow, if you would?" The Dragon bowed to Willow, and the Wolf did the same to Sage.

Sage looked at him in alarm. "What's going on? I thought we were done with the formalities?"

"Don't panic," the Hawk reassured her. "The king just wants a word. We're to escort you to him."

He smiled and offered me his arm, then led me to the white carpet. The Dragon lined up behind us with Willow, and the Wolf and Sage behind them. My heart pounded with nerves.

Okay, so this was both good and bad. Good point: I didn't have to walk down that long white carpet on my own. This way, if I got so nervous that I tripped over my own dress, there'd be someone to catch me. Bad point: a buzz of conversation was rising in the room as everyone speculated on why we were being singled out like this. I felt the weight of a great many unfriendly glances as I walked down the white carpet on the Hawk's arm.

When we arrived at the dais, the king came down the steps to greet us personally, which caused another stir of comment among the watching fae. Apparently, Rothbold's

Court had been a more formal place in the past. Was this a new direction for the king, or just a mark of favour to these young women?

I dropped into the perfect formal curtsey my mother had taught me, and the king took my hand to raise me to my feet. He looked much better than he had last time I'd seen him, his face smooth and unlined, his posture upright. Come to think of it, he'd walked the length of the long room with almost a spring in his step, so the physical effects of his long confinement had obviously worn off. It helped to have magic healing at your fingertips. I wondered if his own magic had fully returned yet, but that was hardly something I could ask in this setting. Or any setting, for that matter.

Several people gasped as the king leaned forward and planted a kiss on my cheek. "Allegra, I have something for you, in recognition of your services to the Crown."

Really? He'd already gifted me the magic to enter the Realms at will. What else could possibly compare with a gift like that? A flunky approached and handed the king a scroll with a deep bow. The king offered it to me.

"This is the title deed to an estate in the forests of Autumn."

This was a what now? An estate? For *me*? Sudden tears filled my eyes, and I could hardly focus on the king's beaming face. I reached out and the king pressed the scroll into my hand.

He said a few more words, but I couldn't take them in. Next thing I knew, he was presenting Sage with a beautiful harp that was surely an heirloom, in grateful thanks for her assistance the night of his return. She took it with reverence and as much awe and excitement on her face as I had felt at my own gift.

For Willow, he had an emerald the size of my fist, on a golden chain that he placed over her head. She thanked him prettily, taking it in her stride, and then the formal part of the proceedings was over. Finally. The king clapped his hands once, imperiously; the white carpet disappeared, and the plain room underwent a fabulous transformation.

Snow began falling from the high ceiling, though none of it touched the floor, disappearing in mid-air just above the guests' heads. Icicles sharp as swords hung from the silver branches of slender trees that appeared all around the edges of the room, growing straight out of the white marble floor.

"It's beautiful," I breathed, holding up my hand to catch a falling snowflake. It lay in my palm, a perfect jewel of symmetry, until it suddenly winked out of existence.

The Hawk laughed at my crestfallen expression and caught another, offering it to me in his strong, tanned hand. I touched it briefly, poking at it with one finger, feeling his warm skin beneath mine.

Then it, too, disappeared, and his fingers closed around mine, drawing me closer. "Shall we dance?"

Was there any expression more romantic? Not when a girl stood in such a magical, glittering ballroom, facing the most gorgeous man in the room. My heart sang as I went into his arms, though there was a brief moment of awkwardness as I tried to put my hand on his shoulder while still clutching my purse.

"Let me put this somewhere." I looked around for a chair or a windowsill, but there were no chairs, and the archways between the trees led directly onto a long terrace.

"Give it to me," Willow said. "I'll find someone to look after it."

"I'm going to try out this harp," Sage said, checking out the musicians, who had begun a waltz. "Have fun, you guys—just make sure you leave before midnight, Al, or the magic will come undone."

I shot her a startled glance, imagining my boobs on display as my dress, grown large again, slipped down my body. She and Willow both burst out laughing.

"Don't panic, Cinderella," Willow said. "This fairy godmother knows her shit."

I laughed, and then I was swooping around the dance floor in the Hawk's arms as if I was treading on air. That was another thing I should have been more grateful for—that my mother had included dance lessons with her Court etiquette instructions. I wouldn't be setting the ballroom dancing scene on fire any time soon, but I was competent enough to follow the Hawk's lead.

He was a good dancer, which made it easy, though I was in danger of being distracted from my steps by the proximity of his body. Circling the garden with my mother was nothing like dancing with a man. It hadn't prepared me at all for the sudden thrill that shot through me as he pulled me against him. Our bodies were pressed so closely together there wasn't a whisper of space between us. I could feel his hard muscles moving, feel his leg slide between mine. It was the most sensual experience I had ever had. The other dancers disappeared. There was only our two bodies, moving as one.

I didn't dare look at him. Hunger for his touch roared through me. I didn't want the dance to end, but eventually, the music stopped. Reluctantly, we separated, though he still kept hold of my hand. I may have been breathing more heavily than normal. Perhaps that was why his gaze slid to my breasts, their tops bared by the low neckline of the strapless dress. Perhaps.

"Would you like a drink?"

I nodded. Together, we squeezed our way through the crowd in the ballroom and through a gap in the silvery, snow-covered trees to a room where a banquet was laid out on long tables. The Hawk ignored the food and headed for the end of the room, where a bar was set up. Servants in silver livery to match the décor were mixing cocktails and serving up drinks with a speed that would have got them a job at The Drunken Irishman any day of the week.

The Hawk snagged two glasses of something sparkling but too golden in colour to be champagne. Whatever it was, it tasted divine, and I drained the whole glass.

"Careful," the Hawk said. His tawny eyes glittered in the soft light from the ice-draped chandeliers overhead. "You don't want to lose your head."

Didn't I? All I knew was that my whole body was still tingling from his touch. Thoughts of my mother and her killer had been buried under a cascade of sexual hunger. I wanted to lose my head. I wanted to spend the night in his arms and not care about the consequences. My head knew how stupid it was to fall in love with a fae, but my heart didn't care. The ballroom might be a frozen wonderland, but my body was on fire, and only his touch could quench it.

I reached around him and took another glass from the tray on the bar. I sipped this one more slowly, watching him over the rim of my glass. He was watching me, too, an answering hunger in his eyes, though he tried harder to disguise it. His gaze slid away and roamed over the crowd behind us.

"Are you looking for someone?" I asked. "Should I be jealous?"

He gave me a sharp look. "Habit. I like to know who is around me. Knights who aren't aware of their surroundings generally don't stay alive for long."

I moved a little closer and put my hand on his silk-clad arm. Any excuse to touch him again. "Surely we're safe here, in the heart of the palace. Let your hair down a little."

"All our enemies are here tonight."

"*Our* enemies?"

"Mine and the king's," he clarified.

I stroked his arm. "The king's? And here I was thinking that you only had eyes for me. Forget about him. He has a palace full of guards to protect him."

He captured my stroking fingers in a firm grip and plucked the half-empty glass out of my other hand. "Let's dance again."

He towed me through the crowd back into the ballroom, where he pulled me into his arms with more force than before. Plastered against his chest, I looked up at him. His lips were so close. Was the alcohol affecting me already, that all I could think of was kissing him?

He frowned down at me. "There's something different about you tonight."

"It's the dress. You've never seen me looking respectable before."

"I would hardly call the way you look tonight *respectable*." His gaze slid from my face down to my creamy white neck and shoulders as if he were looking for somewhere to bite, then lingered on my cleavage. His hand on the small of my back tightened, pulling me even closer to him. With a visible effort, he forced his eyes back to my face. "*Delectable*, maybe. *Stunning*, definitely. But I'm not talking about your appearance. There's something else ... If I didn't know you were a changeling, I'd say there was a trace of magic about you."

Maybe the alcohol was affecting him, too. Usually, his self-control was iron—you'd barely suspect there was a feeling heart beating beneath that broad chest. I'd never seen him so ... uninhibited. I had to say, I liked this new, wilder Hawk. I caught a hint of dark wings upswept in the air behind him—another sign that he was losing control, which produced more giddy butterflies in my stomach in response.

"Maybe you can feel the magic the king gave me."

Again, the music ended long before I was ready. I didn't

want to leave the circle of his arms, but a page appeared out of the colourful crowd, and murmured something into the Hawk's ear.

The Hawk nodded, then released me. "Please excuse me for a moment. The king wants a word. I'll be right back."

I nodded, watching him walk away until he was lost in the crowd. I was so busy staring at him that I jumped when a voice spoke right next to me.

"All alone? May I have this dance?"

I turned to find Kellith, Lord of Summer, bowing gracefully, hand outstretched for mine.

Oh, hell. This arsehole again. I'd rather punch him in the face than let him touch me again. I had hoped he'd forget, but I could hardly refuse him without starting a diplomatic incident. At least my current status meant he actually had to *ask*, not just issue commands. The fae didn't always treat changelings like actual, thinking beings with minds and wills of their own.

I put my hand into his, wishing that the Hawk hadn't disappeared at precisely that moment. A tightness in my chest suggested I was going to need my asthma puffer soon, which was odd. Exercise usually didn't bother me. Maybe I was allergic to Kellith.

Resisting the pressure of his hand on my back, I kept some distance between our bodies. He wasn't physically unattractive—there were no ugly highborns. You had to go looking for trolls or goblins or the like before you found a fae male who didn't look better than a Hollywood superstar. Nevertheless, the white hair and pale blue eyes were a look that was definitely an acquired taste. His eyes were so light it was like looking into a clear pool of water. Kind of creepy, actually. I only met his gaze once before turning my own back to the colourful whirl of dresses surrounding me. I could do this. I just had to control my revulsion for a single dance. But his single-minded extermination of the people of an entire Realm showed that he was the kind of man who executed first and asked whether the victim was guilty later, and every moment in his arms made my skin crawl.

"You should wear blue more often," he said. "It suits you."

"Thanks."

He was wearing blue, too, of course, since blue and silver were the colours of the ruling house of Summer. I wondered if that was why the queen was decked out in silver tonight. Perhaps that was a political comment. The king's colours were gold and green, and it seemed odd that the ball to celebrate the return of the king was not awash with the king's signature colours. Probably, it meant nothing. If the king was like most men, he'd have left the decorating decisions to his wife, and it was possible she'd chosen the wintry theme simply to go with her dress.

Kellith led me through a spin. "I was sorry to hear that your mother has disappeared. Has there been any sign of her yet?"

"No." I made the mistake of meeting his eyes, and looked away at once. His face wore a very proper expression of concern, but his eyes told a different story, hard and uncaring, and rage boiled inside me.

"It must have been an idyllic childhood, growing up in a little cottage in the woods, just the two of you."

"Yes, it was." Though it was no business of his where I'd grown up, and it concerned me that he'd taken the trouble to find out. I did *not* want to get on the radar of a man like the Lord of Summer. Although I guess it was too late for that—I'd already scuttled his scheme to rule the kingdom.

He spun me through another turn, and my head was still spinning as I rolled back into him. Despite the wintry decorations, it was warm in the ballroom among the press of dancers. A scent like gardenias was growing stronger, and I glanced around at the other dancers, wondering who was wearing such a heavy perfume. Several of them were looking back at me, including a dark-haired woman in light blue who was dancing with Jaxen and glaring daggers at me.

"I daresay she'll turn up. I assume Eldric is making enquiries?"

"Yes."

"Try not to worry, then. I hate to see such a pretty girl looking so glum."

He thought I looked glum? Couldn't the idiot tell the difference between miserable and unwell? At least, not unwell, exactly, but very odd. The room was still doing a slow spin around me and I was starting to feel lightheaded. Those drinks must have been a lot stronger than I'd thought. The tightness in my chest had passed, but there was definitely something wrong. My whole body felt weirdly tingly, like pins and needles all over.

"Who is that woman dancing with Jaxen?" They were

snuggled very close, but she didn't appear to be enjoying herself. Every time I looked at her, I found her black scowl staring straight back.

He glanced over. She was still glowering at me, but nodded when she met the Lord of Summer's gaze. "That's Blethna Arbre."

Oh, Lord. Dansen Arbre's widow, who was determined to blame me for the death of her husband. I hoped she wasn't going to make a scene. I really didn't feel up to it.

I searched the room for the Hawk, hoping to find his dark head moving through the crowd toward me. It would be beyond embarrassing if I fainted in the Lord of Summer's arms. I could hear the sniggering now, about how the poor inferior mortal couldn't hold her fairy liquor. And apart from the personal embarrassment, it probably wouldn't reflect well on the king, to have his changeling pet disgrace herself at his ball. Rothbold had enough to deal with without that.

"Your eyes are like a meadow of cornflowers," Kellith said, startling me out of my thoughts. Surely he wasn't trying to crack on to me? But when I looked at him, there was no admiration in his eyes. More puzzlement, as if he saw something that he hadn't expected.

"Sorry?" The smell of gardenias was stronger than ever, almost cloying. Don't get me wrong, I liked gardenias as much as the next person, but I wanted to dunk whoever had worn that perfume in a bath of acid. It was making me feel most peculiar.

"I've never seen eyes that particular colour before.

They're very unusual." He raised his head like a hound questing for a scent, and his eyes widened. "The king has been especially generous to you, hasn't he?"

"The king is most gracious." What in the name of the Lady was he talking about? I suppose he thought me and my cornflower eyes should be serving in the kitchens, not twirling around the ballroom with the bright and noble.

"My Lord," said a voice that had me sagging with relief, though its polite tone was as cold as the wintry landscape we danced in. "May I cut in?"

Kellith relinquished me to the Hawk with a graceful nod, and the Hawk swept me away into the dance, leaving him standing there, looking after us.

"Just in the nick of time," I said, staring up into his tawny eyes. My knight in shining ... pirate costume. "Things were starting to get uncomfortable there. Was everything all right?"

"With—?"

"With whatever you went to do."

He brushed that aside. "It was nothing. You didn't enjoy your dance with our Lord of Summer?"

"You don't like him much, do you?"

He shrugged. "You mortals have an expression, *I wouldn't piss on him if he was on fire*. That about sums it up."

"I hope I don't have to talk to him again this evening. I have the horrible feeling he was about to make a pass at me. Kept going on about my eyes." My head was still spinning uncomfortably, but it didn't seem such a problem now that it was the Hawk's arms around me and not Kellith's. I snuggled in a little closer. "Which reminds me—I've been meaning to ask you. You told Jaxen you were my protector—but what exactly are you protecting me from? Undesirable dance partners?"

I was smiling up at him, but his gaze was serious. "Anything that might harm you." He lowered his voice, though surely no one could have heard him over the music anyway. "You don't know everything that is going on."

"Then tell me."

"It's not my place. But I fear that your service to the king has made you a target, and I'm at least partially responsible for dragging you into that, so now it's my duty to protect you."

"Your duty? Is that all it is?"

His arms tightened just a little. "I didn't say it was an unwelcome duty."

The scent of gardenias surged around us, and my lightheadedness returned in full force. He caught me as I missed a step and stumbled awkwardly, losing the rhythm of the dance.

"Are you all right?" he asked.

"I feel a little wobbly," I admitted. "Would you mind if we went outside and got some air?"

"Of course not." He guided me off the dance floor and through an arch between the trees. Icicles hanging from the branches overhead tinkled like wind chimes as we passed underneath them. I hoped the king had magicked those suckers to stay put—one of them falling on someone's head could kill them.

Outside was a wide terrace, looking out over a wild garden of climbing roses and little hidden pools among the groves of trees. A path, gleaming white in the moonlight, led off invitingly into the greenery. There were no seats on the terrace, but the Hawk led me over to the broad stone balustrade, made of the same shining white stone as the rest of the palace, and I leaned against it, taking a few deep breaths. The moonlit garden wavered oddly in my vision and I dropped my head almost to the balustrade, so close I could feel the cold radiating off the stone.

A few other people shared the terrace with us— including Jaxen and bloody Blethna Arbre. Was she stalking me? But it was big enough to give us all some privacy, though I caught a few curious looks from the corner of my eye as the Hawk hovered over me solicitously.

"Maybe I need my purse back," I said, and he ducked inside to find it. After only a couple of minutes, he was back. I pulled my puffer out and took two deep drags of the medicine. It didn't feel quite like an asthma attack, but I was dizzy and a little short of breath. It certainly wouldn't hurt to take an extra dose, and I'd rather not be the centre of drama at the ball. I focused on calming my breathing.

"Would you like a drink of water? Your face is flushed."

"Yes, please."

The scent of gardenias drifted past my bowed head and I leaned over, checking the bushes beneath the terrace. Not a gardenia in sight. That woman, whoever she was, must have dowsed herself in a whole bottle of her stinky perfume.

"Are you hot?" His hand brushed briefly against my cheek.

"Smokin' hot," I said. "It's the dress."

He strode off to find me some water, and I took a deep breath and straightened, gazing out over the gardens. After a few moments, I felt almost back to normal and wished I hadn't worried him. The whole thing had been a fuss over nothing. It must have just been the stuffiness of the ballroom, combined with whatever that drink had been. I'd have to watch out for it in future. That stuff was potent.

I turned, leaning back against the balustrade, and watched the dancers swirl past the openings into the ballroom while I waited for the Hawk. It was like something out of a movie—the glittering crowd, each more beautiful than the last, the unearthly music drifting out into the dark garden, all set in the winter wonderland of the magical ballroom. For a moment, it struck me how lucky I was to be here, when I'd never expected to be able to return to the Realms. Hoped, yes. Expected, certainly not. I was well aware that no changelings who'd already been rejected by their fae parents had ever made it back before.

And now here I was, at Whitehaven itself, basking in the king's favour—and the personal attentions of his leading knight. It would have been truly sweet, except for my mother's death. And I'd just been dancing with the man who was singlehandedly responsible for beginning the vendetta against Illusion that had most likely caused her death. No wonder I'd felt a little queasy.

A familiar figure appeared on the terrace, stepping out from an archway off to my right. His jaunty steps—almost a swagger—drew the eyes of everyone he passed along the terrace. He wore black and gold, and the intricate gold embroidery on his jacket sparkled in the light from the ballroom as he approached.

"Raven. I didn't expect to see you here."

He flashed his white teeth in a grin, then swept into an exaggerated bow. "Why? Am I not good enough for you, now that you're the king's darling? Too proud to slum it with an old friend?"

"The Hawk said it was mainly fae nobility on the guest list." He was hardly an old friend—I'd barely known him a month—but, like the Hawk, he'd saved my life, so I was prepared to overlook that. I was still unsure of his motives, but that didn't stop me being grateful.

"Not the disreputable types that hang out in the Wilds? Maybe I sneaked in through the kitchens."

"I wouldn't put it past you." Though I was sure the kitchen entrance would be just as well guarded as the main entry, I was half inclined to believe he had scammed his way in somehow. "Disreputable" wasn't quite the right word, but there was something a little too laidback about him, a certain disregard for the rules, shall we say, that made his inclusion on the official guest list improbable. "But it's good to see you again. How are Thing One and Thing Two? I've missed them."

"They miss you, too. They don't get fed cabanossi anymore."

His ravens had kept an eye on me for months before I'd

discovered they were anything more than the ordinary ravens that they'd appeared. And a good thing they had. Without them, I would have died when the house I was living in exploded.

His nostrils flared, and the smile dropped away from his face. "What has happened to you?"

I stared, taken aback. Did I really look that bad? "Nothing. I'm fine. I felt a little odd—it must have been the wine—so I came outside to get some air. But, really, I'm fine."

He moved so close I would have backed away, but I was already hard up against the cold stone of the balustrade. He breathed in deeply, his nose practically in my hair. I could have sworn he was *sniffing* me. "Where is Jamison?"

Of all the questions he could have asked, that one caught me completely by surprise, so that I stared for a moment like a gasping fish before finding my tongue. "Jamison? I doubt he was invited to the ball. What's he got to do with anything?"

"Take your medicine. You have it with you, yes? The medicine that Jamison makes for you?"

"Yes, but I just took some. And I don't need—"

"*Take* it. Beak and claw, woman, before someone sees you!"

What in the name of the Tree had gotten into him? I'd never seen him so strange before. I dug into my purse, just to calm him, and took another lungful of my puffer under his watchful eye.

"How did you know Jamison made medicine for me?" I asked slowly, unable to shake the feeling that something was seriously off with this whole scene. I supposed he could have found out through his little bird spies, but why was it so important?

I caught another whiff of gardenia as he watched me with barely concealed panic in his eyes. He was making me feel panicky, too. I had the distinct feeling he was waiting for something, but I had no idea what, and I hated not knowing what was going on.

"Give me that." He all but snatched the puffer from my hands, turning it over with a look of suspicion on his face, then holding it up to his nose and smelling it. "This is human medicine."

"What? No—Jamison makes it for me specially." We both stared at the offending cylinder, with its factory printing on it. I recalled my own doubts when the girl had handed it to me. She must have mixed up my medicine with someone else's. Maybe the sticky note with my name on it had fallen off the correct tray and someone had picked it up and put it on another one.

"This is the wrong medicine," he insisted.

I couldn't understand his urgency. His eyes were darting around, checking out all the other people on the terrace. "How would you know? Are you a doctor now? But I don't need it, anyway. I'm fine now. I'll go see Jamison tomorrow and get it sorted out. Relax."

"Relax?" He gave a short, unhappy laugh. "You don't know what you're talking about."

First the Hawk, now him. Everyone had secrets they didn't want to share.

"Then tell me what the problem is. You're acting weird." Was he on drugs? "Or don't, I don't care. Maybe I'll just head back inside and go find the Hawk. He's a lot more fun than you."

"You can't." He caught my wrist in an iron grip.

I pulled, hard, but couldn't get free. I was glad, now, that there were other people on the terrace. He was starting to scare me.

"If you go in there, you'll die."

If I kicked him in the balls, he'd let go fast enough, but the situation wasn't quite that extreme yet. I tugged again, more firmly, but he held fast.

"Let go." I kept my voice calm but firm. If I went into the ballroom, I'd die? I'd spent an hour in there already and I was perfectly fine. The drugs theory was looking more and more likely. Best to just keep him calm until the Hawk returned.

"Let's go for a walk in the gardens." He began urging me along the terrace toward a broad flight of steps that led down to the white path through the trees.

"Let's not." I held back, but he was stronger than me, and dragged me to the top of the steps. There, I began to struggle for real. Once he got me among the trees, no one on the terrace would be able to see us. The Hawk wouldn't know where I'd gone. And I was suddenly very reluctant to be alone with Raven. "Let *go* of me!"

At that moment, the Hawk reappeared on the terrace, a glass of water in his hand. I breathed a sigh of relief and relaxed ever so slightly. The Hawk's eyes widened, then he dropped the glass and drew his sword, all in one fluid movement. The sound of glass shattering brought Raven's head whipping around.

Black wings burst from Raven's shoulders, and he snatched me into his arms, leaping skyward.

12

I should have kicked him in the nuts when I had the chance. I screamed and struggled against his pinioning arms, until he said, "Do you *really* want me to drop you?"

When I looked down and saw how high we were already, I stopped fighting and started clinging to him instead. The palace was rapidly dwindling, its white glow fading into the darkness. Below us, the Hawk was climbing in pursuit, his gold-tipped wings beating hard, a determined expression on his face. He was gaining, too. Raven had had a head start, but he was carrying extra weight, and the Hawk was unencumbered.

The Hawk still had his sword in his hand, and I had a horrifying mental image of him slicing Raven's dark wings to ruin, and me tumbling out of the sky. It was the tumbling bit I found horrifying, of course. He could slice Raven to kingdom come as far as I was concerned. I'd never been so angry in my life.

"What in the name of the Lady do you think you're doing?" I shouted. "Take me back right now."

"Not a chance, darling. You're safer with me." He was breathing hard with the effort of climbing, and his words came in short gasping rushes.

"Safer being kidnapped by a madman?" I had to yell to be heard over the thunder of his labouring wings, and the rush of wind against my face. Fortunately, I was in a yelling mood. "What the hell is wrong with you? The Hawk is about to cut you to ribbons—this is your last chance to turn around."

He glanced behind him and saw that the Hawk had indeed come closer, and he swore under his breath. At least, I thought it was swearing, until a mist boiled up around us, hiding us from view. I screamed as loudly as I could, hoping the Hawk would be able to follow the sound of my voice, and Raven swore for real.

"If you don't shut up, I swear I'll drop you," he growled.

A wind sprang up from nowhere, blowing the mist away. I glanced back at the Hawk, willing him on. He made a pushing motion with his hands, and the wind buffeted Raven, shoving him sideways in the sky. I screamed as I was nearly jerked from his arms.

Raven responded by folding his wings and dropping like a stone, arrowing down towards the town that sprawled around the knees of Whitehaven's castle. The Hawk plummeted after us, though he didn't try to use his Air magic again. I was grateful for that as the ground rushed up to meet us. One wrong move, and I'd be wiped all over the pavement like jelly.

Raven swooped through an archway over the street, and

a familiar tingle swept over my body—the feel of passing a magic barrier. All of a sudden, the town was gone, and the moonlit forests of the Wild rushed by below us instead. Behind us, the Hawk burst into view out of thin air—either he'd managed to track us, or he'd guessed where Raven was going. He was even closer, now, and that sword would soon be in slicing distance. I clung to Raven's neck, my eyes fixed on the Hawk, as Raven followed a Greenway from above.

Raven glanced behind, too, and saw that his nemesis was still on his tail. He whistled, a piercing sound that shivered through my body. There was magic in that sound, and in a moment, I knew what the magic had wrought.

A storm of ravens burst into being in the sky all around us. At first, I didn't realise what had happened, since they blended so well into the dark. It was as if the night had suddenly broken into pieces; sharp pieces with stabbing beaks, and claws that ripped and tore. I couldn't tell how many of them there were, but it was a lot—more ravens than I'd ever seen in one place before.

And all of them converged on the Hawk.

He struck out with his sword, and feathered bodies fell from the sky like black rain, but there were always more to take their place. He threw his arms out, and ravens tumbled around him as he whipped up a tornado. So many birds surrounded him that I could barely see him through a whirl of black bodies and flying feathers. I screamed, but I couldn't even hear my own voice above the thunder of wings and wind.

Raven took advantage of his distraction to streak ahead,

folding his black wings and diving again. I shut my eyes, certain we were about to smash into the ground, but he pulled up and skimmed just above it, hugging the Greenway as we fled through the darkness.

I looked over his shoulder, desperately searching for a sign of the Hawk in the sky, but the trees that overhung the path blocked my view. Was he safe?

Seeing how close we were to the ground, I hauled back and slugged Raven in the side of the head as hard as I could. He jerked violently, one wingtip grazing the trees beside the path.

He caught my hand with a snarl, and I struggled violently, determined to get away from him. He had fae strength, which made it hard, but he was also weary from the long chase through the sky, and I held nothing back, wriggling and kicking like a mad thing.

I managed to work my arm free again as the tingle of a gate shivered over my skin. Streetlights lit our way as I threw myself backward and brought both knees up, slamming them into his chest. He doubled over, the great wings missing a beat, and I tumbled free, falling on concrete.

I rolled, grazing my elbows and one bare shoulder. Willow's beautiful dress protected my legs. I sprang to my feet, fists up and ready to fight, wishing I had a knife. Fists weren't going to be much use against fae strength.

Raven hunched over with his hands resting on his knees, his breath coming in deep gasps and his great wings drooping around him. I'd well and truly winded him. I wasn't too upset about that.

I thought about running, but it was hard to outrun a man with wings. As I stood there, glaring at the top of his bent, dark head, I cursed myself for ever trusting him. Why was I such a lousy judge of character? Every crappy boyfriend I'd ever had paraded through my mind, taunting me with all the bad decisions I'd made. And now Raven. I'd thought he was one of the good guys. Seemed like there was only the Hawk left in that category now.

I hoped those birds hadn't given him too much trouble. There didn't seem much chance that he'd find me now, so I was on my own here. I looked around, sizing up my surroundings, and was surprised to find myself on familiar turf. We were standing right outside Jamison's Pharmacy.

It was dark inside, now, of course. I had no idea what time it was, but the night had the still quality of the very early hours of the morning, when even the late-night party-goers have gone home but the daylight world is not yet stirring. No one was on the street except us. There weren't even any parked cars.

Impatiently, I wiped my bleeding arm on the once-beautiful ballgown. "Why have you brought me here?"

He panted for a moment more, then slowly straightened, folding his wings back and letting them disappear. It looked as though the movement hurt him. Good. I hoped he was one massive bruise tomorrow. My skinned arms were stinging something awful, and I had no sympathy to spare for him.

"Remind me not to do you any more favours," he said.

"Favours? You kidnapped me, you feathered arsehole,

and set your bloody birds on the Hawk. Are you drunk or just criminally insane?"

He sighed wearily and rolled his shoulders as if they ached. "Neither, as it happens, though a drink would go down nicely right now. Perhaps that can be our next port of call."

"I'm not going anywhere else with you. Not until you tell me what the hell is going on."

His dark eyes glittered as he bared his teeth in something approximating a smile. He was angry, too, though what he had to be angry about I didn't know. No birdbrained psychopath had just kidnapped *him*. "That might prove a little difficult."

"Try."

He turned to contemplate the window display of the pharmacy. "It's a pity your friend Willow isn't here."

That was the first sensible thing he'd said, though I couldn't see the relevance until he spun and slammed a kick straight through the glass of the pharmacy's front door. I flinched at the unexpectedness of the move.

He reached through the hole in the door and unlatched it. "I've heard she's a useful companion for breaking and entering. Come on."

I followed him inside, uneasy. Was he still obsessing over my asthma medicine? Smashing the front door of Jamison's shop seemed a poor way to repay him for his help over the years. "Couldn't this have waited until the morning?"

"Not if you want to live to see it."

He led the way to the back of the shop, where the door to Jamison's sith was. It was closed, of course. He would hardly leave it open for anyone to wander in accidentally. That didn't stop Raven. He grasped the handle and laid his forehead against the door, murmuring to it in the language of the High Fae.

To my surprise, the handle gave under his touch, and he pushed the door open. Most siths were much harder to gain entrance to than that. In fact, it was usually impossible unless you already had permission from the owner and the door spell recognised you. I had a hard time believing Jamison would have given that permission to someone like Raven. I followed him in, feeling the familiar tingle on my skin as I passed the barrier.

Inside was dark, which was no surprise. Jamison would be in bed at this time of night, since he was one of those fae who had adapted to the daylight routines of the humans. All of us who lived in the mortal world spent at least some part of the day awake, and he liked to work in the business, which necessitated being awake when his customers were. There was an odd smell in the room, which I couldn't quite place.

Raven closed the door and snapped his fingers. Faelight bloomed on his fingertips, rising into the air like a soap bubble and expanding until it hung below the wooden rafters like a full moon. It wasn't very bright, but it was enough for our night-loving eyes to see clearly.

What I saw stopped me dead in my tracks for a moment—but only for a moment. Two legs sprawled on the floor, sticking out from the other side of the big work table in the centre of the room. With a cry of horror, I rushed around the table and sank to my knees.

In a pool of his own blood, Jamison lay there, his throat slit from ear to ear.

13

"Rot and ruin, woman, don't touch him." Raven hauled me to my feet with a vice-like grip on my upper arm. The hem of my ball gown trailed in the blood, which was sticky and slowly congealing, and I had two round patches where my knees had rested in it.

"Why not? I don't think it's catching." I jerked my arm out of his grip, rubbing broodingly at my bicep where he'd crushed it. "We should at least close his eyes."

Poor Jamison had been such a well-put-together person in life, always smartly dressed, his white lab coat neatly pressed. He would shudder if he could see himself now, drenched in blood, sprawled on his kitchen floor like a puppet whose strings had been cut.

"You don't want to leave traces of yourself at a murder scene."

"Have you been watching too much *CSI*? No mortal detectives are going to be combing the scene for DNA."

"I'm not talking about mortal detectives. You led a

sheltered life in that cottage of yours, didn't you? You have no idea what magic is capable of."

"How long do you think he's been dead?" The thought of him lying here, unloved, his death unnoticed, tore at me. And I'd never gotten to tell him I was sorry for all but calling him a liar the night he had tried to help my mother.

The silver globe dipped lower, though Raven gave no command, throwing a ghastly light across Jamison's waxen features. He crouched down, inspecting the body without touching anything. "No more than an hour, I'd say. That blood isn't fresh, but it hasn't been out of his body long enough to dry, either." He sniffed doubtfully around the gaping wound in Jamison's throat. "No magic's been used here—or if it has, the smell of blood is hiding it."

"You don't need magic to slit someone's throat," I pointed out.

"No, you don't. But perhaps you need it to persuade your victim to let you in so that you can kill them in their otherwise unassailable sith."

"You got in all right."

"That's because Jamison knows me well. *Knew* me. Damn it! They must have followed Anawen when she fled here, to find him after all these years." He stood abruptly and strode to the nearest shelves, where he started searching through jars and boxes, opening cupboards and poking around inside.

"What are you doing?"

"Looking for another one of those things of yours. What do you call them? Puppers?"

"Puffers." Indignation grew in my heart as he tossed Jamison's house, pulling things out of cupboards willy-nilly and leaving them on the floor. "You can't just help yourself to his things."

"Why not? He won't be using them."

"You're robbing the dead! It's not right. Oh, for God's sake, will you stop it?" I demanded as a jar tipped over, spilling white powder over the shelf. "What is this obsession of yours with my asthma medicine? You're like a dog with a bone."

I didn't see why it mattered. How long had I been taking the wrong medicine? Three days? Yet I felt fine. Maybe I was human enough that human medicine worked on me after all, and all these years of seeing Jamison for a personalised version had been wasted.

But, apparently, my mother had thought it necessary. She was the one who'd brought me here. I'd been bored that first time, a seventeen-year-old with better things to do with her time than sit around in a dusty apothecary, anxious to get back home to Autumn. I'd explored the shelves to kill time, checking the labels on anything that looked interesting, while Jamison and my mother conducted a low-voiced conversation at the table.

And then I'd gone outside to look at his herb garden and my mother had left. Stupid, naïve kid that I was, I'd thought she'd only left the room. I hadn't realised she'd gone for good, abandoning me to the mortal world, until Jamison had had to explain to me that she was never coming back, and I was stuck here, in the mortal world that

I hadn't seen since I was a baby. He'd been so distressed by my tears, patting me awkwardly on the back as I howled, head down on the kitchen table. He'd fussed around and made me a cup of tea, but I couldn't drink it.

In the end, not knowing what else to do, he'd taken me to Edgar's house. Edgar was a changeling, too, the oldest one I'd ever seen. Seventy-two years old, he lived alone with his fat, ginger cat. He had a gentle way about him that soothed new arrivals, and it fell to him to shelter most of them, explaining their new reality to them. I hadn't heard a word he'd said that night. My mother had walked out without a backward glance, abandoning me among strangers in a strange world. It had been days before I could function again.

"Do you *want* to die?" Raven's voice jerked me away from my memories, back to the room where it had all started. It reeked of blood, now. In the dark, lit only by Raven's silvery globe, it had an eerie quality, and a shiver ran down my spine as I looked around. Maybe Jamison's killers were still here, lurking outside in the garden, watching us through the windows.

"Who's going to kill me? You?"

"Don't be a fool. I'm trying to help you. Your mother's dead, now Jamison's dead; surely even you can see that you could be next."

"Yriell thinks my mother was killed because she was from Illusion. I'm just a changeling, a human, and Illusion was gone before I was even born. There's no reason for anyone to go after me."

He ran a hand through tousled dark hair in a gesture of frustration. "It's like you *want* to die of iron poisoning. Do you have any idea what a painful death that is?"

I opened my mouth to argue that no one had poisoned Jamison, then stopped. How did *he* know that my mother had been poisoned by iron? I'd only just found out myself, and I doubted Yriell was blabbing the news around.

A terrible suspicion entered my mind. He'd been acting so strangely all night. I'd thought he was my friend because he'd helped me before, but really, what did I know about him? I didn't even know his real name. And after his treatment of the Hawk tonight, I had trouble considering him a friend. Had *he* been the one to poison my mother?

"How do you know how my mother died?"

He paused, a pottery jar in one hand, the lid in the other, but he didn't turn around, as if he was racking his brain for an appropriate answer. The moment stretched horribly before he said, "The birds hear a lot of things."

That was bullshit. There were no birds inside this sith, or Yriell's house. A chill crept over me, and I glanced around for a weapon. A knife block sat on the bench, but he was closer to it than I was. Once again, I lamented the impossibility of carrying weapons with a ball gown. This was why I liked to live in jeans and jackets with lots of pockets and room for concealment. The damn dress didn't even do a decent job of concealing *me*, let alone anything I might have liked to carry with me.

Noiselessly, I backed up toward the door that led back

into the shop, but he turned around and saw me with my hand reaching for the door.

"Going somewhere?"

I took a deep breath, calculating my chances of reaching the street before he caught me. Maybe there was something in the shop I could use against him—a walking stick? A paper weight?

"You poisoned her, didn't you?"

"I can't believe you just asked me that."

"Are you going to kill me, too?"

His eyes narrowed. If he'd been angry before, now he was furious. "Are you mad? I'm trying to stop you from … stop you from being killed."

I had the strongest feeling that he'd been about to say something else. "Then tell me how you know my mother was poisoned. Straight out. No dancing around the truth or fae trickery."

He slammed the jar he was holding back on the shelf with such force I was surprised it didn't shatter. "Fae trickery? Rot and ruin, you ought to know who your friends are."

"How, if you won't tell me anything? And don't think I haven't noticed that you're still refusing to answer the question. Once and for all, did you kill my mother?"

"*No.*"

They say that fae can't lie. Like most things to do with the fae, it's not as cut and dried as that, but for the most part, if you ever manage to get a straight answer out of one of them, you can be reasonably sure that it's true. Some of my tension seeped away at the force behind that "no", as if he was affronted at the very idea.

"Okay, then." I let go of the door handle and folded my arms. "Then what is your interest in me? Why are you panicking about this medicine? For that matter, why did you sic Thing One and Thing Two on me in the first place?" I'd never met him before our encounter in the Wilds a few weeks ago, yet he'd been keeping tabs on me for months, watching me through the eyes of his ravens. Who did that to some random changeling? Something more was going on here.

Outside, the thin wail of a siren sounded, still distant but moving this way. We both looked at the body on the floor in the same instant.

"We don't have time for this right now," he said, striding past me to the door. "We need to get out of here before they come to investigate the break-in."

Impatiently, he indicated I should leave the sith, but I hesitated. "What about Jamison? We can't just leave him lying there."

"I'll send someone to bury him and observe the proper rites later." He shut the sith door behind us and murmured something to the wood. I was willing to bet that it was locked again, and any mortals who opened it would only find the tiny staff kitchen behind it. "For now, we need to go. Your safety is more important."

We hurried through the dark shop and out onto the street. There was no one in sight, but someone must have called in the smashed door. Someone could be watching us from concealment even now. The wail of the siren was so close it must only be around the corner.

"The only threat to my safety around here is you," I said, striding down the street with him still glued to my side. "Leave me alone. I'm going home."

"You can't," he said.

"Watch me."

A cop car passed us, heading toward the store. Maybe that was a good thing—Raven could hardly coerce me in full view of the human police.

Turned out I was wrong about that. He caught my face between his hands and looked straight into my eyes. "Sorry about this."

And then the world went black.

Black wings beat at my face. Claws raked at my skin, and I threw up my arms to protect myself, struggling to break free of the suffocating wings.

With a gasp, I woke up and found myself tangled in heavy blankets. The grey light of very early morning was seeping into an unfamiliar room through a gap between the curtains. I blinked in confusion at a high ceiling which was painted dark blue and dotted with shimmering constellations, then pushed back the blankets and sat up. The stone walls were hung with tapestries in vivid greens, mostly depicting forest scenes. Heavy, dark blue velvet drapes covered the window.

My feet sank into thick, luxurious carpet as I padded across to the window and pulled back the curtains. The window was tall and thin, but still wide enough for me to fit through, if that became necessary. Any plan of escaping that way died when I saw how high up I was—three or four storeys. It was misty outside, but the view was mainly trees, like the tapestries, with an occasional roof peeking through. None of the other buildings I could see were anywhere near as tall as the one I was in. Or as large. A huge wing of it stretched off to my left, complete with towers and crenellated battlements. Probably the same castle Raven had taken me to before, though this view of it was unfamiliar.

I left the window and opened the panelled door of the bedroom. There was no sign of the dress I'd been wearing last night. Someone had put me into a nightgown that looked like something Little Red Riding Hood's granny might have worn—long-sleeved, it fell to the floor and buttoned up to the neck. That someone had better not have been Raven.

I'd been more than half afraid that the door would be locked, but it opened easily under my hand, into a lounge room where the green theme continued. A group of comfy-looking armchairs upholstered in green and brown sat before a fireplace, and a small dining table stood at the other end of the room. There was a desk, too, under another large window. The curtains here were open, showing grey, misty sky.

My bare feet sank into the soft carpet as I opened another door and found a bathroom tiled in dark green, with gold fittings. It was small and there was no shower, but the bath was large, one of those old-fashioned claw-footed ones. Not that it mattered. I wasn't planning on staying here long enough to enjoy long, soaking baths. I strode to the only other door and yanked on the handle.

This one was locked.

Damn. So I was a prisoner. I'd hoped I wasn't, but what other conclusion was a girl supposed to draw when someone used magic to knock her out and abduct her? Raven had told me not to go home, and he was clearly prepared to do whatever it took to make sure I didn't. I tested the king's gift of magic, reaching for the Wilds, trying to open a way through. I wasn't too surprised to discover I couldn't. Most fae had wards set up to prevent people gating in and out of their homes.

If Raven thought that meant I was going to meekly accept my captivity, he was sadly mistaken. Sure, his magic gave him a great advantage over me, but I wasn't a helpless damsel. First priority was finding some clothes. It was hard to stand up to your enemies wearing Grandma's nightie.

Back in the bedroom, I checked the carved wardrobe. It held a range of simple dresses in the fae style, long and flowing, which didn't suit my purposes at all. Fortunately, the drawers offered a pair of jeans and a selection of T-shirts. That was more like it. I pulled them on, and they adjusted themselves to fit. Fairy wardrobes were handy like that—any size could be catered for with a sprinkle of magic. There was even a pair of sneakers, which magically shrank to hug my feet. I felt my confidence return with the clothes. If only I had a weapon to go with them.

The desk seemed the most likely spot to find something useful, so I went back into the main room. A letter opener would be ideal—something long and sharp suited my mood at the moment. I'd never been kidnapped before, and didn't care to ever repeat the experience. Rage at being swept up so highhandedly, as if I were no more than a handbag to be carried around for its owner's convenience, simmered under the surface of my methodical searching. Raven had better hope that his servants had been smart enough not to leave me anything I could use against him, because I'd stab the bastard without a second thought if I had the chance.

Sadly, the desk drawers revealed nothing more lethal than some notepaper and pens. None of the mess of ink and quills here—they were modern pens from the human world. One of them even had the name and logo of a popular hotel chain on it.

Momentarily stumped, I looked around the room, but nothing presented itself. A vase of flowers stood on its own column between the two windows. I could always bash someone over the head with that, but I'd hoped for something a little subtler, something that I could carry with me, hidden away.

A flock of birds swooping and dipping above the trees caught my eye. The mist was clearing, burned off by the rising sun. There was something odd about those birds, and I shaded my eyes and squinted into the light. I was used to seeing ravens around their master, but these weren't ravens.

In fact, they weren't birds at all. One broke away from the flock and zoomed toward my window, and I realised, with a thrill of delight, that they were tiny dragons.

The little dragon, completely fearless, landed right on my windowsill. I stood stock still, afraid to scare him away, and stared at him. He wasn't much bigger than a raven. How could a dragon be so small, even a baby one? They were the size of aeroplanes, huge and awe-inspiring. The tiny thing staring boldly back at me would surely never grow that big.

He was green, with tiny, knobby lumps over his skin instead of scales, lumps that sparkled and caught the light. A line of larger knobs—spikes, almost—formed a ridge up his spine. He had large, golden eyes with a vertical pupil like a cat's, and he stared at me without blinking until my own eyes watered in sympathy. His tail, wrapped neatly around his feet, ended in a vicious spike, but the rest of him didn't look particularly ferocious. He was shaped more like a cat than a lizard, though his head was horse-like in a way that was reminiscent of seahorses, save for the tip of his long snout, which had a sharp, beak-like curve on it.

In short, he was one cute little guy. It was only the wings, now folded neatly against his back, that had made me think of dragons. Evidently tired of staring, he leaned forward and tapped with his beak on the glass, then sat back, watching to see what I would do.

I was seriously tempted to open the window for him. That little knock had been so polite. He seemed friendly enough, but that beak looked sharp, and I wasn't sure I wanted a wild dragonet flapping around the room. But then a knock, much louder than his, sounded on the door to the room, and he took flight, startled.

"I'd let you in," I yelled at the door, "but that feathered arsehole has locked the door."

I was annoyed that my visitor had spooked the little dragon. I hoped it was Raven; I needed an outlet for my anger. There was no reply, but I heard a key turn in the lock, and then the door opened.

Willow stood there, precariously balancing a full breakfast tray in one hand, the key in the other. This was even more astounding than the appearance of the little dragon on my windowsill.

"Holy shit! What are you doing here? Did he kidnap you, too?"

She gave me a quizzical glance as she came in, shutting the door behind her with one foot. "Do you think I'd be serving you breakfast if I'd been kidnapped?"

"I just—" I shut my mouth, aware that I was gaping at her like an idiot. But it was so unexpected. Willow was the last person I would have expected to find here, in Raven's castle. "I'm just surprised to find you serving anyone. It's not really your style."

My attempt at humour didn't even raise an answering insult. She concentrated on settling the heavy tray on the table and setting out the cup and saucer. I mean, I'd seen her serve people food before, but the surreal feeling grew as she carefully arranged the cutlery on each side of a plate heaped with bacon, eggs, and tomatoes, tucking the napkin under the fork just so.

Then, to top it all off, she pulled out the chair and waited expectantly for me to sit.

I stared at her. "Well? Aren't you going to explain what you're doing here?"

She shrugged. "You seem to think Raven is a villain. He thought it might help to see a familiar face."

"And so you came? Just like that?" Something wasn't adding up here.

"Why not? We're friends."

Was she as crazy as Raven himself? Friends didn't help reassure their friends that their jailer was a nice guy. Friends busted their friends out of prison. This was so out of character for her. And besides ...

"You vowed you were never coming back to the Realms until Sage was also welcome. What happened to that?"

Her glance slid to the side, then back again. "Desperate times call for desperate measures."

"Okay, fine." I folded my arms across my chest. "Then tell me why it's so important that I stay here. Why couldn't I come back to your sith?"

Again, the eyes slid away before she replied. I'd never seen anything so dodgy. Willow was nothing if not direct. If she had something to say, she'd say it to your face and no apologies. "I think Raven can explain that better. I just wanted to reassure you that everything was okay. I'll go now."

She moved toward the door, pulling the key from her pocket. She was seriously going to lock me in again. This was nuts.

"Wait, Willow." An odd suspicion was growing in my mind. Maybe it was all the talk of Illusion lately—but Willow knew my feelings about tea first thing in the morning. I mean, she wasn't a details person, but I had to start the day with coffee or it ruined everyone's morning. That kind of thing was hard to forget. And yet, there stood the teapot, as if every breakfast we'd shared together had never happened. "Aren't you going to pour my tea? You know how much I love tea with breakfast."

"Sure," she said, moving back towards the table.

That settled it. This wasn't Willow. I launched myself across the room, tackling her to the floor. She shrieked—a very un-Willow-like noise—and flailed ineffectually at me. I wrenched the key from her hand and pinned her to the floor with the weight of my body.

"Who the hell are you?" I snarled. "What have you done with my friend?"

"What do you mean? Get off me!"

She tried to wriggle away, so I let go with one hand long enough to slap her face. She stared up at me in shock, her eyes filling with tears.

"You're not Willow. Who are you?"

She blinked, and tears leaked from the corners of her eyes. A bright red handprint was forming on her cheek, but I had no sympathy for her. Seeing the resolution on my face, she blinked again, and in an instant, Willow's face was gone, and a stranger lay gazing miserably up at me.

15

She looked young, barely a teenager, maybe twelve or
thirteen, and from the way the tears still rolled, I
guessed that that was her real age and not some Glamour
of youth. This was no old and experienced fae.

"Who are you?" I demanded again, stifling a feeling of
guilt for slapping a little kid around. "What have you done
with Willow?"

"I'm Lirra." She sniffed, staring up at me defiantly
through her tears. "How dare you slap me?"

"I'll do a lot more than slap you if you don't answer my
questions." I wouldn't really—I drew the line at abusing
kids, even if they were working for the enemy, but she
didn't need to know that. If she thought I meant it, she'd
be more likely to tell what she knew.

She was pretty, of course—she was fae, it went without
saying—with the same blue-black hair as Raven. Her tear-
filled eyes were green, and her face was delicate, though her
cheeks were still rounded with baby fat. She wasn't very

strong, since I, a mere mortal, was having no trouble keeping her pinned to the floor—or perhaps she wasn't much of a fighter. Her outrage at being slapped certainly suggested she wasn't used to a rough-and-tumble lifestyle.

"What have you done with Willow?"

"Nothing." She squirmed, and I released the pressure on her a little, though I didn't let her up. "I don't even know any Willow."

"That's crap. How could you mimic her so perfectly if you've never met her? Where is she?"

"It's true," she insisted. "I used the dress."

I frowned. She'd better start giving some real answers soon. "What dress? What are you talking about?"

"The dress you were wearing when you got here. It belonged to someone else, didn't it? This Willow person?"

"Ye-es."

"I only have to touch someone's possessions to be able to take on their appearance."

I stared at her for a moment. "You're from Illusion, aren't you?"

She rolled her eyes, and I had to fight the urge to slap her again. Maybe it seemed obvious to her, but this was all new to me. There weren't even supposed to be any survivors left from the old Realm. Everyone thought Summer had killed them all. Now they were popping up everywhere—first my mother, possibly Jamison, and now this girl, Lirra. How had they all managed to escape the purge for so long?

I got up, dragging Lirra with me over to the bed. In fact,

if Lirra was as young as she looked, there must be more of them. Her mother, at least, must have survived the fall of Illusion in order to give birth to her.

With my free hand, I picked up Grandma's nightie, then spun Lirra around and shoved her face down on the mattress. Before she could recover, I ripped one of the sleeves from the nightie.

"What are you doing?" she cried, as I pulled her hands together behind her back and tied them.

"What does it look like? I'm escaping."

I hauled her up and used the trailing end of the sleeve to tie her to one of the bedposts.

"I'll scream."

"Then I'll slap you again. Harder, this time."

"Don't you know who I am?"

"Do I look like I give a crap?"

I ripped the other sleeve off the nightie, and her eyes widened.

"What are you going to do with that?"

"I'm making an anti-screaming device."

She struggled as I gagged her, lashing out with bare feet, but I managed to avoid getting kicked. She glared at me over the gag, her green eyes livid. Too bad. Pretty little princess Lirra would just have to bear the ignominy for a little while. I wondered if she was Raven's little sister, since they shared the same dark hair, and I couldn't see why else a teenager would be roaming his castle. Was Raven from Illusion, too?

Not that I really cared. I would be just as happy never

to see Raven again. He'd actually kidnapped me. I'd been right to think there was something dodgy about him. If only I'd been a little less trusting, I might have spent the night dancing in the Hawk's arms instead of trapped here.

I snagged the key to the door from the carpet where I'd dropped it, thoughts of the Hawk only increasing my anger at Raven. He'd sent his birds against the knight last night as though he were an enemy, after all his solicitude for the Hawk's health and pretending to be his friend. That was okay, though. Two could play at that game. Raven would find I didn't make a good enemy.

I slipped out of the room, locking the door behind me and pocketing the key. They might have to break their pretty carved door down to get to Lirra. Cry me a river. The long hall was lined with doors on both sides and watched over by a gallery of stern-looking portraits. I carefully opened doors until I found what I was looking for—a small, winding staircase at the very end of the corridor.

The stairs were so steep and spiralled so tightly that they must have been meant for servants. Hopefully, that meant I wouldn't run into Raven on the way down to freedom. After half a turn, I reached a tall, slitted window that showed a view over a green-roofed town built around a small lake. More of the tiny dragons splashed in the lake and flitted in the skies above it. I frowned as I continued down the stairs. This was nothing like the castle I remembered from my last visit with Raven. How many castles did the guy own?

I'd passed another window and a door when I heard the

door at the bottom of the stairs open, and male voices echoed up the stone walls toward me. Shit. I hurried back up the stairs to the door I'd just passed and slipped through, pulling it closed behind me as quietly as I could. Fortunately, the long corridor I found myself in—a twin to the one on the floor above—was empty. I could still hear the faint sound of footsteps on the stairs, so I opened the first door I came to and ducked inside. I didn't want to get caught in the open if they were coming to this floor.

And of course, the way my luck was running lately, they were. I eased the door shut behind me just as the door to the stairwell opened. Turning, I found myself in a library with a massive desk and chairs at one end, and a small grouping of lounges in front of a fireplace at the other. In the hallway outside, the voices were getting closer. Were they coming in here? I darted into hiding behind an overstuffed brocade lounge, whose long, ruffled skirt hid the fact that I was crouching behind it.

The door opened again, and two men came in. At least, I couldn't see them, but I guessed by their heavy tread that they were men, and as soon as one spoke, I knew it was Raven.

"I panicked, okay?" he said, as he shut the door behind them. "Where else could I take her? Back to my home? That's the first place the Hawk would look."

"And now he'll look here instead, and we'll be exposed. Why couldn't you leave her back in the mortal world? We all agreed that that was safest." The man settled into an armchair at the other end of the room. "It was what Anawen wanted."

Anawen was my mother's real name. This guy knew her? The urge to peek around the lounge to see who Raven was talking to was almost overwhelming, but I managed to control myself. I didn't want to get recaptured now. All I had to do was remain hidden until they left, and I could escape.

A chair creaked as Raven sat down, too, followed by a thud that sounded like his boots landing on the desk. "I can't let her loose until I can find an apothecary who understands human medicine as well as Jamison did. We need to mock up something convincing enough that she'll keep taking it. The minute anyone sees her like this, the secret's out—and she's the king's pet. Someone *will* see her."

What was he talking about? Sees me like *what*? I looked just the same as I always did.

"If only she hadn't got involved in the king's affairs," the other man said with a weary sigh.

"That damn Hawk has a lot to answer for," Raven agreed. "I thought blowing up her house would be enough to dissuade her from that little adventure."

"Her line isn't easily dissuaded," his companion said dryly, but I was hardly listening. My mind was reeling with shock. *Raven* had blown up my house?

All this time, I'd been so grateful that his little pets, Thing One and Thing Two, had stopped me going back into the house just before it exploded. So grateful that he'd been watching over me, this unknown benefactor of mine, and had managed to save me from whoever was trying to kill me. And now it turned out that *he* was the one trying to kill me.

It hadn't made sense at the time—if someone was trying to stop us looking for the king, why go after the powerless changeling? My death wouldn't have stopped the Hawk from looking—hell, the Hawk had been looking for twenty years. Nothing short of his own death would have stopped him. So why not attack him instead of me? But we'd been so caught up in events, that little oddity had been swept aside.

Why hadn't Raven wanted the king found? But if he hadn't wanted the king found, why had he helped the Hawk and me later, in the Wilds, when we could so easily have been killed? None of this was making sense.

I tuned back into the conversation, aware that I'd missed some of their talk in my shock. This was no time to lose focus; I needed as much information as I could get.

"… could use her as an emissary to the king," Raven was saying. "We may as well make use of the fact that she's the flavour of the month at Court."

"Do you really believe that Summer will stop hounding us now the king has returned? Who do you think killed Anawen and Jamison? There are so few of us left, I'm not prepared to risk it."

"But we could expose Kellith, have him removed from the game. If not now, when? How long are your people prepared to hide?"

"As long as it takes. And you're naïve if you think the king will cast down his own brother-in-law. He married

Ceinwen in the first place because he needed that alliance. He's in no position to repudiate Kellith."

"Besides, if you cut off that snake's head, there are others ready to take his place," said a new voice, a woman's. I jumped in surprise, not having heard her come in with the others. "Are we any better off with Merritt as Lord of Summer? He takes after his father in more than looks."

"You're making a mistake," Raven said. His voice moved across the room. I hoped he was only pacing to the window, but I shrank a little smaller behind my lounge anyway, as if I could hide better that way. "The king is back, ready to take the kingdom in hand again. Do you think he's prepared to forget twenty years of imprisonment? Hand him an excuse and he'll be only too happy to take Summer down."

"If we lose her now, then everything Anawen sacrificed was in vain," the woman said, a bitter note in her voice. "Only being a changeling protects her. If we ask her to speak for us, that only cements her link with Illusion in our enemies' eyes. It puts her in more danger. I'm not prepared to take that risk yet. We should keep her here."

"But the king will be searching for her," the other man said. "We *can't* keep her here."

I liked this guy; he seemed keen to get rid of me, and I was all for being sent back to the mortal world. Not that I was going to wait around hoping he'd win the argument.

"And the Hawk," Raven added.

The other man scoffed. "Then we have at least twenty years before he finds her."

"Don't underestimate him. He knows who I am."

Yeah, you tell him, Raven. The Hawk would find me, sooner or later. He was not the kind to give up. Not that I was waiting around to be rescued. I was perfectly capable of getting myself out of this mess.

The man sighed. "Then perhaps you're right. We should tell her and enlist her help."

"How good is she at keeping secrets?" the woman asked. "Are you really prepared to trust our survival to her?"

The man started to argue, but there was a knock on the door, and someone came in. "Lord, your guest has disappeared."

"What?" Raven left the window and strode across the room. The other two followed him out, the man muttering something under his breath.

I waited until the door had closed behind them and silence had settled on the room. I was almost certain the woman had gone with them, but she'd fooled me before, sneaking around on noiseless feet. After a few moments, I risked a peek around the corner of the lounge, and found the room empty.

Lirra certainly hadn't wasted any time getting free. I'd thought to have more time before the alarm was raised. Still, perhaps it was for the best. Those three seemed as though they could have argued forever, and I would have been trapped behind the lounge, listening to them.

The corridor was quiet when I opened the door. I assumed Raven and his friends had taken the stairs to my former room to see for themselves what had happened. I hurried down the stairs in the opposite direction, towards the outside world and freedom.

There were two doors at the bottom of the staircase, one leading into the building and the other opening into a small courtyard planted with a herb garden. On the other side of the courtyard, a heavy door stood open, without a guard in sight, though I could clearly see a path leading away to the distant town through it. That seemed odd, but I was happy to take whatever luck I could get.

I slipped through the door and tried again to reach for the Wilds. Still nothing. Damn. That seemed overly paranoid of Raven, since I was technically outside his walls, but some fae were like that. I'd have to keep going until I found the limits of the spell—I just hoped it wasn't too far. Now they knew I was missing, it wouldn't be long before they came after me. I ignored the path leading so invitingly down the hill to the town, and headed instead for the nearest trees. Fortunately, I knew a thing or two about slipping through the woods without leaving a trail. With a bit of luck, I'd be free and clear.

The woods near the castle were more open than the forests of Autumn, which could be a problem. Large trees stood spaced well apart, with little undergrowth between them. It would be a lovely wood for a leisurely stroll, but it wasn't so great for finding hiding places when you were being hunted.

A raven cawed somewhere behind me and I froze. Those damn birds of his. I started moving faster, keeping under the spreading branches of the trees to make it harder for them to spot me from the air. Up ahead, the trees thinned even further. Dammit. That was the last thing I needed, but I kept going, almost running now. I had to get away.

Then I burst out of the trees and almost ran right off the edge of the world.

16

Lady save me. I stared, unable for a moment to make sense of what I was seeing. Far below me—so far that it looked like an illustration from a book—a patchwork of tiny fields spread out. In the distance, a mountain range towered above the fields, with rocky foothills climbing to meet the highest peaks. I steadied myself with a hand on the nearest tree trunk. The view was disorienting.

In front of me, the land simply stopped. I wasn't standing on the top of a mountain—I was way too high for that. There was simply nothing beyond where I stood. I looked back, open-mouthed, at where the towers of the castle emerged through the trees. This whole thing—castle, town, lake, woods, and all—rested on a floating island.

It was the biggest one I'd ever seen, though, admittedly, I hadn't seen that many. But it made Oldriss, the island that the Hawk called home, look like a tiny pebble in comparison. If I had needed any convincing about the power of magic, this island would have been prime evidence. Keeping something this big afloat must require an enormous amount of power.

My heart sank as I realised that my escape plans were screwed. Raven doubtless had the whole island warded against gating in and out. Unless I grew wings, there was no way out of here.

I'd have to go back and hope that the grumpy dude managed to convince Raven to let me go. It was either that or wait here until they found me, and be dragged back. I'd rather walk back in under my own steam than as a prisoner.

A winged shape darted in my peripheral vision, and I still flinched, even though I'd more than half-talked myself into returning to the castle. What did it matter if the ravens found me now?

But it wasn't a raven.

One of the tiny dragonets perched on a tree branch that hung out over the void, regarding me with its little head tipped to one side. Was it the same one as before? It was the same shimmering green colour, but I couldn't tell. It certainly shared the same fearless curiosity. I wondered if it really was a baby, or if it was some tiny species of dragon I hadn't heard of. There had been so many of them in the skies above the lake—surely there couldn't be that many babies? And where were the adults, if so?

Maybe I didn't want to know. I didn't need to add dragons to my current list of problems. Though perhaps if one swooped down out of the skies, I could ride it to freedom. This little guy certainly couldn't give me a lift.

He warbled at me, an oddly tuneful sound.

"Hello," I said. "Have you come looking for me?"

It wouldn't have surprised me if the dragonets were spying for Raven as much as the birds were, though I hoped not. There was something so endearing about a pocket-sized dragon that I preferred to believe that he found me fascinating, rather than that he was doing Raven's bidding.

He hopped down off the tree and crept a little closer, slinking on all fours like a cat, his huge golden eyes fixed on me. I crouched down, diverted from my troubles by his cautious approach. He was so cute that I wanted to scoop him up and cuddle him, but I wasn't stupid. Just because he seemed friendly didn't mean he'd accept that kind of treatment.

I held out my hand to him, the way you'd do to a strange dog. "You are the cutest little dragon I've ever seen." I almost didn't care if he was spying on me for Raven. In all my time in the Realms, I'd never seen such a fairytale creature. Nightmarish, yes—I certainly wouldn't have been offering my hand to those dharrigals that had attacked us in the Wilds—but never one so wonderfully, undeniably magical.

He passed through a patch of sun and I saw his hide wasn't merely green. It shimmered through all the colours of the rainbow, like mother-of-pearl. All at once, I realised how slow I'd been.

"You're a rainbow drake, aren't you?"

I should have realised as soon as I saw the jewel-like bumps on his leathery hide. My excuse was that I'd only seen them before on a tiny patch of skin, not on a living, breathing creature. He was far more beautiful than I'd imagined from the descriptions I'd heard of the creatures. "Little flying lizards" didn't do justice to his shimmering skin, delicate head, and bright, intelligent eyes. He stalked with sinuous grace across the leaf litter toward my outstretched hand, much more like a cat than a lizard, his spiked tail waving in the air behind him.

Why was I so sure the little drake was a male? I had no idea, yet I was convinced I was right. He was almost close enough to touch before I wondered if he might breathe fire like his bigger relatives, but he didn't seem at all hostile, so I let the thought go. Yriell had mentioned poisonous spurs once, too, but that didn't seem important anymore.

His beaked snout slid under my hand, then his head pushed gently, urging me to pet him. His skin was warm and surprisingly smooth to the touch, as if he'd been oiled, as I cupped my hand over his head. My skin tingled at the contact, and a huge delight welled up inside me. I knelt, then sat back on my heels.

The little drake climbed into my lap and sat up on his haunches, resting his dainty clawed front feet on my chest. He half-opened his wings for balance as he clambered up, and light streamed through them as though through stained glass. He was the most gorgeous creature I'd ever seen. Nothing about this felt strange or alarming, though wildlife was certainly not in the habit of treating me like a climbing frame. He rubbed the top of his head against my chin, and again, I felt an explosion of happiness. I stroked the little creature's back, though his wings made that difficult. I was afraid to touch them, as the skin seemed so delicate. He made a soft cooing noise, as if there were nowhere else in the world he would rather be than in my lap.

The tingling in my palms had spread, little shivers of delight running up and down my arms. It felt as though bubbles were bursting under my skin. I sat, engrossed, unable to tear my gaze from this enchanting little creature and his inexplicable affection. If he was spying on me for Raven, he was the strangest spy I'd ever heard of.

I still couldn't believe that Raven had blown up my house and then pretended to be my friend, but I'd heard it from his own mouth. Yet I was no longer as upset about his betrayal as I'd been mere moments before. Somehow, this golden-eyed beauty had bathed me in such love and happiness that it no longer seemed so important.

A raven's harsh call broke up our little lovefest. I looked up, but there was no sign of the bird. Yet. It was only a matter of time before one of them found me. It was a big island, but there were only so many places to look, and they had to know I couldn't have gone far in the short time before they discovered I was missing.

I sighed, and gently eased my new friend back onto the ground, though he squawked in protest and tried to climb back onto my lap. I had to stand up to forestall him.

"I may as well head back to the castle and give myself up," I said.

The rainbow drake tipped his head to one side, as if listening intently.

"If only you were a bit bigger, hey? You could give me a

ride out of here. I can't see any other way of getting off this island."

Did floating islands ever land? I didn't think so, but, like so many things in the Realms, I didn't know that much about it. What went on in the other Realms hadn't seemed important when I was living a simple life in the forests of Autumn. If I'd known I was going to get caught up in the affairs of the king, I might have paid more attention to the lessons my mother had tried to teach me. She'd taught me to read and write, and given me a basic grounding in the history and politics of the Realms, but I'd spent a lot more time gazing out the window daydreaming than I had following the intricate twists and turns of either fae history or politics.

I was a little better at geography, which had seemed to have at least some practical application. The mountain range I could see in the distance could only be the Gievrah Mountains, since they were the only heights worthy of the name "mountain" in all the Realms. They divided our world. The peaks themselves formed the Realm of Winter, apart from the two volcanoes that belonged to Fire. On one side lay the Realm of Night, and on the other, every other Realm except for Ocean and Air. The terrain below us might have belonged to either side, since the only Realm I was familiar with was Autumn.

Not that it mattered. If I couldn't get off this island, it didn't matter which Realm was below me. I heard the ravens again, but it sounded as though they were headed away from me. Probably checking out the town. No doubt they'd be back soon enough.

"Do you think if I jumped off, I could open a gate to the Wilds before I hit the ground?" I asked the rainbow drake.

He gave a high-pitched shriek and a feeling of dread swept over me, leaving me shaking. Was that *his* fear I felt? How was the little creature able to project his feelings to me like that? Truly, the Realms were strange. He moved closer and twined his spiked tail around my ankle, as if determined to stop me throwing myself into the void. No fear of that—it was a long way down, and I wasn't feeling lucky today.

A rush of air and wings behind us had me whirling around, expecting to find a flock of beady-eyed birds, or even Raven himself.

"I wouldn't try it, if I were you," said the Hawk, his massive, gold-tipped wings still outstretched.

"Kyrrim!" I cried, and threw myself against his broad chest.

His arms enfolded me. His wings did, too, cupping us in a warm, feathery darkness. I sighed, and relaxed against him, until an insistent squawking at my ankles made him release me.

"I wish you were always this pleased to see me," he said. It wouldn't have done his ego any good to hear that I *was* always this pleased to see him, but I usually managed to exhibit a bit more self-control, so I said nothing. He looked down at the rainbow drake, which had his tail curled possessively around my ankle once again. "And who is this?"

I shrugged helplessly. "A new friend. I think he's adopted me."

His eyebrows rose, but all he said was, "Curious."

The rainbow drake stared up at him, flaring his wings as if to show that he wasn't intimidated by this larger-winged creature.

"How did you find me?" I asked. I mean, I had expected that he would, eventually, but this was much faster than I'd hoped.

"Raven doesn't have as many secrets as he thinks he does."

"What does that mean?"

"It means that I found you. Did you doubt that I would?" It felt as though his gold-flecked gaze was penetrating my soul. "I would move heaven and earth to find you, Allegra."

My name on his lips was a caress. He leaned closer, and I held my breath. His face filled my vision, until he was the only thing in the world for me.

The harsh caw of a raven from somewhere nearby broke the spell.

"We should leave." He swept me up in his arms, despite the little drake's attempt to hold onto my leg. "Ready?"

"Yes."

He leapt skyward with a downbeat of his mighty wings that sent leaves and twigs boiling up from the ground in the backdraft. The rainbow drake squawked in protest and leapt into the air after us. He was surprisingly fast for his size, and soon caught up, slotting into the slipstream created by the Hawk's passage.

Behind us, a raven cawed, then another, and soon a whole flock was crying out. I looked over the Hawk's shoulder and saw them wheel above the trees and chase after us.

As soon as we cleared the edge of the island, the Hawk folded his wings and dropped like a stone. I screamed in surprise and clutched at him as we fell.

"It's all right. I've got you." His words almost disappeared in the rush of wind as we plummeted earthwards.

I squeezed my eyes tight shut, and so I missed the moment when Oldriss came into view. When the Hawk's massive wings spread wide and arrested our fall with a clap like thunder, I opened them again and saw his personal floating island lurking in the shadow of the larger one, like a baby whale nestled beneath its mother's sheltering flank.

He drove toward it with strong strokes of his wings, but the ravens were gaining fast. It was a smallish flock, only about a dozen birds. Surely the Hawk could deal with that many. His Air magic would blow them away. And then I saw Raven clear the edge of the island, diving in pursuit. He was shouting something, but the wind tore his words away.

"Raven's on our tail," I said.

The Hawk nodded, focused on his goal. The rainbow drake peeled off, beating to gain height. I felt a small pang of disappointment. Was he going to report to his master after all?

The ravens ignored him in their rush to catch us— which turned out to be a big mistake. I watched, open-mouthed, over the Hawk's shoulder, as the drake fell on them from above, tearing at them with his claws and lashing them out of the sky with his tail, wielding it like a whip. A couple of birds tried to fight back, but their claws and beaks made no impression on the drake's tough hide. And those fragile-looking wings? Turned out they weren't fragile at all. When half the flock had been vanquished, the rest fled back to the safety of the island, and the drake folded his wings and dived to catch up with us.

"How did you get a whole island here without being seen?" I asked. Oldriss was a small island, only big enough for the Hawk's house and a small grove of trees, but it was still hard to miss. Even a small island drew the eye when it floated through the sky.

"Came in last night under cover of darkness," he said.

And then he'd cleverly hidden right underneath the bigger island. We landed on a small clear patch between the trees and the house. The rainbow drake swooped about our heads, shrilling triumphantly, and I felt the exhilaration of the little creature's successful battle against the birds as if I'd participated myself, adrenaline pumping through my veins.

The Hawk set me down and drew Ecfirrith. I glanced up; Raven was closing fast, and I could make out some of his words now—he was calling my name, and begging us to stop. As if. The Hawk slashed the air with his sword, and the familiar rent in reality appeared—a doorway to another place.

He took my hand, and together, we stepped through.

17

I ducked as something screeched and zipped past my head. In the first, shocked instant I thought it was a raven, chasing us through the gate, but then I realised that the bright green streak zipping around our heads and scolding us was the rainbow drake. His fear flooded me with adrenaline, and I caught a hint of reproach, too, that I had tried to leave him behind.

"Storms, what's wrong with that creature?" The Hawk raised his sword, ready to face this new menace.

I caught at his arm, my heart in my mouth. "He's just upset. Don't hurt him."

The little drake screeched again, flying loops of the room, waves of fear and confusion rolling off him.

"It's okay," I soothed, holding out my hands towards the terrified creature.

We were in a large, sunlit room that looked out over a neatly landscaped yard. A pool glittered in the sun outside. Inside, an enormous TV hung on one wall, in front of a modular lounge in tasteful beige leather. The drake whizzed around and around, looking for somewhere safe to land in this strange place. I wondered if he had ever been to the mortal world before.

I didn't recognise the place either—I felt sure I'd remember if I'd ever been in such a luxurious house before. Through an enormous archway, I could see a modern kitchen that would have any serious cook drooling in envy. Everything was clean and shining, with nothing out of place, as if we were standing inside a show home rather than in a house where someone actually lived.

"Where are we?" I asked.

"My house," the Hawk replied, still eyeing the frantic drake askance.

I was worried that the poor creature would fly at the windows, mistaking the sparkling clean glass for open sky, and brain himself. Finally, he stopped his panicked circling and settled on my still-outstretched arm.

That hadn't been my intention, but whatever worked. I stepped back in surprise as his weight settled on me, his talons cutting into my skin. It only took a moment for blood to begin welling up.

"If you're going to make a habit of that, I'll have to start wearing my leather jacket everywhere," I told the little creature. My arm was already shaking from the effort of holding up the drake's weight.

Golden eyes blinked their concern at me. He half-opened his wings a couple of times, seeking better balance, then flooded me with remorse. He ducked his head, then walked up my arm, carefully picking his way as if I were a tree branch he was shuffling along until he found a more secure perch on my shoulder. Once settled, he nuzzled my cheek apologetically, and I reached up and rubbed his breast, unconcerned by the vicious beak so close to my face. I knew he wouldn't hurt me.

"I think we're good now," I said to the Hawk. It felt weird to have such a weight on my shoulder. How did pirates manage? Parrots were probably a lot lighter, though. I found myself wanting to hang on to him, in case he fell off, but his balance was good, and he seemed perfectly secure as I took a few experimental steps. I beamed in delight at the wonder of it. I had a tiny dragon on my shoulder.

The Hawk didn't look anywhere near as delighted. His face was grave as he stared at the two of us, and I got the sinking feeling that something was terribly wrong.

"He followed me home," I said, awkwardly trying to bring some humour to the situation, to lift that dark cloud from the Hawk's face. "Can we keep him?"

"He certainly appears determined to keep you." His stern expression didn't fade. "What mischief is this?"

"What do you mean?" The drake rubbed his head comfortingly against my cheek again, as if he could tell I was disturbed. Our emotional link must run both ways.

He shook his head. "I must take you to the king. He'll know what to do."

He reached for my hand, but I backed up a step. The little dragon, catching my uncertainty, hissed at him.

"Wait. What do you mean, he'll know what to do? What's wrong? Is it the rainbow drake?" Was there something wrong with this bond that appeared to have formed between us? Maybe rainbow drakes were sacred to the king or something, and I'd unwittingly committed a faux pas by befriending this one. Although it seemed to me that most of the befriending had come from the little drake itself, and I hadn't actually had a lot of choice. Surely the king couldn't blame me for that?

He laughed, but it wasn't a happy sound. "The drake. This." He waved a hand that seemed to indicate that "this" meant my whole body.

"What? I don't understand." A strong scent of gardenias rose around me, and the little drake hummed. It rubbed its head across my cheek again, leaving a damp trail behind. Distractedly, I raised a hand to wipe whatever it was off. Dragon spit? "Please tell me what the problem is, because I don't have any idea what you're talking about."

"Your magic." The Hawk caught my hand, inspecting my fingertips. They sparkled, as if I'd rubbed them through glitter glue. Then he stared intently into my eyes while his own went colder than I'd ever seen them.

"What magic?" The only magic I possessed was the little the king had given me, to allow me to pass between the worlds. Had something gone wrong with it? Why was he looking at me with such anger and disgust? "The king's?"

"Why did you pretend to be human?"

What? "I'm not pretending. I *am* human."

He ignored me, intent on his own line of thought. "But

why would Raven take you? And the drake ..." He shook his head, as if he'd come to a decision. "No, not the king. Yriell."

His hand tightened around my wrist and the little drake hissed ferociously again. I projected reassurance at him, and he settled down with a last, defiant flap of his wings.

"We're going to see Yriell?" I asked, as he strode through the house and down a set of stairs to a huge garage, dragging me behind him like a puppy on a leash.

"Yes." His voice was cold, his grip on my hand impersonal. "Every word that's spoken in the palace flies straight to Kellith's ears. Yriell will be safer. Though why I should care about your safety, I do *not* know."

We got into his car, the drake flapping and warbling in distress at finding himself trapped inside such a strange box. The Hawk cast an impatient glance at him but didn't suggest leaving him behind. Considering how tightly the little creature was clinging to me, he probably figured it would be a waste of breath.

I struggled with the seatbelt, trying to juggle the drake and getting thrown around as the Hawk backed out of the garage and roared off down the street.

"But why?" I asked, once I'd got myself sorted. The drake huddled in my lap, his spikes lying flat against his back, projecting distress and confusion. Or were those feelings mine? The Hawk's bewildering anger filled the small space, making me feel small and hurt. "Why do we need Yriell? What's the matter?"

His lips pressed together in a hard, straight line. I

thought he wasn't going to answer, then he burst out, "No man is an island, you said."

I blinked. I remembered that conversation well—he was so closed off, so self-sufficient, as if he'd learned over the years not to rely on other people. I'd only meant to point out that it wasn't healthy to shut yourself off from others, that everyone needed friends. But what did that have to do with anything right now?

"I trusted you. I let you … But you were lying to me the whole time. This probably isn't even your real face." He was gripping the wheel so hard that his knuckles were white. His voice was flat, emotionless.

"I'm not lying! What is *wrong* with—"

"I preferred it when people laughed at me to my face," he cut in. "At least they were honest in their contempt."

Tears pricked at my eyes. I couldn't bear the ice in his voice. "I'm not—I don't—"

"Spare me the protests. You're fae, as full-blooded as I am. I'm handing you over to Yriell because I have a duty to keep you safe, and I will not neglect that duty. But after that, you're her problem. I don't know what this game is that you're playing, and I don't care. I'm done with your lies."

The rest of the drive passed in stiff silence. He refused to answer any of my questions, so I stroked the little drake and stared out the window, trying not to cry. My stomach roiled, and I felt physically ill. Why was he suddenly so convinced I was fae? Was it because of the drake? But the Hawk hadn't seemed upset by the little creature's presence when he'd found us together on Raven's island. It wasn't until we returned to the mortal world that he'd turned so ice-cold and hostile.

It was strange how quickly the Hawk had wormed his way into my heart. I'd come to rely on him, just as I did on Willow and Sage. He was a true friend—or so I'd thought. Real friends didn't turn on each other without warning. Why wouldn't he believe me?

It wasn't until we arrived at the entrance to the national park that I realised that tiny, dragon-shaped creatures could be a trifle hard to explain away in the mortal world. My heart jolted into my throat as we pulled up at the ticket booth and I looked around frantically for a jacket or something to throw over the drake, now curled into a tight ball on my lap.

"What a cute dog!" the woman on duty said, bestowing a fond smile on him.

I looked down uncertainly and found a fluffy ball of adorable where the drake had just been lying, though the skin beneath my hand felt just as knobbly as before. The Hawk must have cast a Glamour on him—the soft fur was only a surface appearance.

"What's his name?" Dog lovers everywhere got that same sappy look on their faces whenever they saw a dog, and clearly the woman was a dog lover. She was still hanging out of her booth, gazing at the drake with rapt attention.

"Umm … Squeak." My head was aching, and my brain just wouldn't function, so I said the first thing that came to mind. I sent a silent apology to the little drake. He did need a name, but I'd like to devote a little more attention to picking one that suited him when I had a moment to think.

The woman handed the Hawk his change without looking at him. It was probably the first time his good looks had ever failed to impress a woman. "He's so cute."

I gave her a weak smile, then we drove off. We parked near the weir and hiked off into the bush, with me carrying the disguised drake until we were hidden by the trees. Then the Hawk let the Glamour drop and Squeak darted off to explore the dusty green heights of this strange new forest, so different from the lush woods of the Realms that he was used to.

When we turned off the path and approached the blasted stump that marked the beginning of Yriell's Aversion, I was surprised to find that it didn't have its usual force. I glanced up at the drake, who was sniffing suspiciously at bright pink blossoms in the gum tree above my head. Did my bond with him protect me from the full effect? Usually, by this stage, I was ready to turn and run, but I followed the Hawk through the thicket to the house with only a mild reluctance. He was striding ahead, making it clear that he didn't want to talk to me. He was probably hanging out to hand me over to Yriell and be shut of the whole mess. I glanced up again at the drake. I did seem to attract problems lately.

Not that I was sorry for this particular one, even if a rainbow drake was going to be a difficult companion to hide from curious mortal eyes. He zoomed down and landed on my shoulder, wrapping his tail possessively around my neck as the Hawk knocked on the door of the cottage. We heard Yriell muttering to herself as she clomped across the floorboards to the door.

"You again," she said to the Hawk. "And with a face as long as a wet week. What's your problem? Got a scratch in your fancy armour again?" Then she looked past him to me, with Squeak perched on my shoulder like a draconian parrot. "Oh ho! Now the cat's among the pigeons. Come in, come in. This should be good."

Only if her definition of "good" was "entertainment at the expense of others" which, come to think of it, it probably was. Inside, the usual mess was scattered about—

bits and pieces of herbs and leaves, a pestle and mortar with some indeterminate green sludge in the bottom, and a row of empty jars to one side, waiting to be filled. A strong stench of ammonia hung over the room, though she had opened all the windows.

"Tea?" She winked at the Hawk. "Or do we need something stronger?"

"Not for me," the Hawk said. "I won't be staying. I've only come to deliver this woman into your care."

This woman? Now he couldn't even stand to say my name?

"Get that stick out of your backside and sit down, boy." Yriell all but pushed him into a chair at the big wooden table in the centre of the room. "I can smell a story here, and nobody's leaving until I've heard it all."

His face darkened, but she was the king's sister, and he was a Knight of the Realms, so there was no gainsaying her. He folded his hands on the table and stared down at the myriad scratches and divots in the wooden surface, outwardly composed.

I took a seat at the other end of the table. "I'll have a tea, if you're making it."

Something calming might help quell my rising nausea. My headache had intensified, too. I had a feeling I wasn't going to like what was coming next, but I felt so bad I almost didn't care anymore. Squeak caught my mood and rubbed his head against my cheek. That seemed to be his go-to form of comfort. It was surprisingly effective.

I should have remembered that Yriell's definition of

"tea" was a little looser than most people's. The steaming cup she set before me after some crashing around in the kitchen, moving her various works-in-progress, was full of a dark green liquid with a bitter smell. There was camomile in it, and a hint of ginger, but I couldn't identify all the ingredients, and took my first sip with some misgiving.

It was as bad as I'd expected, but I swallowed it anyway. You couldn't really spit out what the king's sister offered you. I was just as constrained by the rules of polite behaviour and the respect due to rank as the Hawk.

"So," said Yriell. She sat down across from me and eyed me up and down. "Looks like someone's been keeping secrets."

"Who, me?" With both of them staring accusingly at me, I felt under attack. "I haven't, honestly."

"You're fae," the Hawk said.

I looked to Yriell for support, but she nodded.

"I'm not." How could I convince them? And why in the name of the Lady had they suddenly both decided that I wasn't human?

Yriell eyed me over the brim of her cup, the steam curling up around her face as she took a sip of tea. Then she laughed and looked at the Hawk as if he'd just said something funny. "She's telling the truth."

"Thank you!" I said. Finally, someone believed me.

The Hawk frowned, looking ready to argue.

"At least, it's the truth as she knows it," Yriell added. "I put something in her tea to help us get to the bottom of this. She can't tell a lie."

"What?" I pushed the evil-smelling brew away, though I felt like dashing it in her face. How dared she? They were both acting as if I were a criminal.

"Relax, girl, it'll wear off in a moment. But we can't have imposters with such access to my brother as you have, can we? We don't want the stupid git disappearing for another twenty years."

I was still angry, but I could see her point. The king's hold on the kingdom was precarious at best. She had to be sure I was who I said I was. But ...

"This doesn't make any sense. I *am* human. Why are you both saying I'm fae?"

"Can smell it on you. You're like a kid hitting puberty. You reek of magic."

The Hawk looked as dumbfounded as I felt. "But how could she not *know*?"

Yriell leaned back in her chair, looking thoughtful. "Well, there's a couple of ways. Someone could have wiped her memory, though you'd need a pretty powerful spell. There's probably only a couple of people in the whole of the Realms who could pull it off. Or ..."

"Yes?" I felt as though I were in a nightmare. Someone could have wiped my memory? But how? And when? I had memories stretching right back into my childhood. Surely I would have *noticed* if something had happened to my memory? "Or what?"

She sighed. "Or ... someone's been suppressing your magic your whole life and feeding you a pack of lies about what you really are. Anyone care to guess who the most likely candidate would be in that little scenario?"

I stared at her, aghast. There was only one person who could have done something like that. "But why would my mother do that?"

If I was fae, there was no reason to throw me out of the Realms at seventeen. I could have stayed instead of having my life ripped apart. And maybe she'd even be alive today if I'd been there. She'd destroyed both our lives, and for what? It made no sense.

"Let's see now. Anawen was from Illusion, fleeing for her life. Refugees were being hunted down and killed. And she had this baby she wanted to protect. Need I go on?"

"But ..." I stared, open-mouthed, so many words trying to spill out that I couldn't manage any of them. *I* was from Illusion? It was a lot to take in at once. My headache was so bad that it was making thinking difficult, but the pieces started to fall into place. Of course I was, if she was. "But why not just pretend we were both from Autumn?"

"Because she stole Livillia's identity, and Livillia had no children. No one would have believed she'd managed to hatch one overnight. That's not the way these things work, you know. Livillia might have been a bit of a loner, but I imagine people would still have noticed a pregnancy and birth. To suddenly produce a child who wasn't a newborn, after no evidence of a pregnancy, would have been impossible. Saying you were a changeling was the only way."

"And the drake confirms it," the Hawk added. "Since they are native to Illusion, and known to form bonds with the fae there."

Squeak warbled comfort in my ear, and I reached up to stroke under his chin. A wave of nausea washed over me. It was all too much. The Lady alone knew what kind of emotions poor Squeak was getting from me, but it couldn't be pleasant for him.

"I guess I can't deny I'm from Illusion with a rainbow drake sitting on my shoulder." My voice sounded a little shaky. Maybe I should have gone for the alcohol option instead of the tea after all. Especially since the damn stuff had been spiked with some kind of fairy truth serum.

The Hawk's chair scraped across the floor as he stood up. At least he was no longer looking at me as if I were the enemy. He was paler than usual, his face a picture of contrition as he took the chair next to me and reached for my hand.

"I'm sorry I didn't believe you." He raised the hand to his lips, and Yriell cackled.

"That's the way! Kiss and make up."

He shot her a hard look, but he didn't let go of my hand. I gave his a little squeeze, grateful that the misunderstanding was behind us. It would have been nice if he'd trusted me in the first place, but I guess the evidence *had* looked pretty damning.

Although—I didn't feel any more magical. What was this power they insisted was so obvious?

"You said I reeked of magic. But I can't do any magic."

"Have you tried?" Yriell lifted an eyebrow, as if that should have been obvious. "Do you even know what kind of magic belongs to Illusion? Your mother seems to have done a bloody good job of keeping you in the dark."

About so many things. I wished she had trusted me. I could have helped her, shared the burden. Our parting needn't have been so awful, if I'd only known the reason for it. All that time, I'd hated her for abandoning me, when she'd actually done it to save me. It must have hurt her as much as it had me. And now she was dead, and there was no way to say I understood, or apologise for hating her for her pain and sacrifice.

I rubbed my face wearily, to hide the sudden tears that sprang to my eyes. I'd literally hated the woman who'd given up her own happiness to protect me. I felt so bad. If only my head would stop hurting.

The Hawk laid his hand on my shoulder. "Are you all right?"

"Actually, I feel sick. Like I'm going to throw up any minute—and I have a splitting headache."

"Balls," Yriell said. "She doesn't have a ward, does she?"

Understanding dawned. I'd started to feel bad almost as soon as I'd arrived back in the mortal world. I'd never needed an iron ward before, when Jamison's concoction had been suppressing my magic. Now that it was free, the iron-drenched mortal world was slowly poisoning me. I had iron sickness.

At once, the Hawk pulled a silver ring off his own finger and put it on mine. It was loose, so he moved it to my index finger and closed his hand around it. An orange glow rose around his hand, and my finger tingled with warmth. Squeak warbled happily and leaned down to inspect the Hawk's magic.

And just like that, all my symptoms disappeared.

I gave the Hawk a grateful smile. "That's better."

He smiled back. "Good. Don't take it off. You'll need an iron ward at all times, now, when you're in the mortal world."

Yriell nodded approvingly. "All right, girl, let's see what you can do."

"You should at least be able to summon light, or cast a simple Glamour," the Hawk said encouragingly. "Those are things that all fae can do, even children."

With his free hand, he clicked his fingers, and a small globe of faelight appeared, floating above his hand. Hesitantly, I copied him. The Lady knew I'd tried this a thousand times as a child. My mother had made it look so easy, I'd been certain that if I only persevered, this magic could be mine, too.

So I wasn't entirely surprised when no ball of light appeared at my summons. I was used to failure. The Hawk, however, looked nonplussed.

"Not like that, girl," Yriell said impatiently. "Do you think your hand's going to explode? Don't be scared of it."

Squeak hissed at her, and I drew myself up. I was not *scared* of magic. Hadn't I wished my whole life that I wasn't a changeling, that I could have some small part in the magic I saw all around me?

She laughed. "Oh, you don't like that? Then don't behave like a frightened baby. You're fae, and magic is our birthright. Act like you mean it."

Act like I meant it. Whatever *that* meant. Okay, I could

do this. Assuming Yriell and the Hawk weren't both suffering from a mass delusion, I was fae. My childhood dream had come true. Magic was at my fingertips, if only I wanted it enough. Squeak hummed deep in his throat, sending a wave of love and encouragement at me. I was fae, and I had a pet dragon, dammit. I could *do* this.

I closed my eyes and took a deep, calming breath. The ammonia smell of the room had disappeared, replaced by the faint scent of gardenias. I was fae. Magic was my birthright. I clicked my fingers, and the little drake's delight flooded through me. I opened my eyes to find a perfect globe of light hovering above my open palm.

Okay, it was smaller than the Hawk's, but damn! Not bad for a first try. I beamed, and Yriell laughed.

"Welcome to the world of magic. You might want to practise that, so you can do it without screwing up your face as if you're taking a dump."

I grinned at her, too thrilled to be offended, and clicked my fingers again. Now that I'd done it once, it seemed easy. I kept summoning and banishing little floating balls of light, just because I could, while Squeak warbled in triumph.

The Hawk watched me, smiling, for a moment. "Do you think Raven knew that she was Illusion?" he asked Yriell. "He's hiding the island of Arlo deep in the realm of Night. There's still a substantial town on it, and a castle, which all looked inhabited, from what I saw of it. There must be several hundred Illusionists there."

"Arlo, eh?" Yriell asked. "I wondered where that had got

to. Seems like he must have—why else would he snatch her like that when her magic manifested?"

"What's so special about Arlo?" I asked, dismissing another globe of light. There were many floating islands, all part of the realm of Air.

"Arlo isn't a natural Air-isle," the Hawk said. "It was actually part of the realm of Illusion, just a regular island in the middle of the River Ivon. On the night that Summer attacked, two Air-isles were visiting Illusion. Arlo was the smallest of the islands that made up the Realm of Illusion, and the Airlings managed to raise it and carry it and all it contained away with them in the night."

I'd heard of that, though I hadn't known the island's name was Arlo. "It must have taken a huge amount of power to raise an island that was anchored to the earth and float it as if it were an Air-isle."

"Indeed," the Hawk said, nodding. "Air lost several strong fae that night, burned out by their efforts. But they managed to save hundreds by their actions."

"And Kellith has been searching for it ever since," Yriell added. "Arlo was a favoured nesting site for the rainbow drakes. He was mightily pissed when Air managed to whiz it out from underneath his nose."

"Why? Because so many people escaped?"

"No. Root and branch, girl, you're slow to catch on sometimes. Did you really think that Summer invaded Illusion to punish them for my brother's disappearance?"

"Well, no ... I mean—" Of course I knew that Dansen Arbre from Summer had actually been responsible for the king's disappearance. And whatever Kellith said, I wasn't buying for a moment that he hadn't been up to his neck in it, too. He wanted that crown. But he'd known perfectly well that Illusion had had nothing to do with King Rothbold's disappearance. Somehow, I'd never thought any further on it, never wondered *why*, in fact, Kellith had been so keen to destroy Illusion.

"Kellith wanted those drakes, and their highly marketable skins. The bastard was prepared to wipe out a whole Realm to get them, too. But the joke's on him. With their favoured breeding ground sailing off into the night, rainbow drake numbers in the remaining isles have taken a nose dive since Summer took over."

"And they don't breed as well without their bondmates," the Hawk added, nodding at Squeak. "Most rainbow drakes seem to prefer the company of people to that of their own kind."

Bondmates? There was a name for this connection between the little drake and me? I'd only just discovered I was fae, and already, I was part of an Illusion tradition. For someone who'd spent her whole life feeling like the outsider looking in at the party, that was a heady feeling.

I craned my neck around to look at the passenger riding on my shoulder. "Are we bonded, then?"

Squeak nipped gently at my ear, as if chiding me for doubting it.

"If he followed you out of the Realms, I'd say so," Yriell said. "You'd better learn how to Glamour him quick smart. He'll be wanting to stay close until he gets comfortable with you."

Maybe I shouldn't have been so quick to leave Arlo. Those people were *my* people. Even the annoying Lirra, who couldn't be Raven's sister if she was from Illusion.

Unless Raven was, of course.

"What's Raven's involvement in all this?" I asked. Surely he couldn't have so openly attended the king's ball if he was an Illusion fugitive.

"Likes thumbing his nose at Summer, I suppose," Yriell said. "Youngest sons never have enough to do to keep them out of trouble."

"Whose son is he?"

The Hawk blinked. "You don't know?"

"Why should I know? I've only met him twice, and we didn't have a chance for formal introductions either of those times."

The Hawk shook his head. "I forget that you've led such a sheltered life. Raven's real name is Bran, which means Raven in Gaelic, so he often uses that instead. He's the third son of Nox, Lord of Night."

19

Right. Of course he was. Another complication was just what I needed in my life. Did Raven's father know his son was harbouring the missing island of Illusion inside his borders? He must do; he was the Lord. Did he also know that his son had kidnapped me? It would be just my luck to have *two* Lords of the Realms interfering in my life.

Not that I had time for Night's scheming. My focus had to be on Summer, and bringing the killer of my mother and Jamison to justice. But, by the Lady, it was getting complicated now. I was a fae—and not just any fae, but one of the few remaining with the blood of Illusion in their veins. I summoned another ball of light, still in awe to find the magic within me, after all this time.

Which begged another question: how had it been disguised, not only from me, but from the world at large? And why had it appeared now? Sure, it was great to discover that I was fae after all, but the timing seriously sucked. The last thing I needed was for Summer to focus on me any more than they already had.

"Raven seemed very keen to replace my asthma medicine," I said slowly, thinking back to that overheard conversation while I'd been hiding behind the lounge in the library on Arlo. "He said he had to find someone who could do it as well as Jamison. He forced me to take some at the ball, even though I'd just had some. He was very agitated about it. And then he watched me as if he was waiting for something that never happened."

"And it was after that that he snatched you?" Yriell asked.

I nodded. "It was very sudden. One minute we were talking, and the next, he just grabbed me and took off."

"That sounds awfully suspicious. Did Jamison make this medicine for you specially? Why?"

"He said my body would have been changed by my exposure to the magic of the Realms. Not much, but enough that human medicine might not work as expected, and it would be safer if he made something that was tailored to my individual needs."

"What a load of bollocks." She made a noise of derision. "Changed by exposure to magic? I've never heard anything so ridiculous. If you were really a changeling, you'd be human, full stop."

"Did you take medicine for asthma when you lived in Autumn?" the Hawk asked.

I nodded. "My mother made it for me. She used to add it to boiling water and I had to stick my head over it twice a day and inhale. We didn't have puffers."

"I'd bet his left testicle that you don't even have

asthma," Yriell said, jerking her head at the Hawk. He looked less than impressed to have his testicles included in the conversation. "Asthma is a human disease. Why would the fae, living in the clean air of the Realms, with their superior bodies, ever suffer from it? That crafty mother of yours fed you this bullshit so she could dose you up every day with something to deaden your magic. And she set you up with Jamison so he could continue the practice once you'd been cast out."

"But now it's stopped working, and her magic is free," the Hawk said. "But why?"

I knew why. I'd been hesitant, when that girl in the pharmacy had first handed me the latest puffer. It just hadn't looked right, but she'd been insistent, even shown me the sticky note with my name on it attached to the plastic tray in which it had come. But sticky notes can come loose, and then get reattached to random trays. Or someone could even have dropped a couple of trays, and unknowingly swapped their contents when they put them back. Either way, it was clear that I'd ended up with a regular human puffer, and someone else had got the special one Jamison had prepared for me.

Which, apparently, had nothing to do with asthma, so I hoped that poor bastard was okay and not wondering why their asthma seemed suddenly so much worse. Hopefully, they'd have the sense to throw the unusual puffer away and demand a new one.

"There was a mix-up at the pharmacy," I said. Somehow, I felt almost as betrayed by the news that I didn't have asthma as I had at the revelation that I wasn't human. All my life I'd been taking that stupid medicine, frightened into it by my mother's graphic tales of asthma attacks, when there was nothing wrong with me. "They gave me a real puffer. No special magic-suppressing sauce."

"No wonder Raven freaked at the ball," Yriell said.

"Yes, but how did he know about the medicine? Jamison or my mother must have told him—but the only reason they would have done that is if they'd known that he was pro-Illusion. And if they knew that, why not just send me to join the others on Arlo, instead of into the mortal world to fend for myself?"

"We don't know the timing," the Hawk said. "You must remember, the Night of Swords was chaos. Summer's soldiers were everywhere, cutting down men, women, and children, setting fire to the buildings. Anawen must have been on one of the larger islands—she wouldn't even have known about Arlo's escape until later. She did well even to get you out of there."

"Arlo moved around a lot in the early years," Yriell said. "You missed all that, boy, since you were having a nap, but Kellith was livid. He searched everywhere, but Arlo was never to be found. I think it probably spent most of the time out over the ocean, only sneaking back to land to resupply. Who knows how long it's been lurking in Night? And if Kellith couldn't find it, with all his resources, Anawen would have had no chance. Most likely, she only discovered it after you'd already gone."

Perhaps that was why she'd left the cottage—she'd heard

that there was a sanctuary for so many of her countrymen and women, and she'd gone to join them. I tried to remember when Thing One and Thing Two had first appeared, Raven's little spies that he'd sent to watch over me. They'd been there all the time I'd lived in the converted garage out the back of Rowan's house—had I seen them before that? I didn't think so, but then, they may have been watching me and just not made their presence known. There were too many pieces of this puzzle missing for me to figure it out.

I sighed, and the Hawk took my hand again, stroking his thumb gently over the back of my hand. I wasn't sure if that was meant to be comforting, or if he was still apologising for doubting me so easily before. Either way, I enjoyed it. I was happy for him to stroke as many bits of me as he pleased.

"What are you going to do now?" he asked, his thumb still tracing lazy circles on my skin.

"I don't know. Raven wanted to use me as a kind of ambassador to the king, but ..."

"But?" he prompted, when I trailed off.

I didn't know what I wanted anymore. I'd been focused on finding my mother's killer, but now ... Should I return to Arlo? Perhaps the people there could tell me more about her most recent movements. Hell, they could even tell me about her past, and my own. Maybe even teach me to harness this strange new magic of mine. Should I go to the king, as Raven had been pushing for, to try to clarify the status of these refugees? Perhaps the whole island could go home. My mother wasn't the only one who needed someone to fight for justice for her.

"But some of the people on Arlo didn't seem too keen on that idea."

"Raven has feathers for brains. Summer already has its eye on you. If you reappear trailing magic like a train, it will only make you more of a target."

"But the king needs to know about this."

"Rothbold's already up to his armpits in alligators," Yriell said. "He won't thank you for throwing another into the pond."

"Those people shouldn't have to keep hiding," I protested, my sense of fair play stung. "They could go home and rebuild their Realm."

"If you believe that, you're stupider than you look," Yriell said. "Kellith's not going to give up the riches of the rainbow drakes without a fight. This could be the spark that sets him off into full-blown rebellion. How about you let my poor brother get a decent grip on the reins first? Time enough to deal with Illusion once he's managed to drive all the snakes out of the palace. They've waited twenty years; it won't kill them to wait a few more months."

I looked down at the table top.

"Go home," she added. "Try to keep out of trouble for a while. I can make you something to hide your magic."

I gave her a doubtful look.

"It's easy enough, especially since I don't have to bother disguising it as human medicine." She grinned. "You might not like the taste, though."

"What if I want to learn to use my magic? Maybe I should go back to Arlo."

She shrugged. "You shouldn't need anyone to teach you. Magic is like an itch waiting to be scratched. If every pubescent fae can work it out on their own, you can, too."

"But I don't even know what I should be able to do! I've never seen anyone work an Illusion, except for that girl in the castle on Arlo. She'd never even seen Willow, but she made a perfect replica of her. How can I just scratch my way into knowing how to do that?"

"Did you ask her?"

I shrugged. "She said all she needed to borrow someone's form was to touch something that had been worn by them."

"There you are, then."

"That tells me nothing! What do I do then? Say 'abracadabra'? How *exactly* do I turn into someone else?"

"How did you make that ball of light?"

"I have to snap my fingers?"

Yriell made an impatient sound. "Are you always this stupid? No, girl; you picture what you want, and then you make it happen."

"That's no better than telling me to scratch an itch," I objected.

"You want an instruction manual? Bah, you've been in the human world too long. Just do it, instead of trying to convince yourself that you can't."

"What, now?" I glanced uncertainly at the Hawk, who shrugged, as if to say *why not?*

"Yes, now." She shrugged off the cardigan she was wearing and tossed it across the table.

I caught it before it slid onto the floor, the wool still warm from her body.

"Turn into me."

Just like that. Talk about getting thrown into the deep end. I kneaded the garment uncertainly in my lap, staring down at it. What was I supposed to do with it now? It was green and, unsurprisingly, had some twigs and burrs caught in the stitching. Yriell's whole wardrobe looked as though she'd just been dragged backwards through the bushes while wearing it. I raised it to my nose; there was an earthy scent to it, the smell of damp soil after the rain, of cool rock caverns far below the surface, of cut grass and fresh sap.

"You going to eat it?" Yriell asked. "Don't think so much, girl. Just do it."

Right. Yriell could star in her own Nike ad, with lines like that. Unfortunately for me, the Nike ads made a whole lot more sense than this did. It was like being handed a ball of wool and a set of knitting needles and being told to produce a fairisle jumper. Sure, it was possible to go from one state to the other. Plenty of knitters could do it. But someone had to show them how to knit first.

I wondered if this was some kind of test. Maybe Yriell didn't truly believe I was fae. I could hardly blame her; I had trouble believing it myself. Or maybe, despite what she'd said, she thought I was lying, that I'd known all along I was fae. If I did somehow manage to pull this off, would this prove in her mind that I must have known how to do it already? Was this all some elaborate "gotcha"?

Damnation. When had I gotten so paranoid?

I tried to remember what Lirra had said, determined to give this a go. The garment had spoken to her, or something like that. No, wait, it had been an aura, right? Damn it, I couldn't remember. Nor had she explained how she'd managed to find Willow's aura, or whatever, instead of mine. How had her magic been able to keep the wearers separate? She was lucky she hadn't come up with some bizarre cross between Willow and me.

Focus, I told myself, reeling my imagination back in. Yriell wouldn't have lent her cardigan to anyone else, so I didn't need to worry about that right now. All I had to do was coax my body into a completely different shape. Nothing major.

I closed my eyes, the cardigan clutched tightly in my fists. A burr was sticking into my right hand, but I ignored the slight prickle. That was part of being Yriell, covered in twigs and muck. Maybe it would help. I breathed in deeply, taking that earthy combination of scents into my lungs. I pictured my skin browning and wrinkling, my hair fading to grey and frizzing about my head.

I opened my eyes to take a peek at my hands. Nope, still smooth. Where was this magic I was supposed to be bursting with, then? How come everyone else could sense it but me?

"I think she's trying to lay an egg," Yriell said in a stage whisper to the Hawk.

I glared at her, then shut my eyes again, determined to show her I could do it.

The Hawk laid his hand over my clenched fist. "Relax. You're trying to force it. Let it well up inside you, then direct it where you want it to go."

Well, at least that was a little better than "scratch the itch", though not much. Relaxing, I could do. Deliberately, I uncurled my fingers and took a deep breath, letting everything relax and soften as I blew it out. Nothing "welled up", but I did notice the scent of gardenias again.

My eyes popped open, searching for the source of that smell. I'd noticed it before, too, but then it had faded away.

"Where *are* those flowers?" I asked.

Yriell gave me a blank look. "Which flowers?"

"The gardenias."

"That's your magic," the Hawk said. "If you can smell it, that means it's surging."

"And that's good?"

"It is if you're planning on using it instead of just stinking up the place," Yriell muttered.

I shut my eyes again and let the sweet perfume wash over me. It was kind of neat. I could go around smelling divine without ever spending another cent on perfume.

"Can you smell it, too?" I asked, without opening my eyes. The magic of powerful magic users, like the Lords, or the Hawk himself, had a scent that could be detected even by completely non-magical humans. But mine probably wasn't strong enough even for another fae to pick up on.

"Of course. That's how I knew you were fae."

Right. That made sense. I took another deep breath, sinking into that delicious scent, letting it well up around me. Squeak warbled encouragement in my ear and rubbed his head against my cheek. I imagined myself looking like Yriell, burrs and all, and felt a gentle flush of heat run over my body. When I opened my eyes, I was just in time to catch the fading of a pale blue glow around me.

"That's more like it," Yriell said, grinning at me. "You've never looked so attractive in all your life."

I reached up and patted my hair. It felt wiry. "Do you have a mirror?"

"Ooh, she's a vain one, this one." But she disappeared into the back room, which I assumed was her bedroom, and returned with a small, handheld mirror.

I nearly dropped it when I looked into it. I mean, I'd been expecting to look like someone else, but I hadn't been prepared for the reality of looking into a mirror and seeing a stranger stare back at me.

"Oh, my God! That is freaky." I touched my face hesitantly and felt the sag of real wrinkles. "Whoa. It feels so real."

"That's the difference between Illusion and Glamour. Glamour is only an outward show—it doesn't change what's really underneath. Here, feel this."

She grabbed my hand and laid it against her cheek. I could see the wrinkles on her face, but her skin was taut and smooth to the touch. "See? That's Glamour."

I nodded. I knew that Yriell's true appearance was far younger and prettier than the face she chose to present to the world. She Glamoured herself to make it easier to live incognito.

"What *you've* got, on the other hand, leaves Glamour for dead," she went on. "Everything is changed, so that the Illusion is perfect. Best of all, it's completely undetectable by magic, unlike a Glamour."

I shoved the mirror back at Yriell, still unnerved at seeing a stranger's face in it. "How do I change back?"

"Same way you got there," she said. "Do I have to teach you everything?"

I bit back a sarcastic retort and focused on returning to my usual appearance, taking a deep breath and letting the scent of gardenias rise around me. I pictured my own face, with its blue eyes framed by short blond hair and its smooth, young skin. Squeak shifted restlessly on my shoulder, chirping in his strangely melodic way.

When I opened my eyes, one glance at the wrinkled skin of my hands told me it hadn't worked. I tried again, focusing on those hands, willing them to take back their youthful appearance. Squeak's chirping grew louder, and he began to butt me gently with his spiky little head.

"Hush, little guy," I said, sending soothing thoughts his way. "I'm trying to concentrate, here."

After several long minutes in which nothing happened, Yriell sighed. "Stuck, are you?"

I raised anxious eyes to her face. Our face. "It's not working."

"Don't get your knickers in a knot, girl. You're going to bust a blood vessel if you keep straining like that. I told you to relax."

"I *am* relaxed. Or I was, at least." I definitely wasn't feeling too relaxed anymore. What if I was stuck like this? "It still didn't work."

Grumbling, Yriell got up and wandered over to her shelves. I watched apprehensively while she pulled a jar from here and one from there, added something else from a drawer, then shoved the lot in her small microwave. At another time, the finishing touch with the microwave might have made me laugh. It seemed so very unmagical, as if she should have been using a smoking cauldron instead. But I wasn't in a laughing mood, and the quicker I got whatever remedy she was cooking up, the happier I would be.

Finally, she passed me a cup half-full of the stuff, whatever it was. "Just take a sip. It shouldn't take much, and you don't want to knock out your magic for a week."

"What is it?" As always with her remedies, it smelled like swamp water, but I was prepared to try anything.

"Probably something very similar to what your mother was forcing on you all those years, and what Jamison was putting in his so-called asthma medicine. It will temporarily smother your magic, which should cause the Illusion to dissipate. Drink it up, now. Down the hatch."

Cautiously, I took a sip. It tasted foul, but I choked it down. They both watched me, the Hawk trying to but not entirely succeeding in hiding a smile at my expense. I checked my hands. Still wrinkled.

"Hmmm," said Yriell. "Better have another sip. It generally works instantaneously, and I can still smell those bloody gardenias."

I swigged another, larger sip, and instantly, I could feel a difference. An energy that I hadn't even noticed coursing around my body was suddenly snuffed out. Sure enough, the smooth skin of my hands showed I was back to normal.

"Give me the rest of that, and I'll bottle it for you," Yriell said, "in case you manage to screw it up again, or if you want to hide the fact that you're a fae temporarily."

Her tone left me in little doubt that she had full confidence in my ability to screw it up. I had to agree with her, so I meekly passed the foul-smelling stuff back to her, glad to have a back-up plan.

20

Back in the carpark, I sank into the luxurious leather seat of the Maserati and blew out a heavy sigh.

The Hawk gave me a shrewd look as he started the car. "This must all come as quite a shock."

"You could say that." Squeak turned round and round on my lap until he had pummelled me into a shape that was pleasing to him, then lay down with his spiked tail curled right up to his beak. I rested my hand on his warm back, and the Hawk's ring flashed in the light. It was a thick, silver band, engraved with vines and blossoms. "I should give this back to you now."

"Keep it," he said, pulling out onto the road.

I kept tugging at the ring. "No, I don't need it now, and I don't want to take your—"

He laid a firm hand over mine. "Keep it."

"I'm sure I can find something else to use as an iron ward without taking your stuff."

"You didn't take it," he said mildly, but with a hint of

steel underneath. "I gave it to you. It's silver mined in the Realms, in the Gievrah Mountains. Nothing makes a better iron ward."

"Oh," I said, twisting the ring around my finger. I had to admit, I was thrilled with the gift. I had to remind myself that the giving and receiving of rings wasn't as significant among the fae as it was among humans. "Thank you. It's beautiful."

"It belonged to my grandmother. It's very old."

He was giving me his *grandmother's* ring? "Oh, but I couldn't possibly take something so—"

"Will you stop arguing? I've never known anyone who argues as much as you do. I want you to have it." In a softer voice, he added, "It can protect you when I'm not there."

"You don't have to protect me, Kyrrim."

That bearded jaw set in a stubborn line. "But I want to. You are very important to me, Allegra."

After the day I'd had, I couldn't take any more uncertainty. "Do you mean that, like, *personally?* Or am I only important to you because the king wants you to take care of me?"

He growled with frustration. "What does the king have to do with our relationship?"

"Everything, I thought. Wait—what do you mean, our relationship? Do we have a relationship?"

"I don't go around giving family heirlooms to every woman I meet, you know." He pulled up at a set of lights and turned to me, laughter dancing in his eyes. "Are you arguing with me *again?*"

God, he was frustrating. "But I thought you weren't interested."

"I told you I was."

"Yes, but ..." That had been weeks ago, the night the king gave me the power to gate into and out of the Realms. Which, come to think of it, I didn't actually need, since I had power of my own. "I thought you'd changed your mind. You were so cold the night you forced me to use the king's gift."

He rolled his eyes. "Did you expect me to be happy that you were kissing other men?"

"But that wasn't—"

He leaned over and kissed me, hard and fast, until the lights changed and the car behind us honked. "Arguing. Again."

I laughed and looked away, unexpected happiness bubbling up inside. After a few minutes of smiling fatuously as I gazed out the window, I realised I didn't recognise any of the roads we were on.

"Where are we going? This isn't the way home."

"You can't go home. You can't let anyone see you like this."

"Like what? My magic is fully repressed."

"Yes, but for how long? Yriell said it could be one hour or a dozen, depending on how strong your magic is."

"What does it matter, anyway? Willow and Sage are my friends. They're not going to turn on me if they find out I'm fae."

"And then what? I take you home and you ... what? Stay

locked up in Willow's sith for the rest of your natural life? Is that what you want?" He didn't look at me as he drove, but I could hear the frustration in his voice.

"I'm sorry I'm such a burden to you."

He breathed out, a sharp, explosive sound. "You're not a burden to me, but one of us needs to think ahead a little. You are from Illusion; therefore, your life is in danger, and you have no idea how to use your power or protect yourself. Let me take you to Oldriss. Please."

It was the "please" that did it. I'd never heard such a note of pleading in his voice. He was desperately afraid for me, though I didn't really understand why—it wasn't as if Lord Kellith could hate me any more than he already did. But the fact that he was so concerned was enough to move me.

Besides, the idea of spending time alone with him while I learned to use my powers—or whatever he thought we'd be doing on Oldriss—wasn't exactly unappealing. My lips still tingled from his kiss.

"Okay. But I have to call Willow first, otherwise she and Sage will panic if I just don't come home."

"As long as you don't tell her the truth."

I shrugged, already dialling Willow's number. God knew what I *would* tell her. Maybe I could say the king had summoned me. It wasn't as though she was running to the Realms every five minutes. She wouldn't know it was a lie.

She picked up after a single ring. "Where the hell have you been?"

"Hello to you, too."

"Don't give me that, Allegra, I was worried sick about you. You just disappeared. What happened to you?"

"Ah ... I got caught up in something."

The Hawk was shaking his head at me and drawing a finger across his throat. *Cut her off. Don't tell her anything yet.* But I couldn't just leave her hanging, could I? She was my friend and, as it happened, she was right to be worried about me. Hell, *I* was worried about me. I'd got caught up in some messy shit, for sure. Somehow, it didn't seem to matter as much now that I knew the Hawk was right there in the mess with me, though.

"Look, I'm sorry. I'll explain it all later."

"No time like the present, Al. I'm waiting."

"Put it on speaker," the Hawk growled.

His face was grim. I didn't want to unleash him on Willow, but I was floundering so, like a pushover, I pressed the speaker button. "Putting you on speaker, Wil."

"Who's with you?" Her voice was full of suspicion.

"It's Kyrrim," the Hawk said.

"Who?"

"The Hawk. Allegra is with me, and she's perfectly safe, but she won't be coming home for a while."

"Why not?"

If he'd hoped to reassure her, he didn't know Willow. She was practically a princess; she wasn't impressed by knights. And right now, her protective instincts were well and truly engaged.

"Because we'll be having hot sex for at least a week."

"Kyrrim! No!" I hit him, but it was like striking concrete, and had about the same effect.

"Right." I could practically hear her voice soften. "Well, aren't you the dark horse? I didn't know you were on first name terms with *Kyrrim*, Al." The way she purred his name was practically indecent, and I felt a blush start somewhere around my nipples and crawl all the way up my neck into my cheeks. "You certainly move fast. Why didn't you say so? But we have a gig tomorrow night."

"Cancel it," Kyrrim said. "She won't be getting out of bed for days."

I groaned and covered my face with my hand.

"Well, I like a man who knows what he wants, but that won't be—"

"Not up for negotiation, Willow. Goodbye."

At his nod, I ended the call. My cheeks were on fire. "Why did you tell her that? We're not going to have sex."

"Aren't we?"

God help me, the man was impossible. "No. At least ... no."

I felt like such an idiot when he laughed. "You don't sound sure. Tempted?"

"Will you be serious? What are we really going to be doing for a week?"

He eyed me, the side of his mouth twitching as he fought down a smile. "What, you don't think you could keep up with me?"

"I can't talk to you when you're like this." Nor could I focus when all I could think of was the feel of his strong body on mine that time in Raven's house. Or the way he'd looked at me as he spun me around, laughing, after we'd brought the king safely home, as if I were the centre of his world.

Finally, he took pity on me. "Much as I would like to hurl you down on my bed, I do have some self-restraint."

"You would? I mean ..." Shit. Now all I could think of was restraints. Mmmm. Wicked images involving tight leather and handcuffs filled my mind. Suddenly, it seemed awfully hot in the car. I stopped hiding my eyes and looked at him.

The car stopped at traffic lights, and he returned my gaze candidly. "Your life is in danger, and neither of us is free to indulge our natural inclinations right now. We have other priorities. My current one is to get you to Raven."

"And after that?" I could hardly believe I was being so daring, but his kiss had made me brave.

He reached out with his free hand and took mine, rubbing his thumb across my skin as he'd done once or twice before. Now, as then, I found the small, insistent pressure intensely erotic, and I drew in a sharp breath.

His gaze was drawn to my lips, and his eyes darkened. "All we can do is take it one step at a time," he said, his voice husky.

His words were non-committal, but the touch of his hand told a different story. He drew my hand to his lips and pressed a kiss on the back of it before letting go as the lights changed.

I stayed silent for the rest of the drive, stroking the sleeping drake in my lap. My life was horrendously complicated at the moment, with the search for my mother's killer, the revelation of my true heritage, and people trying to kill me.

But not all the complications were bad.

21

We stepped through the gate formed by three slashes of Ecfirrith, and the Hawk closed it behind us. Ahead, at the top of a small rise, my childhood home sat among its overgrown gardens. Even in its dilapidated state, it did my heart good to see it again.

"Why did you pick here for the meeting?" I asked as we walked up the slope, the long grasses brushing against my jeans.

We'd only stayed on Oldriss for a few moments. A certain raven had been lurking in the trees there. The Hawk must have known, because as soon as we set foot on the island's soft grasses, he'd walked straight into the tiny wood.

"I know you're there," he'd said, "so make yourself useful. Take a message to your master to meet us at Anawen's home in Autumn in one hour. Tell him to come alone."

Thing One had taken off with a raucous cry, and the

Hawk had formed a shimmering gateway in the air with his sword. Squeak had led the way, swooping through as the Hawk took my hand in his.

"It seemed a neutral spot," he said now, in answer to my question. "I didn't want to meet on Arlo, where he's surrounded by his own people."

"They're my people, too, apparently," I said mildly. I was keen to get back to Arlo, now that I knew the truth, and see what they could teach me, both about my new powers and my heritage.

It was funny—I'd gone all my life believing that I'd been stolen from a human couple as a baby and, though I'd wondered about them, I'd never had a burning desire to meet them. I guess it was because I knew it was impossible. But now, anything was possible. If Anawen truly was my mother, and not just the woman who'd stolen me from my parents, then I could find out who my father was. I might even have siblings, or aunts and uncles. Grandparents, even. My imagination served up a whole happy family to me, even though I knew it was likely that they had all died in the purge of Illusion.

"Raven may be a Lord's son, but he's as slippery as they come. If we want to pin him down and get the truth from him, it would be better not to hand him the advantage." We reached the cottage and he held the door open for me.

"Let's stay outside," I said. "It's such a beautiful afternoon."

"As you wish."

I sat on the front steps, and he sat down beside me, his

thigh pressed against mine. The sunlight caught the russet highlights in his hair and brought his high cheek bones into sharp relief. He was a thing of such beauty, I couldn't help staring at him.

He captured my hand and began to play with my fingers. A surge of pure happiness filled me, and Squeak, who was soaring and diving over the garden, trilled in response. I wished this moment could last forever.

Naturally, Raven chose that moment to arrive. Dressed head to toe in black, he came strolling through the trees at the bottom of the meadow and made his way up the slope towards us. Squeak arrowed down towards him and landed on his shoulder, warbling away at him.

"I gather he's happy to see you," I said when Raven reached us, the little drake still perched on his shoulder. The sparkly traitor was even rubbing his little head against Raven's cheek in evident fondness, his feelings of pleasure coming strongly down the bond between us. "That makes one of us."

"I've spent a lot of time on Arlo lately," Raven replied, ignoring my dig. "The drakes treat me as one of their own."

The Hawk had let go my hand as soon as Raven had appeared, and now he stood. I remained seated. It was warm in the sun, and I was comfortable, and I was damned if I was greeting Raven like a long-lost pal. The kidnapping still rankled. Not to mention the destruction of my home, which he'd apparently blown up simply to warn me away from the investigation into the missing drake skins. He could have tried a less extreme method of communication first, for God's sake.

"You were quick," the Hawk said.

"I never like to keep a lady waiting." He grinned. "And besides, the king's losing it. He's been sending furious messages to my father, who's liable to disown me if Allegra doesn't reappear in short order."

I shrugged lazily. "Not my problem."

Raven flopped down on the grass and stretched his long, booted legs out in front of him, so the Hawk sat back down, too.

"Did you tell him you didn't have her?" he asked.

"Of course. But he didn't believe me."

"Gosh, I wonder why," I said.

Raven wagged a finger at me. "Now, now, miss, none of your sarcasm. I may not be the most upstanding citizen of Night, but I never lie to my lord father. I have no wish to die."

"You should have come to me last night," the Hawk said. "I could have found some way to get her out of that ball without all this drama."

"How was I to know that you had such a vested interest in her?" His smirk made me wonder if he'd seen our intertwined fingers when he arrived. "I thought you were just following orders. And you have to admit, it's a pretty big secret."

"It will have to come out, now, anyway, unless you want the king invading Night to find her."

I shuddered at the thought. Trouble with another one of his Realms was just what the king didn't need. His grasp on power was already precarious, and Summer was enough trouble to handle at a time. But I was touched that he cared enough about me to risk it.

"He can't afford to do nothing when his new favourite is kidnapped from under his very nose," the Hawk went on. "It makes him look weak."

Right. It wasn't about the king's personal feelings about me. It was just politics. Of course.

"So what do we do?" I asked. The Hawk seemed to have all the answers so far. Maybe he could see a solution.

"We could just sneak her in to see the king, couldn't we?" Raven asked. "If we prove that she's okay, he can settle things with my father."

The Hawk shook his head. "Just because you can't feel her magic now doesn't mean it's under control. Yriell gave her something, but the effect is only temporary."

"Can't we just tell him I'm from Illusion?" I asked. "We could tell him about Arlo, too. Wasn't the Lord of Illusion his best friend? He deserves to know the truth. And how long are they supposed to stay in hiding? Surely, now the king is back, this is the time."

The Hawk looked unconvinced. "He needs time to consolidate his power again. Everything is in flux right now. Throw this into the mix, too, and it could all come crashing down—Summer won't meekly give up their stolen territories."

That's what Yriell had said, too, but it didn't sit well with me. What about justice for Illusion?

Raven sat up straighter. "Or it could be the thing that strengthens him against Summer. He needs allies. I have a whole island full of them, just waiting to support him." His face lit with excitement as he warmed to his theme. "And some of the other Lords would welcome the return of Illusion as a power. I know my father is worried by Summer's continued ascendancy. Kellith has a stranglehold on this kingdom. We need something that will break it."

We both turned pleading faces to the Hawk.

He rubbed a hand over his eyes in a weary gesture, then took my hand again. "I can't countenance anything that would endanger you."

I could see he was weakening. He must want the king to regain control of the kingdom more than anyone. He certainly had no love for Kellith and his minions.

I cast around for a way to make this work. "I could take the rest of that potion Yriell made and go see the king."

He was shaking his head before I'd even finished the sentence. "Too risky. We don't know how long its effect will last. The last thing we need is for your powers to manifest in front of half the Court."

"I took Jamison's twice a day, and that was enough to keep it under control."

"Yes, but Jamison knew what he was doing. He was probably guided by your mother, who'd had your whole childhood to experiment with the dosage. We can't afford to experiment now."

"I just need long enough to get to the king—"

"No." His grip on my hand tightened.

Damn, he was stubborn. Half of me wanted to punch him for thinking he got to tell me what I could and couldn't do, and the other half felt an odd frisson of pleasure at the idea that somebody cared enough about me to want to protect me. For someone who'd been kicked out of home at seventeen to fend for herself, that was a powerful feeling—one that I hadn't experienced in a long time.

So, I bit back the automatic challenge to his assumption of authority over me and set my mind to considering the problem. "What if I used the cloak of shadows that Raven gave me? I could get into the palace without anyone seeing me."

"That sounds like a fast way to get yourself killed," the Hawk said. "The guards are all on high alert since the king returned. You'd only have to brush against someone, or knock something over, and it would be swords first, ask questions later."

I sighed. Maybe there was another way to go about this—to set my magic to work for me? If it was too risky to appear before the king as someone who wasn't supposed to have magic but did, what if I instead went to him in the guise of someone everyone knew had magic?

"What about this…?" I said slowly, still thinking it through. Yes, there could be other benefits to doing it this way. I could kill two birds with the same magic stone. No one but the murderer knew that my mother was dead. "I do what Lirra did when I was on Arlo. She managed to turn herself into Willow, just from touching Willow's dress. This house is full of my mother's clothing."

Raven's eyebrows shot up. He had a very expressive face. "That's pretty out there. I like it."

The Hawk was slower to respond. I could tell he was running the idea through his mind, looking for anything that might put me in danger. "Your mother's killer knows that she's dead."

"Yes, but what are the chances that the killer will be at the Court when I drop in to see the king? I mean, we're pretty certain it's someone from Summer, but Summer's a big place." As far as I was concerned, discovering the identity of the murderer would be a plus, but I knew I couldn't sell it that way to the Hawk. He was too concerned for my safety. "You said yourself I can't show my face at Court, reeking of magic. But no one will be suspicious if my mother turns up smelling of magic. Even if they don't know her—and most people won't, let's be honest—she's clearly fae. And I'll be with you, so I'll be perfectly safe. You can get me in to see the king, and we can tell him the whole story. Please, Kyrrim." I tried the same trick he'd used on me, putting all the emotion I could into my plea.

He closed his eyes for a moment, clearly finding it as difficult to resist as I had. "I still think it's a bad time."

That wasn't a no, so I counted it as a win. I took his hand in both of mine. "I want to help the other Illusionists. They're my people, and this injustice has been allowed to go on for long enough. It's time they got back their rightful place. It's time they went home."

He gazed down at our joined hands, then squeezed mine. "Very well."

Feeling very daring, I leaned forward and grazed my lips across his bearded cheek. His tawny gaze was so serious, I couldn't tell what he was thinking.

"Hey," said Raven, "where's my kiss?"

"You don't deserve one. You're a kidnapper. And you blew up my house."

He blinked. "Who told you such a lie?"

"You did. I overheard you telling someone about it while I was on Arlo."

His look of shock was immensely satisfying, but he quickly recovered. "What else did you overhear?" He tried to sound casual, but I could tell from the sudden tension in his pose that he was intensely interested in my answer. It made me wonder what else he was hiding from me.

"Oh, this and that. Enough to know I shouldn't trust you as far as I could throw you."

"Told you I wasn't an upstanding citizen."

"Not much point telling me that *after* you've blown up my house and kidnapped me. I actually had it figured out by then."

"Will they help her?" the Hawk cut in. "The Illusionists on Arlo?"

A cautious expression replaced the smile on Raven's face. "Help her how? Most of them are afraid to leave the island."

"She's having trouble controlling her magic. Someone who knows what they're doing needs to guide her. Someone from Illusion."

"Ah." The cautious look cleared. "I wondered why you wanted to meet with me. I'm sure we can manage that. I know just the person."

I rose, releasing the Hawk's hand with reluctance.

"Guess I'd better go find some of Mum's clothing, then."

Raven got up, too. "Need a hand?"

"Why? So you can add perving at girls while they get changed to your list of misdemeanours? No, thanks."

I went inside and shut the door firmly behind me. Sunlight streamed in the front windows, laying golden beams across the warm wooden floors. Dust motes danced in the beams, and I sighed, remembering how neat and tidy my mother had always kept this place. I crossed the main room and went into her bedroom. It looked just the same, though a light film of dust lay on every flat surface. There was even still a pile of books on her nightstand, testament to her love of reading. The bed was neatly made, the quilt tucked in and smoothed over. Her wardrobe doors were shut, and I felt like a child again as I turned the smooth wooden handle and opened the door where her dresses hung. I'd often sneaked in here when I was little, to try on her shoes and drape myself in the soft scarves she wore in winter.

Most of her clothes were gone. Only two brown dresses that she'd never really liked hung there, next to her working apron. I reached out to touch the apron, a thousand memories crowding into my mind: my mother shelling peas on the back doorstep, peeling vegetables at the sink, pushing those stray strands of hair that always seemed to escape her bun by the end of the day out of her face. Mum in the garden, where she spent hours every day; weeding, mulching, watering, or just contemplating the plants with quiet satisfaction.

A scent of gardenias rose around me, and it took a moment before I shook free of my memories of the garden and realised that the aroma was my magic returning, and not some strong remembrance of days past.

I pulled the apron out and slipped it over my head. It was made of calico, yellowed with age, and had half a dozen pockets across the front. Those pockets had held a multitude of things in their time—eggs, freshly collected from under sleepy hens; pegs for the washing; a great range of kitchen and garden implements. This apron was like a tradesman's tool belt, and my mother had worn it every day.

The corpse I'd so carefully reburied in the little clearing outside had worn an apron just like this one.

My magic stirred again in response to the tangle of emotions I was feeling—already, Yriell's potion was wearing off. So many memories, good and bad, were tied up in those apron strings.

My hands trembled as I tied the strings on either side. It was hard to believe she was gone. Harder still to know that I'd never really known her. Our lives together had been a lie, but I couldn't hate her for that. She'd only been trying to keep us both alive, the best way she knew how. It didn't stop me from mourning the lost opportunity to know her better, though, or from feeling sad at the sacrifice she'd had to make. Imagine having to abandon your own child in a strange world, knowing you might never see them again. Knowing that they'd probably hate you for it, but you couldn't tell them why. All to keep them safe. It must have been agonising for her.

Now came the hard part. I let my magic rise around me, breathing in the scent of gardenias. Just as well I liked gardenias, because I would be smelling them a lot now. Imagine if my magic had smelled like three-day-old fish, or dog poo. That would really suck.

Stop putting it off, idiot. Focus. I pulled my wayward thoughts back into line and bunched the apron in my hands. I stared at my face in the mirror on the inside of the wardrobe door, but that was too weird, so I shut my eyes. The magic filled me, and dimly I sensed Squeak through our bond, pushing love towards me. I focused on the shape of my mother's face, the severe hairstyle she always wore, the way her eyes crinkled up at the corners when she smiled. I had a thousand images of my mother stored away in my memories, and I let them all out, seeing her laughing, or focusing on a tricky bit of needlework, watching her face in all its moods.

And then I opened my eyes, and couldn't help a yelp of surprise. Livillia stared back at me, as real as the last time I'd seen her, when she'd walked out of Jamison's Pharmacy, leaving me behind forever. It wasn't Anawen's real face, but I'd never known that woman. It was the face that had sung fae lullabies to me, the face I'd spent more time with than that of any other person in either world. The face of the one person I would always love, whatever she had done or not done, despite all those years of exile when I'd tried to convince myself that I hated her for abandoning me.

The beloved face of a woman who was now dead. I watched as the face in the mirror crumpled, screwed up in pain, and tears began to leak down its cheeks.

"Are you hurt? What's wrong?" The Hawk was beside me in an instant, though my crying had been almost soundless.

His eyes met mine in the mirror, and understanding dawned in them. Gently, he turned me around to face him and wiped the tears from my cheeks. Then he bent down and pressed a kiss on my lips, so tender that it made me shiver, and renewed tears welled in my eyes.

"This is hard for you," he said, kissing the tears away. "But your mother would be proud. If you can be the means to restore Illusion's people to their home, your pain will have been worth it."

I nodded, scrubbing tears away. I had never seen this gentle side of the Hawk before. He was a complicated man. I must look a sight, but it didn't seem to bother him that I was tear-stained and sniffing. Or even that I didn't look like myself at all.

"Hey, no kissing my mother." I tried for some levity, but my voice wobbled alarmingly.

He drew me closer, his big hands almost meeting around my waist. "It doesn't matter what you look like. It's what's in here that counts." He tapped my breastbone.

Somehow, coming from him, that didn't sound corny. Had anyone ever said anything to me before with such sincerity shining in their eyes? Let alone anything so nice?

Raven cleared his throat, and I tore my gaze away from the Hawk with some difficulty. He was lounging in the doorway, checking out my new appearance with evident approval.

"If you two lovebirds would pay attention to the plan, we have a Realm to save."

22

Together, the three of us—plus Squeak, of course—gated back to Arlo as the sun was setting. The Illusionists had modified their wards to allow us entry. It was strange to be back here so soon. Only this morning, I'd been desperate to escape this place, and now I couldn't wait to meet the people who lived here. My people.

All my life, I'd been No One of Nowhere, a changeling who could never know her birth family; a creature tolerated in Autumn, but never truly part of it. And now I was a trueblood, as fae as anyone else, the survivor of a shattered Realm. My stomach fluttered with nerves as we entered the castle I'd so recently escaped from. Someone on this island could be a true blood relative of mine. I tried not to get my hopes up, knowing how many from Illusion had died in Summer's attack, but it was possible.

"So, this isn't your castle, right?" I'd assumed it was another of Raven's homes when I had first woken up here, but Arlo was part of Illusion, even if it was currently hiding in the Realm of Night. "Whose is it?"

"It was the home of Lord Perony's brother, Veynar, and his family," Raven said. "Sadly, none of them survived the Night of Swords. They were all at Lord Perony's home on the main island, meeting with their guests from Air and Summer, who had come to offer their help in the search for the missing Lord. Of course, we all know how that turned out. Veynar's servants still live here and keep the place, but now it functions as a kind of town hall for the residents of the village, and a place for their leaders to work."

"And also as a place for the sons of Night to stay when they visit," the Hawk added.

"That, too," Raven agreed. "Though it's just me. Quinn wouldn't put his inheritance at risk by doing anything to upset Father, and Paxyl is just too busy painting to have time for any of that political nonsense. It's the biggest fear of his life that something will happen to Quinn and he'll have to become the heir." He paused as he nodded to the guards and led us through into the castle courtyard. "And the biggest fear of mine is that they'll both die and *I'll* be left as heir."

The courtyard wasn't very big, but then, Arlo wasn't the biggest island, either. Nor was it much of a castle, as far as defences went—more an overgrown manor house, with windows opening right in the outer wall on at least two sides. It would have been a hard place to defend effectively. The Illusionists had probably never expected to have to defend it, safe on its island in the middle of the river, and it made my blood boil to think of that night of betrayal.

Raven led us up a set of stone stairs to a modest wooden

door. Squeak trilled and launched himself from my shoulder as we went inside, climbing up into the open air. Perhaps he didn't like enclosed spaces, or maybe he'd decided to go say hello to his family. Inside, a spiral staircase took us up to the next level, where we ran into a man in servant's livery.

"Lord Bran." The man bowed politely. Obviously, everyone was very used to seeing Raven coming and going.

"Grindel, could you let Morwenna know that we're here?" And Raven must spend quite a bit of time here, if he knew the names of the servants.

Grindel bowed again and opened a door to reveal a small sunlit parlour. "Wait here, my lord, and I'll find her."

I sat down in a chair by the window and checked the sky, hoping to catch a glimpse of Squeak in flight. From here, I could see the lake, with the village nestled around this end of it. A few rainbow drakes hovered in the skies above the water and, as I watched, one folded his wings and dropped like a stone, arrowing down into the water. A moment later, he reappeared, a fish in his mouth. Two other drakes saw and gave chase, but the first drake was determined not to share. He powered away toward the village. I lost sight of them once they'd dived among the houses, but it made me smile. I could just imagine that drake fleeing to his bondmate for protection from the would-be thieves.

The Hawk sat down opposite. "Who's Morwenna?"

"She's the leader of the people here," Raven answered. "She and her husband, Tirgen, took charge when Illusion fell. It's thanks to Morwenna's powers that Arlo has managed to remain hidden all these years. Her Illusions are very strong. Once, when Summer was very close to finding it, she actually managed to cloak the whole island in the Illusion of a cloud."

I tried to imagine how much power it would take to cast an Illusion on a whole island, even a small one like Arlo. I was already feeling a little tired from holding my mother's appearance. "You said someone here might be able to help me control my power better. Did you mean Morwenna?"

"She's the strongest here. She doesn't lead because of her lineage, you know. She's just a healer. But there are no nobles left—they all died on the Night of Swords."

That was fine by me. I'd grown up in a country cottage. Nobles made me uneasy.

The door opened, revealing a dark-haired woman. She was beautiful, of course—all fae were beautiful—and had the resting bitch face also typical of so many of them. She reminded me of someone.

When Lirra came in behind her, I realised who. Surely, she must be Lirra's mother.

"Morwenna, this is Allegra," Raven said, rising to greet her.

She stiffened in surprise at my name and raked me with a cool stare.

"She left our hospitality too early to meet you when she was here earlier."

The Hawk rose, too, with his natural politeness.

I got up as well, not wanting to anger her more than I

probably already had, considering what I'd done to her daughter. "Hi."

"Lirra told me." Her hard eyes stared impassively at me for a moment before she transferred her attention back to Raven. "Grindel said you needed me."

Right. None of that time-wasting chitchat for this lady.

"Have a seat," Raven said, flopping back into his own chair with a vague wave of his hand at an empty couch. "This could take a while. It's a bit of a long story."

He launched into a summary of our plan to use the Illusion of my mother's appearance to get in to see the king without alerting our enemies, so I could tell the king the truth about this island and its inhabitants.

"So, the three of you have decided to reveal our existence without even consulting with us?" Her tone was arctic.

"Tirgen agreed with me. He wanted Allegra to speak for Arlo to the king." Raven, full of enthusiasm for our plan, looked a little taken aback by the hostility in her voice.

"My husband doesn't make the decisions around here."

"Morwenna, look at her. Who will recognise her like this? It's the perfect opportunity. The Hawk will escort her straight to the king. She can set up a meeting for you with Rothbold—we can even bring him here, if you think that's safer. But it's time to do *something*."

She stared at him for a long moment. "I know you, Bran. There is some flaw in your plan, or you'd be at Whitehaven already."

"I'm having trouble controlling my magic," I said. "Once I get to the king, I want to be able to change back to my own form. I can create an Illusion easily enough, but dispelling it is harder."

Impossible, actually, but I wasn't going to tell her that and risk a sneer. I could tell she was the sneering type.

She tipped her head to one side and considered me, as if I were a rather distasteful specimen she'd been asked to dissect. "Try changing back now."

I gathered my magic around me, comforted by the now-familiar scent of gardenias. Lirra nodded encouragingly at me as I focused on the picture of my own self in my head and tried to will my form back into those familiar lines. It wasn't easy to concentrate with everyone staring at me like that.

Feeling a little panicky, I struggled in silence for what felt like eternity, but my form refused to budge. Finally, Morwenna sighed and waved an exasperated hand at me. Blue light flared, and my skin tingled as her magic washed over me. A tart ginger scent flushed away my gardenias, and I was my own self again. The apron, which was real, looked bizarre over the top of my jeans once the Illusion of my mother's dress had vanished.

"Now try to retake your mother's form."

I closed my eyes this time, to block out the sight of all those expectant faces. Well, the expectant ones and Morwenna's, which was more bored than anything else. I summoned my magic, and this time I could feel the change creep over me. That was odd. I hoped it didn't look too creepy for the others to see my features slowly morphing into someone else's.

I opened my eyes to confirm what my magic had told me. My hands were my mother's again, with longer fingers than mine, slightly roughened from years of working in the garden.

"How did you change me back?" I asked, my curiosity driving me into conversation with her. "Can anyone do that?"

"Only Mum," Lirra said, with obvious pride, before Morwenna could answer, "and a couple of others. Lord Perony could do it, too. You have to be really strong to break other people's Illusions."

"Can you do it?"

"Not yet." She glanced at her mother almost shyly. "But maybe one day."

"Why can I only change in one direction?"

"That often happens when power is untrained." Morwenna's tone implied that it was somehow my fault for not being trained. "That's why we like to bond our youngsters early, so that their drakes can help them."

That didn't really explain anything. She seemed to have taken an instant dislike to me. As a changeling, I'd been used to being greeted with disdain, but my blood was just as good as hers now. Either she was holding the fact that I'd tied her daughter up against me, or she was still annoyed that she hadn't been consulted on our plan.

"She has a bondmate," Raven said helpfully.

"Really?" The look she gave me made it seem as though she questioned Squeak's choice.

"Yes," I said, feeling defensive. I didn't really care if she sneered at me, as long as she helped me, but I wouldn't put up with her looking down that long nose at Squeak. His love was pure and freely given. I felt a surge of it down our bond, as if he'd picked up on my resentment and was sending soothing feelings.

I had no idea how a rainbow drake, even one as loving as Squeak, could help me use my magic better, but I wasn't about to give her the satisfaction of asking. Maybe it would have been better if Raven had asked Lirra to help me—at least she hadn't seemed to dislike me on sight, despite our last meeting. But here we were.

"Let's go outside," Morwenna said, and I followed her meekly to the doors that opened onto the balcony. Everyone else stayed inside, though I left the door open behind me so they could hear our conversation if they wished.

This place had definitely not been built for defence. It was more of a pleasure palace than a castle. The balcony looked over beautiful gardens immediately below us, but beyond the castle wall, a view of the lake, darkly glittering in the last rays of the setting sun, opened up. As usual, several rainbow drakes circled in the sky above the lake or darted above the town nestled on its shore, occasionally diving down and disappearing into its paved streets.

Morwenna said nothing, only stood there, looking out at the view, but I realised when one of the drakes arrowed towards us from the lake that she must have called her bondmate to her silently. She held up her arm as the drake backwinged and landed neatly on it, then fluttered up to her shoulder, where it lay its scaled head against her cheek. It was a beautiful creature, bluer than Squeak was, with silver tips to the spikes that currently lay flat against its neck, and huge golden eyes. In that moment, rubbing her cheek affectionately against her drake's head, Morwenna looked a far more pleasant person than I'd seen any indication of up until now.

She must have felt my eyes on her, because she looked up, and it was as if a shutter came down over her face, rendering it cold and unapproachable again. Then, in the blink of an eye, I wasn't looking at Morwenna anymore, but at a much younger woman, dressed casually in T-shirt and jeans with strawberry-blond hair cascading down her back.

"Now I'll perform a beginner's transition back to my own form." Even her voice had changed—it sounded younger and lighter in tone. "Listen with your magic as well as your ears."

Listen to what? She hadn't made any noise at all when she'd assumed the Illusion of this girl's form, whoever she was. But I obediently summoned my magic, wondering how on earth you "listened" with it. Maybe something would come to me.

She hummed the first bars of a lilting melody that put me in mind of a song by The Corrs, though it was nothing I'd ever heard before. The beautiful blue drake's eyes lit up, and it nudged her cheek again with its head, leaving a glittery smear that quickly faded as if absorbed into Morwenna's skin. Then it crooned back to her, puffing up its chest and spreading its wings a little for balance. Its voice joined with hers, entwined in the same lovely melody, before breaking into a harmonisation. I was so fascinated and delighted by the impromptu concert that I almost forgot what we were here for, but a surge in the smell of ginger reminded me, and I tentatively reached out with my magic as the music swelled.

Morwenna glowed softly blue, and then her real form was back, eyeing me with disapproval. "Did you catch it? Did you feel the magic in the music?"

I nodded tentatively, not sure if I had. I'd felt *something*, but that didn't mean I could replicate it.

"The greatest singers in the Realms have traditionally come from Illusion," she said. "Music is an integral part of our magic. Now, call your bondmate and try it yourself."

I reached out to Squeak, and he soon appeared, arrowing down out of the darkening sky. Already, I could tell him apart from the other rainbow drakes, though they were all a similar size and colour. And yet, they were all individuals. The shape of his head was different, as was the way his spikes lay against his glowing green neck. I felt a surge of love as he landed neatly on my shoulder and wound his tail around my neck affectionately.

I reached up to stroke his head, and he closed his eyes and ducked his head against my fingers, a blissed-out expression on his mobile little face. He warbled softly, and it sounded like a purr.

"Now let him oil your face."

I stared at her blankly. Oil my face?

She sighed. "They have a gland on the top of their heads that secretes a special oil. It's part of their bonding rituals. It strengthens your connection to him, which allows him to boost your native magic."

"That glittery slime is magic?" That must be why Squeak had been trying to wipe it all over me back at Yriell's. He'd been doing his best to help me with my Illusion. Yriell had told me once that she thought rainbow drakes had a poisonous spur that was somehow linked to Illusion magic. Guess she'd gotten the details wrong.

I stopped rubbing Squeak's head. On cue, he butted it against my cheek. And here I'd been thinking that was his way of begging for pats.

We're supposed to sing, I said to him in my mind, though I doubted he could understand my words. How, exactly, did we do this? Did he just have some innate understanding of what was required? Would he join in if I started to sing?

I realised that the idea of singing was making me nervous. Ridiculous. I sang all the time in the band. How was this any different? And yet, it was. I stood here, in the Realms, next to a judgy witch who was watching me impatiently. It was nothing like performing surrounded by my friends.

"Go on, then," Morwenna prompted. "What are you waiting for?"

"My mother used to punish me for singing." Damn, why had I told her that? It was hardly relevant, now, and it certainly wouldn't earn me any compassion from this woman.

"And rightly so," she said. Of course she would approve

of my being punished. Briefly, I wondered how happy Lirra's childhood had been. I could well believe that Morwenna would be even stricter than my own mother had been. "She may not have trusted her medicine to keep your power blocked if you encouraged it with singing. In her place, I would have done the same. Singing may even have attracted a drake, which would have been dangerous for both of you. But now, you are free to sing."

She waved in an imperious manner that said "get on with it" loud and clear.

Feeling horribly self-conscious, I cleared my throat and began to hum one of Rowan's songs. Its lilting melody reminded me of the one she had hummed. I didn't know if the kind of song made any difference. Guess I'd just have to figure it out on my own, since I wasn't willing to give her the satisfaction of seeing just how ignorant I was.

Rowan had always said this song was catchy enough to make the Top 40, if we ever got a record deal. Squeak certainly seemed to like it. He sat up straighter, his shoulders swaying ever so slightly in time to the rhythm, his body thrumming with excitement. Then he stretched his head out and began to warble a counterpoint to the lilting melody.

Wow. Rowan had to hear this. Maybe we should get Squeak into the band. The harmony seemed to come to him instinctively. It was so beautiful, and fitted so exactly with the song it was hard to believe that it wasn't already part of it, yet Squeak had never heard this song before. I almost lost the thread of the part I was singing, I was so lost in admiration of Squeak's harmonising.

"Good." Morwenna's voice recalled me to the moment. "Now focus on your magic. Let your form slide and make the change."

This part had always come relatively easy, so far, but the transition to my mother's form seemed to happen without effort this time, my magic rising up in response to the magic Squeak and I were making with our voices. A soft blue glow rose around me and the change rolled over me like putting on a comfy old sweater.

Morwenna inspected me, probably for mistakes, and I kept singing. She hadn't told me to stop, and I was enjoying it so much. Squeak's voice was pure and unearthly. It was like having an angel singing on my shoulder.

"Now dispel the Illusion and let your real form rise to the surface again." Her voice was clipped, her face expressionless as a rock. She reminded me of a drill sergeant barking orders at a bunch of disappointing recruits, which was ruining my good mood and the magic of the moment, so I closed my eyes to block out the sight of her stony face.

Instead, I focused on the smell of gardenias that filled my nostrils, and the glory of Squeak's harmony winding around my melody. A shiver of magic washed over me.

The sound of clapping broke the spell, and I opened my eyes just in time to see the blue glow fade, stopping mid-song. Squeak warbled on a few notes more, then butted his head gently against my face, as if to ask why I'd stopped. Raven stood just inside the open door, grinning hugely at me, and I realised that my own self was back.

Well, it hadn't been easy, exactly, but certainly a lot

easier than it had been without Squeak. I stroked his neck gratefully.

Predictably, Morwenna still looked as though she could smell something rotten, even though her teaching had been successful. "You need to practise," she said. "The transition should be instantaneous. Once you have mastered it with your bondmate's help, you will need to work on dispelling the Illusion on your own."

"But it should be much easier now that she's done it once, shouldn't it?" Raven asked, giving me an encouraging smile.

Morwenna shrugged, still frowning. "Possibly. But it's equally possible that her power is stunted from being suppressed so long. She may never amount to much."

And with that, she swept past him and stalked across the room to the door, clicking her fingers at Lirra to follow as if she were no more than a dog. Squeak squawked indignantly at her, the spikes of his neck flaring. He could feel my resentment. Stunted, indeed. She was pretty full of herself.

She took no notice of him, of course, just as she didn't appear to care that Lirra didn't immediately leap to follow her. I came back in from the balcony and Lirra took my hand almost apologetically.

"Don't take any notice of her," she whispered, patting my hand consolingly. "You did well. She'll be better once she gets to know you. At the moment, all she can see when she looks at you is her sister, and it hurts her."

"Her sister?" I repeated stupidly.

"Anawen," the girl said, then she slipped out of the room in Morwenna's wake.

I stared after her, thunderstruck. Morwenna was my mother's sister? Then why was she treating me like I was something nasty she'd stepped in? She was my *aunt*, for God's sake. And that meant Lirra was my cousin.

Well. Somehow, I'd imagined meeting my family would go a little better than that.

23

I stared at the closed door in shock. "Wait, what? Morwenna is my aunt?" I whirled on Raven. "Why didn't you say anything?"

"Does it matter?" His gaze slid away from mine. "There'll be plenty of time for family reunions after you've seen the king."

"Does it *matter*? You are a complete jerk, you know that? Of course it bloody matters. I have a *family*!"

Squeak launched himself from my shoulder and flew straight at Raven's head.

"Hey!" Raven threw up an arm to protect his face as Squeak lashed his spiked tail at him.

Rage still boiled through my veins, but I called the little drake back to me. He landed on my shoulder and wrapped his tail around my neck, rubbing his head comfortingly against my cheek.

Raven looked shaken. "I can't believe he attacked me. There's nothing wrong with the strength of your bond, at least."

Squeak hissed at him.

I projected love and reassurance through our bond, stroking his jewelled hide to calm him. "And *I* can't believe you kept something like that from me. Do you know what it's like to have no one?" I actually had a family, and he hadn't thought that fact was important enough to share.

The Hawk took my hand. "Morwenna didn't bring it up, either, did she? Only the child. Perhaps you need to give her some time."

"Yes," said Raven, seizing on this with eagerness. "Talk to her later. Right now, you have an appointment at the palace."

I gave him a filthy look, but the Hawk nodded and drew his sword. "Can you retake your mother's form?"

It took me a couple of tries, but I managed it with Squeak's help. As soon as my Illusion was complete, he slashed a gateway in the air with Ecfirrith. Squeak chirped and sat straighter on my shoulder.

"You'll have to leave the drake here," the Hawk said.

Squeak's cheerful chirping changed to confusion and then protest as I unwound his tail from my neck and tried to encourage him to take flight. "Stay here with your friends," I told him. "I'll be back soon."

He leapt into the air, and I thought he was heading for the open balcony door. Instead, he darted through the glowing gateway and disappeared. The Hawk muttered a curse under his breath.

"It's dark," Raven said. "No one will see him."

"Make sure he stays away from you," the Hawk growled at me, "or he'll give the game away."

I nodded, hoping the little drake would listen to me. I reassured myself that I still had Yriell's potion in the pocket of my apron—just in case I got stuck again and couldn't change back to my own form without him.

Hand in hand, the Hawk and I stepped through the gate and arrived outside the gates of Whitehaven. The guards came to attention at the sight of the knight, and we marched through without challenge. They couldn't have recognised me in this form, so clearly the Hawk's presence was enough to vouchsafe me entry. No one was pointing at the sky or doing anything to suggest they'd just seen a rainbow drake, so I sent very stern instructions down our bond that Squeak should hide himself somewhere and crossed my fingers.

The winding path through the gardens was just as lovely as I remembered, but I was too nervous to appreciate the beauty this time. As we climbed the marble steps to the grand entry, the Hawk stopped a man who was hurrying past and asked him if the king was receiving in the throne room.

"Not tonight," the man replied, his gaze sliding over my unfamiliar face with a supreme lack of interest. "He's hosting a dinner for the seasonal Lords in the blue dining room."

The Hawk thanked him and strode on, and I followed close behind. I got a few odd looks from servants we passed in the halls. I probably looked like a servant myself in my humble apron, more like someone who should be working in the kitchens than wandering the marble halls of the palace in the company of so illustrious a personage as the Hawk. Having him was as good as an access-all-areas pass. No one did more than raise a discreet eyebrow as we passed.

Not even the guards at the door of the blue dining room hesitated for more than a second. Clearly, the Hawk was someone who was allowed to interrupt the king, whoever he was entertaining. One of them opened the door at a curt gesture from the knight, and we entered.

Immediately, I could see where the dining room had got its name from. The walls were still as white and shimmering as in the rest of the palace, and the white marble floors as pale, but on the wall opposite the door, an enormous blue tapestry hung. It showed a typical fae hunt, with lords in feathered hats and ladies in beautiful dresses astride horses of silver and midnight black, racing through a dark forest by the light of the full moon. Whatever they were in pursuit of wasn't shown, but the hounds streaming in front of the horses made it clear that the prey was almost within the hunters' reach. The whole thing was done in shades of blue. It was the biggest tapestry I had ever seen. I couldn't imagine how long it must have taken to weave. It covered the entire wall and dominated the room.

Directly in front of the tapestry stood a long table on a dais, at which the king and queen sat with a group of other fae. The seasonal Lords and Ladies, I assumed, judging by the finery of their clothes. I took them all in at a glance. The lords of Summer and Autumn I already knew. That man with the wild red hair bore such a strong resemblance to his daughter that I knew straight away he must be the

Lord of Spring, which left the other man as the Lord of Winter.

Four other tables below the dais seated perhaps a dozen each. These must be the favoured retainers of the lords. So much for a small, intimate dinner.

The king looked up at our entrance and smiled at the Hawk. At his side, the queen looked less pleased—though, for all I knew, that was her habitual expression. Her brother, Kellith, was on her other side. I watched for his reaction, but his gaze slid over me just as that of the man outside had done, immediately dismissing me as someone of no importance.

I could hardly believe it. I had expected a guilty flinch. A double-take, perhaps, at seeing someone he knew to be dead walking around, still breathing. Could he be that good an actor? I'd been so convinced that he was the man behind my mother's death, but he acted as if he'd never seen her before.

Quickly, I checked out Jaxen. I'd spotted him at one of the lower tables. I'd discarded him as a suspect earlier, but maybe I'd been wrong. But he was looking at someone on the Summer table, his brow creased in confusion.

I followed his glance. Blethna Arbre stared at me, eyes narrowed. Her face flushed a furious red as our eyes met and she half-made as if to rise, then fell back into her chair.

Oh. My. God.

Was it her? Had she killed my mother?

All this had taken a bare millisecond. I followed the Hawk between the tables, towards the king, my mind spinning. It would make sense—and meant that I'd been looking for motive in all the wrong places. This wasn't about the fact that my mother was from Illusion. It was about revenge.

I stopped in front of the dais, but the Hawk mounted the steps with an easy stride that spoke of how at home he was here. I felt like the one thing in a game of "one of these things is not like the others" among all these noble fae in their jewels and silken clothes. My simple dress and humble apron stuck out like a sore thumb.

The Hawk bowed, then approached the king and bent close, saying something into his ear. The king cast me a speculative glance, then murmured something back, and the Hawk came back to lead me from the room, his hand on my elbow.

"I told the king you were Livillia and you had information about his kidnapping," he said, once we were safely in the hallway again. "I didn't want to mention Illusion in front of everyone. I'm sure the queen, at least, was eavesdropping. He said to wait for him in the small drawing room and he will meet us after dessert."

I nodded, hardly even listening. My feet moved automatically, keeping pace with the Hawk as he led me through the maze of corridors to a small room, furnished with comfortable lounges. I sank into one of the chairs, replaying that look Blethna Arbre had given me over and over. It had been pure venom.

Had she truly killed my mother just to get back at me? Why did the crazy bitch hold me responsible for the death of her husband? Technically, it had been Yriell who had killed him, by closing the gate between her home and the fae Realm when he was halfway through. A more effective way to slice someone in half would be hard to imagine. I shuddered as I recalled it.

"Cold?" the Hawk asked. "Let me build up the fire a little."

I shook my head, but he was already bending to his task. I stared at his strong back, the movement of the muscles beneath his shirt as he lifted a heavy log onto the fire, but my mind was elsewhere. She wouldn't take up a vendetta against the king's sister for her husband's death. Yriell was too powerful. So was the Hawk. So, who else was there to blame but the changeling who had uncovered her husband's plot and led the rescue of the king? No wonder she hated me.

And from hating me, it wasn't a giant leap to finding a way to make me pay. A life for a life. I swallowed hard as bile rose in my throat. It made sense, in a twisted kind of way. In her mind, I was responsible for her husband's death, so she had found a way to make me suffer the same agonies of loss as she was going through.

She had killed my mother. I was sure of it.

The Hawk jabbed at the fire with the poker a few times. When it was burning to his satisfaction, he sat down opposite me. "You're very quiet."

I nodded, not sure I could speak. Emotions roiled inside me: fury, hate, agony. The pain of my mother's loss cut even deeper now that I knew she hadn't rejected me at all.

"Blethna Arbre," I began, but the opening of the door cut me off.

A servant bowed to the Hawk. "Excuse me, sir, but the queen desires your presence in the dining room. Immediately, sir." We both stood up, but the servant shook his head. "Just you, sir. Your companion may wait here."

The Hawk turned to me. "Will you be all right on your own? The Lady alone knows what she wants. I could be a while."

I nodded, eyes on the carpet. "I'll be fine."

I even managed to sound normal. He followed the servant out and I sank back into my chair as the door snicked shut behind them.

The log he'd put on the fire shifted, and sparks flew up the chimney. Watching the flames soothed my distress, though the fury remained. I would tell the king and demand retribution. He had no great love for Summer— surely he would take action? But what proof could I offer him, except my own certainty that I was right? The flames leapt and writhed in the fireplace, and I turned my face to their heat, but found no answers there.

After a time, I leapt up and paced to the window. She'd probably killed Jamison, too. I couldn't just let her get away with it, but what could I do? Take justice into my own hands? I stared out the window, seeing not the lamplit gardens but Dansen Arbre's gruesome death play out again in the dark glass. Was I the kind of person who could do something like that? I shook with fury now, but could I really take someone's life in cold blood?

A winged shape passed across the moon. A bat, or Squeak? I leaned my head against the cool glass, my night vision shot by the brightness of the room, and tried to rein in my emotions. I didn't want to upset him again. But I was lost in a world of anger and regret. If I hadn't become involved with the king, would my mother still be alive? Had saving him been worth losing my mother?

It seemed like a message from the goddess when the door opened and Blethna Arbre slipped into the room. Here she was, ready for me to kill while my blood still boiled with hatred. Instinctively, my hand went for my knife, but there was no knife in the voluminous pockets of my mother's apron—only the small bottle Yriell had given me with the remainder of her magic-deadening potion.

Blethna held her hand out, as if telling me to stop, but something shot out of her palm. Only my quick reflexes saved me as I hurled myself behind the nearest couch. A blast of heat to rival the flames in the fireplace whooshed over my head, and the top of the couch blistered and blackened.

"How many times do I have to kill you, bitch?" she snarled.

Another wave of heat hit the couch, and it burst into flames. Shit. I was toast—literally. She was between me and the door, and she had Summer magic and I had nothing to defend myself with. I rolled away, closer to the window. Could I get out before she roasted me alive?

She came after me. I had no time to open the bloody window and climb out. What was I thinking? I picked up a small side table and hurled it at her, hoping to throw her off balance. I needed to distract her, to stop her using her magic. The table, like the couch, burst into flames as the air shimmered with heat. Her Summer powers were strong.

I dodged the next wave of heat—thank God she could only manage tightly focused blasts, otherwise the whole room would go up and I'd be charcoal on the floor—and snatched up the poker. Maybe I could use it to break the window. Or better yet, break the bitch's head.

Sweat sprang out on my forehead as I dodged around the furniture, though she looked as cool as ever. It was getting mighty hot in here. I took a swipe at her with the poker, but she danced out of reach, so I used the momentum to slam it into the glass of the nearest window, which shattered.

Hopefully, the noise would bring the guards running. She sent another blast of shimmering heat at me, and I had to hit the deck again, scrambling behind an armchair. At this rate, there wouldn't be any furniture left in the room soon, and I'd be out of things to hide behind. Did she never tire?

Something swooped in through the broken window with a shriek of fury. Squeak! His rage was an inferno that rivalled Blethna's magic. She screamed as he slashed at her face, his claws tangled in her hair.

I sent abject gratitude down my link with Squeak. His timing was perfect. I leapt up to take advantage, swinging my poker at Blethna while she was distracted. The thud as it connected with her back was the most satisfying sound I'd ever heard.

She screamed again, and lashed out with her magic. But not at me. Squeak shrilled in agony, even as a wave of pain slammed through our link. I dropped to my knees from the shock of it.

Squeak fell to the floor, whimpering piteously.

I had to protect him. Gritting my teeth, I forced myself back to my feet and slammed the poker into Blethna again. This one wasn't such a solid hit. She staggered, but brought up her hands again. I was too close to her and there was nowhere to hide. She was going to fry me.

I hurled myself at her, bringing her down in a tackle that would have done a footy player proud. We crashed through another of the delicate side tables, reducing it to matchsticks. The king really needed to invest in some more robust furniture for this place.

Momentarily winded by landing on her back with me on top of her, she gaped up at me, struggling for breath. Her open mouth gave me an idea, and I whipped out Yriell's bottle from my pocket. Thank the Lady it hadn't smashed. I pulled out the stopper and upended the bottle into the bitch's mouth. She gasped and spat most of it in my face, and I felt my own magic desert me as a few drops entered my mouth, my skin tingling as the Illusion dissipated. I prayed that she'd swallowed enough.

She got an arm free and punched me in the side of the head, hard enough that my vision darkened. My disorientation gave her the chance to shove me off and scramble away.

"You!" she snarled, then thrust both hands out at me. "You need exterminating."

Nothing happened. The look on her face was comical.

I took advantage of her confusion and snatched up the poker again. This was more like it. No magic, just muscles and my trusty poker.

"Why did you kill my mother?" I circled around, making sure I was between her and the door. She was not getting away now.

She raised an eyebrow, though the move wasn't so elegant now. Her elaborate hairstyle was a mess, her face still red from our tussle on the floor. "Filthy Illusionist. She needed killing. Just like you."

"Bitch, the only one here who needs killing is you."

She backed away toward the window, and I followed, making sure to keep her away from Squeak. He was still keening, a sound of such pain that my heart constricted with fear for the little guy. I could feel it, too, every fibre of my being vibrating in agony. Only the adrenaline was keeping me on my feet. I risked a quick glance at him, but he was curled up around himself, his back to me, so I couldn't see the extent of the damage. I sent a quick prayer to the Lady for him.

My opponent was built like a fighter, long and lean. I'd already discovered there were muscles under that pretty dress. My whole body throbbed, and I wasn't keen to tangle with her again, even with my poker. Where the hell were the guards?

"Of course, since she was your mother, I made sure to make her death extra painful."

She's lying, I told myself. *Don't let her rile you.* She just wanted me to lose my head and make a mistake. I gripped the poker a little tighter.

"If only I'd had time to do the same for the little apothecary she ran to. It would have been quite poetic, don't you think, considering he even sold it in his shop? Do you know how marvellous human pharmacies are?" A nasty smile twisted her face. "You can buy iron in a bottle, right there off the shelf. Imagine it! Enough to kill a dozen fae, and all perfectly legal."

I drew in a slow breath, trying to calm myself.

She laughed. "Your mother was very bad. She didn't want to take her medicine."

She leapt for the broken window, but I was moving, too. She wouldn't escape me now. I swung the poker and caught her on the leg. She stumbled, but managed to turn the stumble into a kick that took me right in the gut. I doubled over, and she snatched at the poker, but I had it in an iron grip.

I elbowed her in the face as we struggled over it, and she fell back, blood streaming from her nose. Good. I hoped it was broken. I took a firm grip on the poker and belted her in the side of the head. She went down like a sack of potatoes.

And of course, the king chose that moment to enter the room, accompanied by his brother-in-law, Kellith, Lord of Summer.

25

The King stopped dead in his tracks, his mouth open in surprise.

"What in the name of the Tree is going on here?" Kellith said, in tones of outrage.

I stepped back, lowering the poker, though I still kept it in my hand. The end was bloodied, and bits of her hair stuck to it. Admittedly, the scene looked bad, with me standing over her bloody body, but the evidence of her use of her magic against me was all around us, too, in the blasted and charred furniture. It wasn't my fault I was the better fighter.

"She's not dead," I said, crossing the room in quick strides and sinking to my knees beside the still form of Squeak. I realised that he'd stopped making noise a few moments ago, and I could no longer feel his pain. My heart was in my mouth as I bent over him. I couldn't have cared less if Blethna *were* dead, but I knew the fae were made of sterner stuff than that. My blow might have killed a human, but she would recover, more's the pity.

Squeak's breathing was laboured, but at least he was still breathing. I hesitated to touch him, but even without moving him I could see that one wing was full of ragged holes, their edges charred, and the paler skin of his belly, which had once been a beautiful soft green, was now an angry red.

"What has happened here?" the king demanded, finding his voice at last.

"Isn't it obvious?" Kellith said, his face livid with rage. "She's attacked Blethna. This is what comes of keeping changelings as pets. She's a rabid animal."

King Rothbold shot him a stern look. "She is not a pet, and I have no doubt that if she did indeed attack Lady Blethna, she had a very good reason. Don't leap to conclusions, Kellith. Let the girl answer." He turned back to me, ignoring the lord who fumed by his side. "How have you come here, and why are you wearing that apron? And why is there an injured rainbow drake in my palace?"

I looked ridiculous, with my mother's apron over my jeans. The king had come here expecting to speak to a completely different woman, but the apron was the only thing that remained, like Cinderella's glass slipper. Why had he brought Kellith with him? And where was the Hawk? I couldn't help finding it suspicious that Blethna had turned up right after the queen had sent for the knight, and now Kellith was here, ready to support whatever story she had intended to spin for the king, to explain why she had killed the woman who was awaiting him in this room.

Except the scene that had greeted him wasn't the one

he'd been expecting. There was malice in his gaze as he stared at me. I had no doubt that if he'd been alone, my end would have come very swiftly. But the king was with him, so he still had to play the game. Though he really needed to work on his acting skills; if the king hadn't been so surprised himself, he would probably have noticed that Kellith's initial reaction had been fury that his pet had lost the fight rather than shock that there'd been a fight at all.

No doubt Blethna had filled him in on the pertinent details before she'd come to accost me. He was probably the one who'd arranged for the queen to send for the Hawk. If she even had. I felt a small twinge of worry—perhaps Kellith had had his thugs waylay the Hawk in the corridors. But Kyrrim was a warrior; he could take care of himself. I needed to focus on my own predicament, and make sure that when the shit hit the fan, I didn't end up caked in the stuff.

I glanced up at the king, reluctant to leave Squeak's side. Rothbold's initial confusion had already been replaced by a sort of weary look that seemed to say, "here we go again". More plots and wheels within wheels. He wasn't stupid; he knew how rare rainbow drakes were. Summer might have controlled Illusion's lands now, but no one would think that this one was here because Kellith was just *that* attractive a personality. I wished the Hawk had had the opportunity to tell the king who "Livillia" really was. Hell, I wished the Hawk was here.

"She attacked me." My voice shook with anger, not only for myself and my mother, but for poor little Squeak. He'd only wanted to protect me—he hadn't deserved to be drawn into a battle he was hopelessly outmatched for. But he obviously had more bravery than brains, and I owed my life to him. And look what his loyalty had brought him— his wings were scorched raw. The left one was more hole than wing. How could he ever fly again, with damage like that?

"Outrageous," Kellith said flatly. "Why would Lady Blethna do such a thing?"

"I think that's pretty easy to figure out, Kellith," the king said dryly. "We all know Blethna has been demanding blood price for Dansen's death and holds Allegra responsible. And Blethna is not known for her forgiving nature."

Kellith snapped his mouth shut, smoothing his expression into acquiescence, but not before I'd caught the poisonous look he'd cast at his brother-in-law. I half wondered whether he'd attack Rothbold right here and now, and whether I was in any condition to do something about it if he did. But then I realised that that wasn't his way. He was a spider that lurked in the background, manipulating his webs to ensnare his victims. He wasn't the type to wield the executioner's axe himself. He would expend a thousand Dansen Arbres to get what he wanted before he would ever lift a finger of his own.

Maybe that was how you had to play it when your sister was the queen. Presumably, his plan was to rule through her—from all accounts, that was pretty much what he'd been doing for the last twenty years—so he couldn't risk doing anything that cast him as anything but the brave and noble Lord willing to step up and help out his grieving sister. Regicide would probably incite the other lords to make a stand against him.

Fortunately, I didn't have to put my theory to the test, as the Hawk chose that moment to reappear, skidding through the doorway with his hand on his sword hilt. Thank God he was okay. My heart lifted as his gaze sought mine, as if he was reassuring himself that I was all right, before he turned his attention to his monarch.

"Sire, I can explain," he said. "I cast a Glamour on the Lady Allegra and disguised her as her mother, Livillia, to see if we could smoke out Livillia's killer."

So now I'd been elevated to the peerage. Nice. But I could have told him he was wasting his time with the Glamour story. I was quite certain that Kellith had already figured out I was from Illusion. Whether or not he'd known before tonight that Blethna had killed my mother, whatever she'd told him when she'd come to finish me off must have included some pretty damning facts in that regard.

Or was the Hawk still trying to protect the king from the truth? He and Yriell both seemed convinced that the king had too much on his plate to be burdened with the truth about Illusion right now. That seemed like a pile of horseshit to me. The truth might sometimes be a burden, but the king had a right to it, perhaps more than anyone in the kingdom, considering what he'd gone through because of Summer's deception.

Rothbold turned to me. "Your mother is dead? I had not heard that. I'm sorry."

"We had our suspicions of Lady Blethna," the Hawk continued, lying with a perfectly sincere expression. I was impressed. I hadn't realised that the noble knight had it in him. "It seems they have been confirmed."

Kellith couldn't contain himself any longer. "Rothbold, this is preposterous. This changeling has bewitched your knight. Where is the proof?" Now he looked smug, because he knew everything had been covered up. Nice try, dirtbag. Shame I had an ace up my sleeve.

"Your sister has a very effective truth serum, if you are in any doubt, sire," I said.

Kellith shot me another of those poisonous looks. If looks could kill, I would have been deader than week-old roadkill by now. I returned his gaze calmly. Try wriggling out of that one, arsehole.

Rothbold cocked his head at his brother-in-law. "What do you think, Kellith? That sounds like an excellent idea."

Blethna groaned softly, and it occurred to me that no one had gone to check on her yet, not even her liege lord. Kellith had less concern for her than I had for the little rainbow drake. Not that I cared what happened to her, but I thought Kellith might have at least pretended to be concerned for her welfare. But no. She sat up, propping herself against the wall, clearly in no hurry to get up.

"I'm sure that won't be necessary." Kellith said, and a look passed between them, promising an eternity of pain if she didn't fall in with his wishes. "Blethna will cooperate fully with any investigations you care to make."

She bowed her head, though whether she was

acquiescing or merely exhausted, I couldn't tell. I should have guessed he'd throw her under the bus—as Sage liked to say—rather than risk having his own plots exposed. I suspected that if the subject of truth serum were raised again, Blethna would suffer an unfortunate and fatal accident. That bowed head suggested that Blethna knew it, too.

"It's true, sire." Her voice was low but sure. "I did kill this woman's mother."

Well, if I'd had any doubt before of what a scary bastard Kellith was, it was gone now. She'd rather admit to murder than try to spread the blame to her liege lord. Maybe that was loyalty, but I suspected it was fear.

"But she was trying to infiltrate the Summer palace at the time," she continued. "Just one more Illusionist with a score to settle. We've had a rash of assassins over the years, sire."

Wait, what? This was bullshit. Or ... was it? Where had my mother gone when she left the cottage?

Kellith sighed. "A veritable plague of them."

"When I caught her, she was wearing the form of one of our guards. I had no choice."

"She poisoned her with iron," I burst out. "Does that sound like a clinical execution to you? She was after revenge. And then she killed Jamison, too, just because he tried to help my mother."

The king hesitated. "Yes, but if your mother was an assassin ..."

"You've only got her word for that."

The king stared at her for a long moment. What was he thinking? He wouldn't let her off, would he? I opened my mouth to protest, but the Hawk shook his head sharply at me. He knew the king better than me—better than anyone, probably—so I swallowed my fury and kept quiet.

"Perhaps I *will* need my sister's services," Rothbold said finally. "But we can settle the question of culpability for Livillia's death later. For the moment, it is quite clear to me that Blethna has attacked a guest in my palace. Guards!"

Two guards armed with swords rushed into the room in response.

"Take Blethna Arbre to the dungeons."

"You would take this changeling's word over Blethna's?" Kellith cried, outraged.

"I would," said the king, a dangerous glint in his eye. "I suggest that you accompany Blethna to the dungeons and counsel her on the perils of lying to her king. I will have the truth from her, one way or another."

Fuming, Kellith accompanied the two guards and their prisoner out. The Hawk shut the door behind them, and I let out a sigh of relief.

"Are you truly unhurt?" The king came to crouch next to me, gazing down with sorrow at poor Squeak's injuries.

"Pretty much, sire." My head throbbed where Blethna had punched me, and I had a few scrapes from diving around the room to escape her magic, but I'd been very lucky. Luckier than my brave rainbow drake.

The Hawk knelt on my other side and put an arm around me. I leaned against him, grateful for the support.

"I don't know what is going on here," the king said, taking my hand. "But I do know this. Rainbow drakes bond with the folk of Illusion. Perony was my best friend, and I spent a lot of time with him and his people." A shadow crossed his face. "I thought nothing was harder than realising I'd missed the first twenty years of my daughter's life, until I discovered that Perony and all his people were gone. I don't believe for one moment that Kyrrim Glamoured you, young lady. Not with a rainbow drake flying to your protection. I beg you, if there are any survivors of Summer's bloodbath—tell me."

His hand tightened on mine, and he gazed at me with such earnest hope that my heart went out to him.

"Indeed there are, sire. That's what I came here to tell you."

He bowed his head, but not before I caught the glimmer of tears in his eyes. The Hawk laid his hand on his sovereign's shoulder. Wordlessly, Rothbold covered that hand, and then he released us both and stood up.

"How many?"

"Several hundred, sire." The Hawk rose, too. "Nox's son, Bran, has been sheltering the island of Arlo in his father's Realm. Allegra comes to you as their ambassador. They want to go home."

"Of course they do. Of course they do." The king still looked as though he might weep. "*Damn* that man and his murderous ambitions."

I knew he meant Kellith. The Lord of Summer was a tumour that needed to be cut out, before he spread his poison across the whole of the Realms.

"It won't be easy," he said to the Hawk. "Kellith won't give up the riches of Illusion without a fight. We will need to handle this carefully."

"That's why we came to you in secret, sire," I said. "Though that didn't work as well as I'd hoped." I gazed down at Squeak, my insides knotting with worry. "Do you think your healers could help him?"

"We should take him back to Arlo," the Hawk said, before the king could reply. "They will know what to do."

"Of course," the king said. "Our discussions can wait. Your bondmate must come first. But how is it that I can sense no magic in you? You feel like a changeling, not a fae."

"That might also have to wait, sire. It's a long story."

"Very well." He called for a servant, and sent him running for wet cloths to wrap the injured drake in.

When the servant returned, the Hawk helped me wrap Squeak. We were as gentle as we could be, but I was glad the little drake was still unconscious.

When I stood, with Squeak cradled carefully in my arms, the king said, "I will pray for your bondmate's recovery."

"Thank you, sire."

"Tell the people of Arlo that their king rejoices in their survival. We will meet very soon, and I will have justice for all the people of Illusion. Including your mother."

26

"He won't let Blethna off, will he?" I asked. The king was the ultimate dispenser of justice in the Realms, but his political situation was tricky. I was afraid he'd go easy on the highborn fae so as not to rock the boat with Summer.

The Hawk had hustled me out of the room. I was exhausted and aching in a dozen different places, as well as sick with worry for Squeak, who was still mercifully unconscious. Now, we were heading for the palace gates.

Honestly, I hardly knew if I was coming or going. It felt as though this day would never end. I'd started the day as Raven's prisoner on Arlo, discovered I was fae, acquired a bondmate and a family and learned to use my power—then got into a fight for my life with the woman who had killed my mother and poor Jamison.

"Did you see Kellith's face when the king suggested he still might call on Yriell's services? If that's the alternative, Kellith will accept whatever punishment the king decides for Blethna without a fuss."

"Even death?" I glanced up at him, strong and sure by my side. Thousands of floating lamps bobbed over the gardens and illuminated his face. I was glad of them. My night vision was good, but I was exhausted, and I felt a terrible responsibility for the little drake in my arms. I didn't want to miss my step in the dark and jostle him.

The Hawk laughed grimly. "Do you think Kellith cares if she lives or dies? She is of no use to him anymore, so she is utterly disposable."

Good. Squeak whimpered, though he didn't seem to be awake. I sent love and encouragement down our bond, just in case. She'd blasted him without a second thought. The world would be a better place without her in it. Both worlds, in fact.

I stumbled a little on the paving stones as we passed through the palace gates, and the Hawk steadied me. Once outside, he drew his sword and formed the now-familiar glowing gateway in the air. Then he swept me up into his arms, careful of the little drake I carried.

"What are you doing?" I demanded. "I can walk."

"You're exhausted," he said, ignoring my protest as he stepped through the gateway.

I let my head fall against his shoulder, enjoying the unfamiliar sensation of being taken care of, even if it was only for a moment. Not that I couldn't take care of myself perfectly well, but it was nice to relax once in a while and let someone else shoulder the responsibility.

The Hawk wasn't even breathing heavily as he climbed the hill to the castle on Arlo. Lights showed in most of the windows. Despite how much I'd crammed into my day, it was still only early evening. I sighed, enjoying the feel of being cradled in his strong arms. If only I weren't so worried about Squeak, I could really savour this moment. But I was too eager to reach the castle.

A dark shape winged down out of the night sky, letting out a squawk as it passed. Another drake, checking us out. Presumably, the ravens were all asleep at this time of night. It disappeared into the dark, but a moment later it came back with a couple of friends at its wingtips, all chirping in distress as they circled our heads for a moment before taking off again.

"They'll have gone to raise the alarm," the Hawk said.

Sure enough, the gates opened as we approached, and Raven strode out, with another man I hadn't seen before.

"He's injured?" the other man called, hurrying towards us, and as soon as he spoke, I recognised his voice. He was the man who'd been arguing with Raven in his library the day I'd escaped, when I'd been hiding behind the couch eavesdropping on their conversation. The one who'd wanted to use me to approach the king. Morwenna's husband, Tirgen—which made him my uncle.

"Burned by Summer magic," I said as the Hawk set me gently on my feet again.

"May I see?"

I nodded. Uncle T was a slim, brown man with a head of thick, dark curls. One of the drakes which had been circling us landed on his shoulder, leaning forward to look as he lifted the edge of the damp cloth covering Squeak with tender care. The drake keened softly in distress as the blackened ruin of Squeak's wing was revealed, and I felt an irrational urge to comfort it. Gently, Tirgen closed the wrapping again, then reached up to soothe his drake, who ducked his head into the man's stroking palm.

"Can you help him?" I asked anxiously.

He nodded. "Bring him to the lake. The wet cloth was a good idea, but he needs to be fully immersed."

Obediently, I turned to follow him, and Raven fell in beside us.

"What happened?" Raven asked.

"Blethna Arbre decided to exact revenge," the Hawk said, still sticking closely to my side. I was glad he hadn't demanded to carry me again; I'd have felt like an idiot, being toted around like an invalid in front of everyone. Squeak was growing heavy in my arms—though he didn't weigh more than a small dog, I'd been carrying his weight for some time now, and my arms were tiring. But I was determined not to move him more than necessary, which meant no one else was touching him until I got him into the water.

The Hawk added a few more details, but I stopped listening, concentrating on putting my feet one after the other on the road down to the village. At least it was downhill. The streets of the town were softly lit, and several people watched us go by. Raven stopped to knock on one door, but I hurried after Tirgen, towards the lake, which glimmered in the dark on the far side of the town. I caught glimpses of it now and then as the streets bent around.

At last, we reached the water. Reeds drooped their heads all along the shore, except for a part that had been cleared around a small jetty that jutted out into the water, with half a dozen boats of varying sizes tied up to it. None were very big. They seemed recreational more than anything.

Tirgen strode straight out into the water, so I followed him, my feet stirring up clouds of sand as they sank into the soft lake bottom. Hurrying footsteps sounded on the path behind us, and Raven appeared with Morwenna and Lirra in tow.

Morwenna had a long length of cloth in her hands, and she quickly took charge. As I lowered Squeak gently into the water, she slung her cloth under his limp body. She positioned me under the overhanging branches of a young tree on the bank, then reached up and tied the ends of her cloth to the branch. After adjusting them to her satisfaction, Squeak was cradled in a makeshift hammock that held him so that he was almost entirely submerged, but he couldn't sink completely and drown. Several other drakes perched on the branch, looking down at him and warbling to each other like a bunch of hospital visitors at the bedside.

"There," she said, regarding her handiwork with satisfaction. "That will help, at least until we can get a better healer here."

"I thought you were a healer?"

She favoured me with a look of intense dislike. "I am, but this will need someone more skilled than me. I can ease the burns, but I'll need help with the wing."

"Will you be able to save it? The wing?" That was my biggest fear, that the little drake would lose the power of flight because of me.

She scowled at me. "It may take some time, but I'm hopeful. Raven has already sent for the healer."

"He'll be fine, I'm sure," Lirra said. "Mum has more healing magic in her little finger than most people have in their whole bodies."

"Thank God," I said.

"You should have taken better care of him in the first place," she snapped. "How could you let this happen?"

"We were attacked with Summer magic," I said, stung at the rebuke. Did she think I would have let this happen if there had been any way to prevent it? "He saved my life."

"Drakes are very loyal." She made it sound as though she thought Squeak's loyalty was a mistake. "Did you at least manage to speak to the king?"

"I did. He was thrilled to hear of Arlo's survival, and promises justice for Illusion."

"Did you set up a meeting?" Tirgen asked. "Is he coming here?"

"We didn't get into the details. I wanted to get Squeak here as fast as possible."

Morwenna shot me another dirty look as we waded out of the water. I couldn't win with her—she wasn't happy that I hadn't set up a meeting, but she would have been furious if I'd stayed to chat with the king and delayed treatment for Squeak.

"That's a good start," Raven said. "Justice has been a long time coming."

"The king's a good man," Tirgen said.

Yes, he was. And he seemed keen on justice, too—except when it came to changelings, apparently. He'd created that injustice himself. Now that I knew his character better, that seemed odd.

I yawned and rubbed at my face.

"Tired?" Raven asked.

"It's been a big day." I needed a pillow, stat, or I would keel over and fall asleep face down in the lake.

"That sounds like my cue to whisk you away to a nice, soft bed," the Hawk said.

"Plenty of beds in the castle," Raven said. "You're welcome to stay."

I glanced down at Squeak, floating in his hammock, then looked at Morwenna. She wouldn't want me to stay. I needed to talk to her, but I couldn't face another challenge tonight.

"We'll keep him unconscious for three or four days," she said. "It will speed his healing. So you don't need to hang around."

Called it. The rejection stung, but hey, I'd lived as a changeling all my life. I ate rejection for breakfast.

"Let me take you home." The Hawk put one arm around me and drew his sword with the other. Three slashes and he'd formed a gateway. Mist billowed out of it, so I couldn't see where he was taking us, but as long as it had a bed, I was down with it.

"You'll let me know if he wakes up?" I asked Morwenna.

"He won't." Grudgingly, she added, "But yes."

The Hawk pulled me through the gateway without further ado. We stepped into his house in the mortal world.

"I could have stayed with Raven," I said.

"I want you with me," he said, in a voice that accepted no arguments. "I'm not giving Kellith a chance to get to you."

"He could hardly have found me on Arlo," I pointed out. "He hasn't managed to find it in twenty years of searching. It's not as though he'll succeed now just because I'm there."

I yawned so hugely I thought I would dislocate my jaw, and his gaze softened.

"You're just arguing for the hell of it, aren't you? I think arguing must be in your DNA."

"I'm impressed you even know what DNA is," I said with another massive yawn.

"You'd be surprised what I've managed to pick up over the years." He sheathed his sword and took me into his arms.

"You know, there's one thing I don't understand about the king." The oddity was still niggling at me, and the Hawk knew him better than anyone, perhaps. "He seems so concerned with the welfare of all his subjects—except changelings. Why does he hate them?"

He frowned. "Who said he hates them?"

"He must do. He passed that horrible law that forces all changelings to leave the Realms by the time they turn eighteen."

"That was born out of concern, not hate. He wanted

changelings who weren't going to become fae to have a chance at a full human life, not grow old alone in the Realms."

"Oh." That still didn't seem quite right to me—why not let people judge for themselves what made them happy?—but it certainly put a more charitable spin on his motivations.

"Anything else I can help you with? Are you hungry? Would you like a drink?"

"You know, I'm quite capable of looking after myself. You don't have to do it."

"I'm not doing it because I have to. I'm doing it because I want to. And you're still arguing."

"Sorry." I gazed at his full lips, now unaccountably close, and the word came out in a kind of breathless squeak. Maybe I was tired, but I wasn't dead, and his hands were moving in long, sensuous strokes down my back and over my butt.

"No, you're not. But that's probably the only time you'll ever apologise to me, so I'll take it."

He bent lower, and his lips grazed lightly over mine. My breath hitched in my throat.

"What else do I have to apologise for?"

"Disturbing my peace." He dropped another kiss on my lips. "Making it impossible for me to do my duties without distraction." His hands tightened on my arse, and he jerked me against his hard body. Distraction? I could hardly breathe, much less think. Who was being distracting now? "Stealing my heart."

His mouth closed on mine again, but he was done being gentle. He devoured me, like a starving man finding food at last, and I melted against him, lost in the kiss. I had kissed a few guys in my time, but I'd never been kissed like that before.

When he finally raised his head, I could barely stand, my whole body throbbing with need, and we were both breathing hard.

"Stealing your heart?" I scoffed, though my own heart was singing, and I couldn't repress a smile of delight. "That's the corniest line I've ever heard."

"Really?" He gave me a look of mock innocence. "But it worked so well on all the other girls."

I punched his rock-hard chest, and he laughed and swept me up into his arms.

"Not this again," I said. "You realise I do have legs?"

"I do," he said, striding through the house. "And I plan to become most thoroughly acquainted with them."

He kicked open the door of a bedroom and put me down on the king-sized bed inside.

I slid over to make room for him, then gave him my most innocent face. "You want me to go to sleep?"

He peeled off his shirt over his head, revealing the muscles of a Greek god. I would be drooling in a minute. He grinned down at me, well aware of the effect he was having on me. "Eventually," he said. "First, I have some other activities planned."

27

I stretched luxuriously, revelling in the feel of silken sheets against my naked skin. When I opened my eyes, the room was dark—was it night again already? I felt as if I'd only just gone to sleep. Still, Kyrrim *had* kept me awake for rather a long time—it had been almost dawn when I'd curled up in his arms.

Not that I regretted a moment of it.

Something that smelled a lot like bacon tantalised my nostrils and I decided that maybe it would be worth getting out of bed to go discover the source of that tempting scent. My clothes lay scattered across the floor, in roughly the order that the Hawk had ripped them from my body— literally, in the case of my underpants, which were no longer wearable. I shrugged and pulled on my jeans, going commando. I would sacrifice my whole wardrobe for a night like that.

Following my nose to the kitchen, I found Kyrrim at the stove, his naked back to me, dressed only in a pair of jeans.

I moved quietly, but his warrior's senses knew I was there, because he shot me a grin over his bare shoulder and held out a hand demandingly.

"Come here."

"So bossy," I complained, but I pressed myself against his warm back, breathing in the scent of him.

He turned and snaked one arm around me, snugging me up against his hip. He had eggs frying in one pan, and long strips of bacon in another. The smell made my mouth water, and it occurred to me that I couldn't remember the last time I'd eaten.

"How are you this morning? Hungry?"

"For what?" I ran my hands over his skin, admiring the taut muscles of his back and chest.

He growled deep in his throat and turned to face me directly. "I meant food, but if you have something else in mind ..."

He drew me against him roughly, his hands sliding up under my T-shirt, and kissed me with a hunger that I thought we'd slaked last night. Apparently not. An answering fire woke in my belly and went roaring through my body at his touch, and I pressed myself against him eagerly, losing myself in his kiss.

Moments later—or was it hours? I lost track of time—the smoke alarm in the hallway outside the kitchen began to beep, and I became aware that the room had filled with smoke. By that time, I was sprawled naked across the kitchen bench, and probably wouldn't have noticed if the house had burned down around me, except for that annoying alarm.

"Kyrrim," I said, pushing half-heartedly at his shoulders. "The bacon …"

"Damn the bacon," he growled, refusing to be diverted from what he was doing.

And since his activities were causing such glorious sensations, I decided that damning the bacon was a very sensible idea, and thought no more of it.

Some time later, he helped me to my feet, since my legs had grown unaccountably shaky, and I got dressed for the second time. While I was doing that, he threw the leathery eggs and the scraps of charcoal that had once been bacon into the bin and opened all the windows to clear the smoke, walking around in unselfconscious nudity.

Shit, if I had a body like that, I'd flaunt it, too.

"You need to put some clothes on, or I won't be responsible for the consequences," I said, when I was decent again.

"You still hungry?" The glint in his eye told me he wasn't talking about food.

"For bacon? Yes. Do you have any more?"

I picked up his jeans and threw them toward him. It was a glorious view, but I would never get out of this house if he didn't get dressed soon.

He pulled another package of bacon out of the fridge and waggled it triumphantly at me. Thank goodness. I was ravenous. How long had we slept?

"What's the time?" I asked him.

He indicated the oven clock with a jerk of his chin as he pulled up his jeans. Eight sixteen. Not as late as I'd thought.

Yes, we'd slept the day away, but I'd been so tired I could easily have slept through until after midnight.

I ran hot water into the sink and began scrubbing the burnt residue off the pans. Kyrrim came and stood behind me, his arms snaking around me. He ground against me, and I could feel that he was ready to go again. By the Tree, the man was insatiable. I felt a stirring of lust deep inside, and resolutely ignored it.

"Do you think it's possible to die of too much sex?" I asked.

"Want to find out?"

That sexy growl of his was almost irresistible, but my stomach chose that moment to emit a loud growl of its own.

He laughed and released me, taking the now-clean frypans from the drying rack. "I can tell you have other priorities."

He turned away and put the pans on the stove again, filling the larger one with strips of bacon, and cracking four eggs into the smaller one. I admired the muscles of his back and shoulders for a moment, then my gaze slid lower and I noticed the rectangular shape in his back pocket.

"Is that your phone? Can I borrow it?"

"Sure."

I slid my hand into his pocket, taking the opportunity to kiss the back of his neck as I leaned closer.

"Do you want breakfast or not, woman? Don't distract me."

"You're very easily distractible."

He pointed the tongs at me sternly as I danced out of reach, phone in hand. "And *you* are very distracting."

"I thought I was just annoying and argumentative."

He grinned. "That, too, sometimes."

"Tell the truth—you didn't like me at all when we first met."

"You grew on me."

"You make me sound like a skin disease."

"Now you're just fishing for compliments. Who are you ringing?"

"Willow."

The phone rang so long I thought she wouldn't pick up, but she finally did. Her tone was clipped and formal, since she obviously didn't recognise the number. "Willow Andrakis."

"Willow, it's me."

There was a lot of noise in the background—people talking, music playing. Was this the night we had that gig at The Drunken Irishman?

"Al?"

"Yeah. I'm back. Don't start that gig without me."

"Really? You can play?"

"Sure." I raised my eyebrows at Kyrrim, who looked dubious, but then shrugged fatalistically. There wasn't much Kellith could do to me in front of hundreds of people at the pub. Particularly not when it was at least three-quarters full of fae. "Why not?"

"I'm surprised you can still walk."

"Wha—oh." I'd forgotten Kyrrim had told her we were

going to have a bonk fest. And then it had come true. I cast him a suspicious glance, but he was innocently dishing out our breakfast. My stomach rumbled again. "I'm just going to grab some food and we'll be there."

"The Hawk's coming, too?" There was amusement in her voice. "What, he can't leave you alone even for a couple of hours?"

"Something like that."

"I'm glad you're back. You need to do something about that diabolical cat of yours."

"Kel's not mine."

"Well, he sure as hell ain't *mine*. The little bastard left a dead mouse in the middle of my bed this morning. I swear, if he does it again, I'm going to wring his furry neck."

"I'll try to find a new home for him soon. See you in a little while."

I hung up and joined Kyrrim at the kitchen table.

"I suppose it's pointless to tell you that it would be safer if you stayed here?"

"Completely pointless," I said around a mouthful of bacon. Man, that was good. My stomach was convinced I hadn't eaten in a week, so I shovelled another forkful in, delighting in the salty explosion of flavour. "Besides, I'll have my own personal bodyguard with me, right?"

He rolled his eyes. "Eat your bacon. You're going to need the energy."

"Playing guitar doesn't take that much energy."

"I wasn't talking about that."

Oh. He laughed at the look on my face. I couldn't

believe the change in him. I had never suspected, when I first met him, that there was this smiling man, full of sexual innuendo and humour, lurking underneath the stern knightly exterior. It was as though he'd had a complete personality transplant, but really, it was probably just that he'd decided to let me in. I remembered our "no man is an island" conversation and marvelled at how far we'd come since then.

Once we'd finished eating, we went down to the garage, where the black Maserati sat in all its gleaming splendour.

"Can I drive?" I asked, without much hope that he'd say yes.

To my surprise, however, he tossed me the keys.

"*Really?*" I jumped up and down with glee.

"Don't make me regret this."

I screeched the tyres taking off, and he groaned and covered his eyes. I laughed, exulting in the deep growl of the engine that vibrated through my feet on the pedals. It handled like a dream, responding to the lightest touch on the wheel, and cornered more smoothly than any other car I'd ever driven. He let me drive it all the way to The Drunken Irishman. I still had a huge grin on my face when we pulled up outside the pub.

It was a perfect night. Being back on stage with the band felt so good, with Rowan's drumbeat pounding in my body like a heartbeat, Sage at my side, and Willow up front in her rightful place in the limelight. I even had a boyfriend out there in the audience again. Kyrrim sat at the bar, one hand tapping along in time to the music. Just like old times—better, in fact, since the Hawk was no cheating snake.

The scents of other people's magic swirled around me as I played. The place was packed tonight, and there were a lot of fae present. The Hawk's eyes roved over the crowd, keeping watch. Keeping me safe.

None of my bandmates had noticed yet that there was something different about me. Among all these fae, it was hard to pick out individual magic scents. But once we finished the gig and started loading Willow's car, they would realise I was fae, and the questions would start flowing. We were in for a long night once that happened. Willow and Sage wouldn't be happy until they had heard every detail.

I glanced again at the Hawk. It was hard to stop myself, as if he were a magnet and I was made of iron, helplessly drawn to him. I grinned, unable to keep the joy I felt inside from bubbling over. It would be a long night, but a very good one, with a man like that to go home with. He smiled that gorgeous new smile at me, the one that had only appeared once the king was rescued, the one that said he was no longer an island.

The one that said he was mine.

THE END

Don't miss the next book, *Changeling Illusion*, coming soon! For news on its release, plus special deals and other book news, sign up for my newsletter at www.marinafinlayson.com.

Reviews and word of mouth are vital for any author's success. If you enjoyed *Changeling Magic*, please take a moment to leave a short review at Amazon.com. Just a few words sharing your thoughts on the book would be extremely helpful in spreading the word to other readers (and this author would be immensely grateful!).

ALSO BY MARINA FINLAYSON

MAGIC'S RETURN SERIES
The Fairytale Curse
The Cauldron's Gift

THE PROVING SERIES
Moonborn
Twiceborn
The Twiceborn Queen
Twiceborn Endgame

SHADOWS OF THE IMMORTALS SERIES
Stolen Magic
Murdered Gods
Rivers of Hell
Hidden Goddess
Caged Lightning

THIRTEEN REALMS SERIES
Changeling Exile
Changeling Magic

ACKNOWLEDGEMENTS

No book is written in a vacuum, and I'm very grateful to the people around me for their support. My family is always ready to lend an ear when I need to talk over plot problems, and Mal and Jen again offered their services for beta reading. My sprinting partner, Melanie, helped me focus and kept me going, and my friends in the Authors' Corner listened to a lot of complaints when things weren't going well. Thank you, all of you, for your support.

ABOUT THE AUTHOR

Marina Finlayson is a reformed wedding organist who now writes fantasy. She is married and shares her Sydney home with three kids, a large collection of dragon statues and one very stupid dog with a death wish.

Her idea of heaven is lying in the bath with a cup of tea and a good book until she goes wrinkly.

Made in the USA
Columbia, SC
24 February 2019